U0015234

大學語言課程教研薈萃
第二語言讀寫教學研究論文集

Research Into Second Language Chinese and English Literacy Instruction

主編 ｜ 李明懿、雷貝利
策劃 ｜ 國立中央大學語言中心
Edited by Mingyi Li & Barry Lee Reynolds
Planned by Language Center, National Central University

中央大學出版中心 ｜ 遠流

目錄

編者序一

　　近年全球在地化的趨勢凸顯了國際競爭和合作的重要性，而語言教育在此競合能力的培養上扮演著極其重要的角色。中央大學自2002年起，首開先河，以提升大學院校語言教學品質為目標，舉辦中／英文為第二語言或外語之閱讀與寫作教學研討會，致力於兩種語言教學專家間的觀摩與交流。「第五屆以中／英文為第二語言之閱讀與寫作教學研討會」立於前四屆的基石之上，在2013年6月登場。是屆研討會發表論文共17篇，工作坊9場，會中討論的火花精彩激盪，豐碩的研討果實孕育出第二本論文集──《大學語言課程教研薈萃》。論文集經雙重匿名全文審查共收錄研討會發表之全文七篇。論文主題內容有：以中／英文讀寫為目標之課程規劃、課堂教學活動設計、學術語言教學、數位工具應用及移民語言教學。

　　本論文集以大一英文課程教學開場。如何強化學習動機始終是一項重大議題，教學發展的熱情和創意是強化學生學習動機的最大動力，中央大學高永銳老師的〈**一個有趣的大一英文之教學活動──大一英文朗讀暖身活動設計**〉（An Interesting Read-Aloud Warm-Up Activity for Freshman English）以朗誦文學作品作為大一英文課堂暖身活動，並在學期初及學期中針對學生的聆聽意願進行問卷及教學意見反饋調查，發現學生不僅聆聽意願提高，更因此而增強其學習動機。台灣的新移民華語教育是近年方興的議題，欣見學者在此園地的育苗逐漸茁壯，本論文集收錄了黃湘玲、林青蓉、許秀娟、鄭淑真四位老師的〈**移民數位華語讀寫課程模式與特色探究**〉（The Inquiry of Immigrants E-Learning Literacy Program and Features），論文針對移民在台生活的公民讀寫素養需求，探討移民華語教師如何使用「來去華語100句」學習平台進行讀寫課程規劃及其課程的特色。此研究發現，教師在規劃課程時，以數位華語學習平台結合紙本教學，並將讀寫學習元素融入原本以口語表達為主的課程。在漢字教學方面，賴秋桂老師〈論對外漢字教學的策略與課程規劃〉（How to Set Up a Curriculum for Teaching Chinese Characters to Non-native Speakers?）提出以不同策略的切入時間點作為關注對象，觀察對外漢字教學策略在學生習字過程中如何調整與配合。論文將漢字教學分為教學法彈性運用、基礎工作、正式習字及進階習字四個時間面向，指出在各時間面向中宜於使用的教學策略以及其間的有效配搭。在英文寫作教學上，吳曉萍（Hsiao-Ping Wu）老師和宋可音（Koying Sung）老師在〈線上及學術寫作字彙密度及文法複雜度分析〉（Lexical Richness and Syntactic Complexity Analysis－From an Online Genre to Academic Discourse）中，試從詞彙量、詞彙密度和句法複雜性來觀察並比較台灣大學生英語線上即時交談時和正式寫作時的語言特性。該研究指出，讀寫的表現因語境和語體而異，學術寫作在結構上的複雜度高於線上交談；而線上交談並不會對寫作能力造成負面的影響，其真實語境有助於提升語言的流利度。近年因大學國際學位生人數的增加，學術華語亦逐漸受到重視。謝佳玲老師和吳欣儒老師的〈華語讀寫能力對學術摘要寫作之預測作用及其教學應用〉（The Predictive Effects of Chinese Reading and Writing Performances on Academic Summary Writing）透過對大學國際學生華語字形辨識、字義理解、理解推理、引導式短文寫作與摘要寫作的檢測，探討前述四項讀寫能力是否能預測摘要寫作的表現。其研究結果顯示，此四項能力與摘要寫作的關連性具跨語言之普遍性，其中短文寫作能力為預測效果最佳的參照指標。資料導向學習（Data-Driven Learning）乃由 John Tims 於 1980 年代所創。主張學習藉由真實語料的接觸，觀察、分析、歸納詞語的使用規則。本次研討會華語和英語各有相關論文一篇。其中，林慧老師的〈平衡語料與中文閱讀詞彙習得〉（Concordances and the Acquisition of Lexicon in Chinese as a Foreign Language）討論利用平衡語料庫來幫助非母語學生閱讀時理解文章中生詞意義與用法的可行性和優點。學習教學方面，則有劉顯親老師和林嶽峙老師的〈引導式語境共現應用於大學生英文寫作之詞彙學習〉（A Study of Guided Concordance Use on English Vocabulary Learning for Writing by Chinese-L1 College Students），研究結果指出非母語大學生在教師鷹架引導下使用共現工具進行英文寫作，其詞彙知識和輸出表現都有明顯的進步，而母語干擾所帶來的偏誤也因此減少了。這篇論文在語料庫應用的效益之外也凸顯了教師在學生的習得過程中所扮演的重要角色。值得一提的是，此次學術語言教學在論文發表篇數中佔相當比重，足見以增進大學院校國際學位生學術語言技能為目標之教學及其研究逐漸受到重視。

《大學語言課程教研薈萃》的誕生必須歸功於許多人的努力和奉獻。除了論文集的作者之外，要感謝李振清教授、葉德明教授、柯華葳教授、信世昌教授、衛友賢教授、陳純音教授、陳雅芬教授、陳俊光教授、張郁慧教授、賴陳秀卿教授、謝佳玲教授、葉修文教授、余綺芳教授、招靜琪教授、JoAnn (Jodi) Crandall 教授、鍾鎮城教授、梁美雅教授等諸位師長期以來不輟的支持和鼓勵。最後特別感謝中央大學語言中心單維彰主任及其所領導的第五屆中／英文為第二語言或外語之閱讀與寫作教學研討會籌備及執行團隊：高永銳老師、劉愛萍老師、黃惠姿專員、張惠琴專員、許馥曲小姐、英文主編雷貝利教授以及語言中心全體同仁。

李明懿 謹誌
國立中央大學語言中心助理教授
2017 年 2 月

Editor's Preface I

The recent rise of glocalization has highlighted the importance of international competition and cooperation, and language education plays a vital role in developing the skills required for these global dynamics. Since 2002, National Central University has been hosting the Chinese/English as a Second Language Conference on Reading and Writing Instruction, paving the way for the improvement of language education quality in universities and encouraging education and exchange among teaching experts of the two languages. Building off the foundation of the previous four conferences, "The 5th Chinese/English as a Second Language Conference on Reading and Writing Instructions" was held in June 2013. During this conference, 17 papers were presented and 9 workshops were held. Lively discussions took place and the research findings from the academic papers were compiled in a second volume—*Research Into Second Language Chinese and English Literacy Instruction*. The papers in the volume have been anonymously peer-reviewed, and the collection includes seven papers that were presented at the conference. Topics cover curriculum design with the aim of achieving Chinese/English reading and writing skills, classroom activities design, academic language teaching, applications of digital technologies to reading/writing instruction, and language education for immigrants.

The first paper in the volume is on teaching English to freshmen. Increasing learner motivation has always been a major issue in education, and enthusiasm and creativity play the biggest roles in motivating students to learn. The paper "**An Interesting Read-Aloud Warm-Up Activity for Freshman English**" by NCU teacher Yung-Kuang Kao proposes reading literary works aloud as a warm-up activity for teaching English to freshmen. Based on questionnaires and feedback given at the start and during the semester, the study discovered that students were interested in the activity, and the activity also increased their motivation to learn. The topic of "Chinese as a Second Language for Immigrants in Taiwan" has gained popularity in recent years, and we are delighted to see papers sprouting from ideas that scholars have planted in this area. The volume also includes the paper "**The Inquiry of Immigrants E-Learning Literacy Program and Features**" written by Xiang-Ling Huang, Qing-Rong Lin, Hsiu-Chuan Hsu, and Shu-Chen Cheng. The paper addresses the reading and writing requirements for immigrants living in Taiwan and provides suggestions for utilizing the learning platform "Lai-Qu Huayu 100 Sentences" to design a curriculum for reading, writing and other subjects when teaching Chinese to immigrants. It was discovered in this study that teachers combine digital Chinese learning platforms with teaching material from books, and incorporate reading and writing elements into lessons that are usually expressed orally when they design their curricula. With regard to the teaching of Chinese characters, Julie Lai's paper "**How to Set Up a Curriculum for Teaching Chinese Characters to Non-native Speakers?**" proposes a curriculum that implements various strategies at different times and examines how adjustment and cooperation can be applied when teaching Chinese characters to non-native speakers. The paper divides the process of teaching Chinese characters into four time periods (flexible application in teaching, basics, current learning, and advanced learning), and points out the teaching strategies and the matching strategies that can be applied at each period. Regarding the teaching of English composition, the paper "**Lexical Richness and Syntactic Complexity Analysis — From an Online Genre to Academic Discourse**" written by Hsiao-Ping Wu and Koying Sung examines vocabulary, lexical density, and syntactic complexity in the online English conversations and academic discourse of Taiwanese university students. This research points out that reading and writing performances varies in different contexts and genres. The structure of academic writing is more complex than online conversations. However, online conversations do not have a negative impact on composition skills as real-life contexts can be beneficial to language fluency. In recent years, the number of international students pursuing degrees in Taiwan has increased, and therefore Chinese for academic purposes is increasingly being taken seriously. The paper "**The Predictive Effects of Chinese Reading and Writing Performances on Academic Summary Writing**" by Chia-Ling Hsieh and Xin-Ru Wu discusses the possibility of predicting summary writing performance through four reading and writing abilities (character recognition, literal comprehension, understanding and reasoning, and guided essay writing and summary writing) used by international university students learning Chinese. The results of this research demonstrate that the link between the four abilities and summary writing contains cross-linguistic universality, with Chinese essay writing as the best indicator of predictive effects. Data-driven learning was coined by John Tims in the 1980s. The concept advocates the use of authentic corpora to observe, analyze and incorporate the rules of word usage. This conference includes both a Chinese and English paper on this topic. Among these papers, Hannah Lin's "**Concordances and the Acquisition of Lexicon in Chinese as a Foreign Language**" discusses the feasibility and advantages of using a balanced corpus to help non-native speakers understand the meanings and usages of unfamiliar words when reading. With regard to education, Hsien-Chin Liou and Yueh-Chih Lin point out in their paper "**A Study of Guided Concordance Use on English Vocabulary Learning for Writing by Chinese-L1 College Students**" that foreign university students, under the guidance of their teachers, use concordance tools in their English compositions, showing significant improvement in their knowledge and output of vocabulary words and experiencing less interference from their native language. This paper highlights the benefits of corpus application as well as the important role of the teacher in the student's learning process. It is worth mentioning that numerous papers on academic language learning were presented at this conference, demonstrating the gradual importance of the teaching and research of academic language skills for university students pursuing international degrees.

Research Into Second Language Chinese and English Literacy Instruction was published thanks to the efforts and contributions of many people. In addition to the authors of the papers collected in the volume, I would like to thank Professor Chen-Ching Li, Professor Te-Ming Yeh, Professor Hwa-Wei Ko, Professor Shih-Chang Hsin, Professor David Wible, Professor Doris Chun-Yin Chen, Professor Ya-Fen Chen, Professor Fred Jyun-Gwang Chen, Professor Claire Hsun-Huei Chang, Professor Jose Lai, Professor Chia-Ling Hsieh, Professor Shiou-Wen Yeh, Professor Chi-Fang Yu, Professor Chin-Chi Chao, Professor JoAnn (Jodi) Crandall, Professor Chen-Cheng Chun, and Professor Mei-Ya Liang for their support and encourage-ment. Lastly, I would like to thank Wei-Chang Shann, director of the Language Center, and the preparation team that he led in the execution of the "5th Chinese/English as a Second Language Conference on Reading and Writing Instructions": Yung-Kuang Kao, Ai-Ping Liu, Cassie Huang, Hui-Chin Chang, Ms. Fu-Chu Hsu, Professor Barry Lee Reynolds (English editor), and all my colleagues at the Language Center.

Li, Mingyi
Assistant Professor

Coordinator, Chinese Language Division

Language Center

National Central University

February 2017

Editor's Preface II

In June of 2013, the fifth International Conference on Chinese and English as a Second Language (C/ESL) was organized and hosted by the Language Center of National Central University. As in previous years, the theme of the conference was Chinese and English second language (L2) literacy. Such a theme seems particularly relevant as the internationalization of Taiwan continues to gain attention. This can be observed not only from the number of internationals coming to Taiwan to study Mandarin Chinese but also in the increasing number choosing Taiwan to pursue newly established English-instructed international degrees or traditional Chinese-instructed degrees. This phenomenon extends outside the classroom into the greater reaches of Taiwanese society where a number of immigrants are in need of Chinese literacy skills. The conference call for presentations resulted in a very interesting and diverse collection of contributions exemplifying that both Chinese and English L2 educators are investigating many of the same issues. This reinforced our initial belief that there were advantages to be gained from bringing Chinese as a Second Language (CSL) and English as a Second Language (ESL) researchers together. Soon after the conference, a call for chapter proposals was sent to the conference presenters. After a strict review of the submissions and much deliberation by the editors, only a select portion was accepted for further revision and final inclusion in this volume. With this in mind, I thank the authors for their continued patience and meticulous revisions throughout this entire process. Without their dedication, this volume would not have been possible. Such a process led to a strict acceptance rate. Reading over the chapters I find three themes have emerged:

curriculum design, academic literacy, and the application of corpora to aid L2 acquisition.

The first three chapters report on research conducted to address specific curriculum design issues. This begins with Yung-Kuang Kao's (高永銚) "An Interesting Read-Aloud Warm-Up Activity for Freshman English" (一個有趣的大一英文之教學活動──大一英文朗讀暖身活動設計) in which she discusses how incorporating English literature through the use of reading aloud in her required university Freshmen English classes has increased students' motivation to learn English as well as having had a positive effect on their willingness to listen to English. This action research was able to bring her students from a point where they considered English class "as naptime or a time for studying other courses" to one in which they felt English "allows [them] to have fun" because it is "[their] favorite subject." She ends the chapter by providing examples of how she extended the read-aloud activities beyond the classroom into the community and provides suggestions to teachers on how read-aloud activities can be tailored to different student groups. In chapter two, "The Inquiry of Immigrants E-Learning Literacy Program and Features" (移民數位華語讀寫課程模式與特色探究), Xiang-Ling Huang, Qing-Rong Lin, Hsiu-Chuan Hsu, and Shu-Chen Cheng (黃湘玲, 林青蓉, 許秀娟, 鄭淑真) report on their investigation of teachers' uses of digital materials to teach Mandarin Chinese literacy skills to immigrants. Besides generating learner interest in the target language through the use of digitalized course materials, they found learners benefited from teachers' flexibilities in providing access to paper-based materials in digitalized forms as well as digitalized materials in paper-based forms. These techniques assisted teachers in gradually increasing learners' digital literacy. Digitalized writing activities also aided learners' in written language production. In addition, teachers were found to select functional writing assignments that they perceived as being relevant to the lives of the immigrants. In the third and final chapter on curriculum design, "How to Set Up a Curriculum for Teaching Chinese Characters to Non-native Speakers?" (論對外漢字教學的策略與課程規劃), Julie Lai (賴秋桂) provides CSL teachers with some guidance on how to aid learners in the mammoth task of vocabulary acquisition. Vocabulary is the component of language that can never be acquired in its entirety. This results in L2 vocabulary acquisition being a lifelong process, causing some adults acquiring vocabulary in a logographic language like Traditional Chinese to become discouraged during early stages of acquisition. Based on the findings gathered from questionnaire data obtained from L2 Mandarin Chinese learners and teachers, suggestions are provided on how teachers can assist learners in improving both their written production and recognition of Chinese characters through task-specific instruction.

The next two chapters report on research conducted to address academic literacy issues. In chapter four, "Lexical Richness and Syntactic Complexity Analysis—From an Online Genre to Academic Discourse" (線上及學術寫作字彙密度及文法複雜度分析), Hsiao-Ping Wu and Koying Sung (吳曉萍, 宋可音) investigated whether Taiwanese English and Applied Language majors' use of instant messaging had any negative effects on their academic writing. Their findings run counter to the argument that engagement in texting and other types of computer-mediated communication leads to a decline in traditional literacy skills. Instead, their results suggest literacy practices are contextual, meaning that the participants in their study were apt at using academic English in contexts where academic English was appropriate and limited their use of "text speak" to instant messaging. The authors go on to claim that instant messaging is useful for encouraging target language fluency development since it provides an authentic language environment. In chapter five, "The Predictive Effects of Chinese Reading and Writing Performances on Academic Summary Writing" (華語讀寫能力對學術摘要寫作之預測作用及其教學應用), Chia-Ling Hsieh and Xin-Ru Wu (謝佳玲, 吳欣儒) investigated whether proficiency in a number of L2 Chinese reading and writing skills (character recognition, definition understanding, inferencing, guided short essay writing) correlated with proficiency in the necessary academic literacy skill of writing abstracts. Their results indicated that the ability to write teacher-guided short essays in Chinese provided the most predictive power for advanced CSL learners being able to successfully write abstracts of academic texts. The chapter ends with suggestions for strategies teachers can employ to assist learners in improving their ability to write short essays and abstracts.

The last two chapters of the volume report research on the application of corpora to aid L2 vocabulary acquisition. In chapter six, "Concordances and the Acquisition of Lexicon in Chinese as a Foreign Language" (平衡語料與中文閱讀詞彙習得), Hannah Lin (林慧) found giving learners access to both a dictionary and a corpus to be more effective in increasing learners' knowledge of unknown vocabulary than just providing a dictionary. She claims that learners often fail to accurately acquire Chinese words due to overreliance on direct translation from dictionaries and suggest CSL teachers provide learners with access to corpora containing example sentences to encourage accurate L2 vocabulary acquisition. The volume ends with chapter seven, "A Study of Guided Concordance Use on English Vocabulary Learning for Writing by Chinese-L1 College Students" (引導式語境共現應用於大學生英文寫作之詞彙學習) by Hsien-Chin Liou and Yueh-Chih Lin (劉顯親, 林嶽崎). A majority of the errors produced by L2 English writers can be categorized as misuse of vocabulary in the form of miscollocations; this may be caused by L1 inference or lack of access to input of example sentences containing the misused words. Addressing this issue, they designed a four-week instructional intervention incorporating concordancing exercises. It was found that the concordance use had a significant impact on the participants' L1-influenced collocation errors. They end their article with suggestions on how ESL teachers can incorporate concordance use into their language instruction.

Without the support of a number of sources, this volume would not have been possible. Grants from Taiwan's National Science Council (current Ministry of Science and Technology), Ministry of Education, and National Central University's Research and Development Office given to the NCU Language Center supported the conference. Thanks to those who offered endless support and encouragement of the conference in various ways: Professor Cheng-Ching Li, Professor Te-Ming Yeh, Professor Hwa-Wei Ko, Professor Shih-Chang Hsin, Professor David Wible, Professor Doris Chun-Yin Chen, Professor Ya-Fen Chen, Professor Fred Jyun-Gwang Chen, Professor Claire Hsun-Huei Chang, Professor Sau Hing Jose Lai Chan, Professor Chia-Ling Hsieh, Professor Shiou-Wen Yeh, Professor Chi-Fang Yu, Professor Chin-Chi Chao, Professor JoAnn (Jodi) Crandall, Professor Chen-Cheng Chun, and Professor Mei-Ya Liang. A special thanks also goes to the members of the faculty and staff of the Language Center that served in the planning and running of the conference: Language Center Director Professor Wei-Chang Shann, Professor Ming-Yi Li, Lecturer Ai-Ping Liu, Lecturer Yung-Kuang Kao, Administrative Assistant Hui-Chin Chang and Administrative Assistant Hui-Tzu Huang. Lastly, for this volume, we owe a debt of thanks to Hui-Chin Chang in providing limitless support in countless administrative tasks for many months before the conference as well as many months after and my co-Editor Ming-Yi Li for the patient and scrupulous Chinese editing of this volume.

This volume has been written and edited by L2 educators for L2 educators. It is our hope that prospective and practicing teachers can find inspiration in the chapters to develop their own pedagogical approach to the teaching of CSL and ESL.

Barry Lee Reynolds

Assistant Professor of English Education

Faculty of Education

University of Macau

February 2017

Macau SAR

編者序二

　　「第五屆以中／英文為第二語言之閱讀與寫作教學研討會」在 2013 年 6 月，由中央大學語言中心規劃主辦。如同往年，本次會議主題為探討「中／英文為二語之讀寫發展」。正當台灣國際化的程度愈發受到重視，該會議主題也就更顯切題。此國際化現象可從下列兩點觀察的到：一、愈來愈多國際人士願意來台學習中文。二、願意來台修讀以英語授課的國際學位或傳統以中文授課的學位人數亦逐漸增長。由於來台移民人士對於中文讀寫技巧的需求量與日俱增，國際化的現象也就從學校教室擴展到台灣社會了。本次研討會徵求論文發表，匯集了相當多有趣及多元研究主題的貢獻。舉例來說，我們發現中文為二語以及英文為二語的學者所探討的議題有許多相同之處。而這也呼應我們舉辦此研討會最初的理念，也就是中文為二語和英文為二語的學者能有所互惠。在此次會議結束後，遂即邀請論文發表學者投稿全文。在對稿件進行嚴謹的審查及經過主編的審議後，僅有一部分的稿件能獲進一步修改及接受，並收錄在本書裡。因此，我由衷感謝作者們在審查過程中，持續不斷的耐心以及思慮周全的修正。他們的奉獻造就了這本書的付梓，也造就我們對稿件接受的嚴謹。在瀏覽本書篇章後，三項議題浮現在我腦海裡，即：課程設計、學術讀寫技巧、及資料庫應用輔助二語習得。

　　前三章為課程設計相關議題之研究發表。首先，高永銚的〈一個有趣的大一英文之教學活動──大一英文朗讀暖身活動設計〉一文裡，探討如何透過放聲閱讀，把英美文學融入在她的必修大一英文課程裡，以提升學生英語學習動機及聆聽意願。她的學生原本認為英文課只是一門「午覺時光」或「修課時間」而已。然而，透過她的行動研究，學生變得喜歡英文課，認為是一堂可以帶給他們歡樂時光的課程。她在結尾時舉出一些她如何把放聲閱讀活動從教室帶入社區的例子，並提供相關建議協助老師根據不同類型的學生特性，利用放聲閱讀進行適性化教學。第二章黃湘玲、林青蓉、許秀娟及鄭淑真的〈移民數位華語讀寫課程模式與特色探究〉一文裡，探討教師如何運用數位教材來指導移民人士華語讀寫技巧。除了透過數位化課程教材的使用來引發學生對於華語學習的興趣，她們發現，不論是紙本教材數位化或是數位教材紙本化，學習者都能在這樣的彈性裡從中獲得益處。而這種技巧亦協助教師提升學生的數位素養。數位化寫作活動亦能協助提升學生的寫作表現。此外，教師也會選擇他們認為跟學生日常生活相關的寫作題材作為他們的學習任務。課程設計的最後一章節，賴秋桂的〈論對外漢字教學的策略與課程規劃〉一文，可提供教學建議給華語為二語的教師，如何協助學生習得漢字。二語字彙的習得是一段終生學習的旅程，也就往往造成成人在學習初期時，容易對漢字的學習產生放棄念頭。然而，字彙的習得是永無止境的。根據華語為二語學生及教師的問卷資料，該文作者提供如何透過任務導向教學法，協助學生增進其書寫及文字辨識能力。

　　接下來兩章節為學術讀寫發展相關議題。第四章吳曉萍和宋可音的〈線上及學術寫作字彙密度及文法複雜度分析〉一文，探討台灣英文及應用英文系學生即時通訊軟體的使用對於其學術寫作表現是否有負面影響。她們的發現與過去爭論通訊軟體或其他以電腦為媒介的溝通會導致傳統讀寫技巧的退步有所出入。反之，她們的結果指出讀寫練習是具有情境的。也就是說，她們的受試者能在學術英文情境裡，使用適當的學術英文，並對即時通訊裡口語文字的使用有所限制。該作者進一步宣稱，由於即時通訊軟體可提供真實的語言使用環境，故對目標語言流利度的發展是有所益處的。第五章謝佳玲及吳欣儒的〈華語讀寫能力對學術摘要寫作之預測作用及其教學應用〉一文，探討華語為二語的讀寫技巧能力（文字辨識度、定義理解度、推論能力、引導式短文寫作）是否與學術摘要寫作的讀寫能力有所關聯。結果指出，中文短文寫作能力可準確預測華語為二語進階學習者是否能成功完成學術摘要的撰寫。該章節於結尾時，提供教師相關教學策略以協助學生增進短文及摘要寫作能力。

　　本書最後兩章節為語料庫在二語字彙習得上之應用。第六章林慧的〈平衡語料與中文閱讀詞彙習得〉一文裡發現，讓學習者搭配使用字典和語料庫在字彙習得的成效上，比起只使用字典還來得有效。她表示，過度依賴字典裡的直接翻譯，會造成學習者對中文字彙知識瞭解的不完整。因此，她建議華語為二語教師應運用語料庫裡的例句來協助學生的字彙習得。本書最後章節為劉顯親及林嶽峙的〈引導式語境共現應用於大學生英文寫作之詞彙學習〉。該文指出大部分英文為二語學習者的書寫錯誤可歸納為搭配字詞的誤用。而造成這種錯誤的原因可能是受到母語的干擾或是缺乏對於語料庫例句的接觸。為了協助學生減少這種錯誤，他們設計了為期四星期的用詞索引教學課程。研究結果發現，用詞索引的運用對於減少受試者因母語干擾所犯的搭配詞錯誤有顯著影響。最後他們亦提出英語為二語教師該如何運用用詞索引在語言課程裡的相關建議。

　　若無上述作者對於此次研究主題的貢獻，本書是無法完成的。本研討會承蒙台灣國科會（現為科技部）、教育部及中央大學經費補助。在此感謝下列人員對於本研討會各方面無窮盡的支持及鼓勵，分別為：李振清教授、葉德明教授、柯華葳教授、信世昌教授、衛友賢教授、陳純音教授、陳雅芬教授、陳俊光教授、張郁慧教授、賴陳秀卿教授、謝佳玲教授、葉修文教授、余綺芳教授、招靜琪教授、JoAnn (Jodi) Crandall 教授、鍾鎮城教授及梁美雅教授。特別感謝下列語言中心教職員規劃及舉辦本研討會：語言中心主任單維彰教授、李明懿教授、劉愛萍講師、高永銚講師、張惠琴行政助理及黃惠姿行政專員。最後，我們特別感激張惠琴小姐在此次研討會前前後後幾個月以來，任何行政大小事務上的無私支持，以及我的共同主編李明懿老師對於本書中文稿件耐心及細心的編審。

本書由二語教育學家編撰完成，亦提供給二語教育學家教學上的建議。我們希望不論是未來或在職教師皆能從本書章節內容中有所啟發，以發展一套自我的華語或英語為二語之教學法。

雷貝利 謹誌
教育學院英語教育助理教授
澳門大學
2017年2月
澳門特別行政區
（高千文 譯）

大學語言課程教研薈萃

第二語言讀寫教學研究論文集

Research Into Second Language
Chinese and English Literacy Instruction

An Interesting Read-Aloud Warm-Up Activity for Freshman English

Yung-Kuang Kao
Language Center, National Central University
kaoyungkuang@yahoo.com

Like universities in many countries where English is a second language, universities in Taiwan require all students to take a minimum number of required English language courses. One negative consequence is that many students have little motivation for participating in the courses. To increase the motivation of my Freshman English students, I have developed an English warm-up activity incorporating the reading aloud of English literature. Results indicate that reading aloud to students and having them read aloud to their peers can be highly effective in motivating their interest in learning English and willingness to listen.

Keywords: Freshman English; Read-Aloud Warm-Up Activity; English Literature; Children's/Young Adults' Literature; Poetry

一個有趣的大一英文之教學活動——
大一英文朗讀暖身活動設計

高永鋧

國立中央大學語言中心

kaoyungkuang@yahoo.com

　　台灣的大學如同其他以英語為二語的國家一樣，要求全校學生在校期間必須修習學校開設的英語必修課程。這項規定造成學生缺乏參與這些英語課程的動機。筆者為了增加大一英文課程學生的學習動機，發展一套在英文文學課程中融合大聲朗讀的熱身活動。研究結果顯示老師對學生進行大聲朗讀，以及讓學生之間相互大聲朗讀的活動，對於增強學生英文學習動機與相互聆聽的意願，有相當良好的效果。

關鍵詞：大一英文、大聲朗讀的熱身活動、英文文學、兒童與成人文學、詩歌

1.0 Introduction

Like universities in many countries where English is a foreign language, universities in Taiwan require all students to take a minimum number of English language courses. One difficulty faced by teachers of such courses is that many students have little motivation to participate. Language Center (LC) teachers at National Central University (NCU) are responsible for the Freshman English courses for students from all departments except the English department. Most of these non-English majors are not very motivated to learn English. Students have told me that English is not important. Many students consider English class as naptime or a time for studying other courses. The only reason these students take Freshman English is because it is required. They do not see the importance of learning English as a second language. In short, these students are not that motivated when they take the Freshman English courses. Hence, as a Freshman English educator, I am constantly thinking about this question: How can I generate interest and motivation among these students to learn English?

To bring back these students' interest and get them motivated, I have developed a warm-up activity for my Freshman English classes. The purpose for this Read-Aloud Warm-Up Activity or RAWU in short is quite clear: to generate student alertness and to stimulate all four language skills. My secret weapon goes mostly back to literature; sometimes I find inspiration in young adults' literature or even children's literature, and I have no discrimination, as long as I believe the content will be interesting to my students. All the read-aloud materials are "carefully selected." By carefully selected, I am referring to a process in which I pick out materials that are not too long and often contain a humorous element, both of which would make them suitable for reading out loud. After several semesters of hands-on practice, this activity has received a substantial amount of positive feedback from students enrolled in my Freshman Reading & Writing and Listening & Speaking English classes. In the sections below, I provide a rationale for why literature and reading aloud can be useful to teaching, detail the process of RAWU, describe the feedback of one class of students, and finally report my future teaching goals.

2.0 Literature Review

There seems to exist a stereotype among some grown-ups that children's literature belongs to some "low class" works not worth their time to read, not to mention study, since they are all "adults" now. In the following, I reflect on the term "children's literature." My goal in doing so is to show that adults can indeed discover numerous good reads in children's literature and ESL/EFL teachers should treat children's literature as an excellent source of input for learners as well.

Most people may confuse children's literature with picture books; therefore, it will be beneficial to provide an explicit definition of children's literature used for this study. According to Tomlinson and Lynch-Brown (1996), "Children's literature is good quality trade books for children from birth to adolescence, covering topics of relevance and interest to children of those ages, through prose and poetry, fiction and nonfiction." (p. 2). Nodelman (1996) further discusses the differences and similarities in children's and adult literature by stating that the differences are less significant than the similarities; he believes that the pleasures of children's literature are not that different from the pleasures of all literature. Specifically, Nodelman (2008) defines children's literature as:

...the literature published specifically for audiences of children and therefore produced in terms of adult ideas about children, is a distinct and definable genre of literature, with characteristics that emerge from enduring adult ideas about childhood and that have consequently remained stable over the stretch of time in which this literature has been produced. Those ideas are inherently *ambivalent;* therefore, the literature is ambivalent. ...It is a plot-oriented literature that shows rather than tells. ...Its texts are internally repetitive and/or variational in form and content and tend to operate as repetitions and/or variations of other texts in the genre. (pp. 242-243)

From these descriptions one may conclude that children's books are much more than mere picture books. The term "children's literature" is actually an umbrella term that includes books for people aged from birth to late teens. With this in mind, Silverstein's (1974; 1981; 1996) works, the *Harry Potter* series (1997, 1998, 1999, 2000, 2003, 2005, 2007), *Goodnight Moon* (Brown, 1947), *The Hobbit* (Tolkien, 1966), *The Adventures of Huckleberry Finn* (Twain, 1959), *D'Aulaires' Book of Greek Myths* (D'Aulaire & Parin, 1962), and *Alice's Adventures in Wonderland* (Carroll, 1865), are all within the scope of children's literature. In the following, I now turn to a discussion of the benefits of children's literature in the context of learning.

2.1 Benefits of Literature/Children's Literature

Children's literature is literature. Hence, all the general benefits of literature can be gained from children's literature. Firstly, Children's literature is plentiful and published at different levels; therefore, teachers can always find something fit for the students' comprehension levels. Furthermore, the use of literature at an early age, especially in relation to learning, may make an impact that continues even until adulthood. Silvey (2009), for example, cites 110 society leaders extoling at least one children's book and how children's literature helped sculpt them as individuals. Lastly, students that have literature read aloud to them will experience a general sense of wellbeing. Krashen (2004) found, for example, Korean teachers and students enjoyed pleasure reading, something that they already considered natural in their native language but not for a studied foreign language. By introducing pleasure reading through reading aloud, teachers can use this opportunity to guide students into the world of foreign language literature, one they may fear or even consider as burdensome.

2.2 Benefits of Reading Aloud

In this section, I now discuss the benefits of reading aloud. I feel that one of the most important reasons for students to read aloud is the noticeable improvement of articulation. Bloom (2000) suggests short poems be memorized for recitation practice by students. Poems can be used to emphasize the rhythm of the English language. Bloom suggests such a process allows for the reader to process the text read. Pitts (1986) further suggests that reading aloud can help in improving reading comprehension for inexperienced readers. I have seen in my classroom that reading out loud helps students improve all four language skills. Furthermore, reading literature aloud to students allows for teachers to immediately assess students' listening comprehension. Lastly, students reading aloud to an audience of peers provide a means to experience an immediate sense of accomplishment. Silverman (2013) claims this is one of the main reasons that many early educators use reading aloud in their classrooms.

3.0 Methods & Procedures

In this section, I describe the methods and materials used for data collection in this study as well as provide a description of a step-by-step sample RAWU activity.

3.1 Participants

The participants of this study were 39 Freshman English students enrolled in a Freshman Listening and Speaking class at the NCU LC. Participants' English abilities were at the basic level, determined by the NCU LC. Although this was a freshmen class, some of the students in the class were retaking the class as sophomores, juniors, or seniors.

The reading materials selected for RAWU activities were all done so with the understanding that both the students and the teacher would be reading them out loud (see Appendix A). A large portion of the materials selected was from the genre of poetry due to the length; shorter stretches of text lend themselves more to RAWU activities than others.

3.2 Willingness to Listen Questionnaire

Listening is one of the skills which teachers often consider as being critical to effective communication. Hence, many teachers provide instruction in listening. However, some learners are poor listeners not because of their lack of listening skills but because of their orientation toward listening (Richmond & Hickson, 2001). Some are just not willing to listen. A Likert-scale questionnaire developed by Richmond and Hickson (2001) was adapted for the purpose of this study to measure students' willingness to listen and to determine whether the RAWU activity developed for my class had any positive effect on their willingness to listen over time (See Appendix B).

Richmond and Hickson's (2001) questionnaire was proven quite reliable with the alpha reliability of 0.85. Students were asked to complete the willingness to listen questionnaire at the beginning and middle of the term.

Scores on the willingness to listen questionnaire could range from 24 to 120. Scores above 89 indicate a high willingness to listen. Scores below 59 indicate a low willingness to listen. Scores between 59 and 89 indicate a moderate willingness to listen. To compute a willingness to listen score, the following steps were followed: Step 1) scores for items 2, 4, 6, 8, 9, 12, 14, 16, 17, 19, 21, and 23 were added together; Step 2) scores for items 1, 3, 5, 7, 10, 11, 13, 15, 18, 20, 22, and 24 were added together; and Step 3) the total score would equal 72 minus the total for step 1 plus the total from step 2.

3.3 Open Response Questionnaire

At the end of the term, students were asked to complete a written feedback questionnaire containing the two following questions: 1) *What have you learned from this course?* 2) *Think of all the course materials (RAWU Reading Materials, Textbook, Homework Sheets, In-Class Video Worksheets, etc.), and choose your favorite. Please explain why you made this choice.*

3.4 RAWU Activity

The time for RAWU activities should be at the beginning of classes. The first 10 to 20 minutes class can be used to get students' attention and infuse a dosage of listening practice. Since many classes in Taiwan have a ten-minute break between two 50-minute class blocks, a RAWU activity can be used at the beginning of the second block to refocus students' attention after the break. Teachers should not feel as if they couldn't ask students to complete other small tasks during completion of a RAWU activity. For example, once I distributed a copy of an illustrated reading material and asked students to circle the picture of all the animals that were mentioned in the story as they heard the animal's name being read aloud. In this specific example, students had to listen and circle more than forty animals.

3.4.1 Sample RAWU Reading

The reading material selected for this RAWU activity was "Stopping by Woods on a Snowy Evening" (Frost, 1969). I greeted the students and then before passing out a handout containing the reading material, briefly introduced the author (Robert Frost) and the type of reading material (poetry). In this particular activity, I asked students to "listen for the rhythm and music that Frost manages to create with words." Then I read the poem aloud to the students. As I read line by line I would paraphrase the poem's meaning. Since this was poetry, I first wanted students to understand the literal meaning of the poem. I, therefore, only paraphrased the literal meaning. Then I played the audio recording of the poem read by the poet. This finished the initial reading of the material. Then I began a question and answer time with students. I asked, "Do you hear the rhythm and the music within the poem?" and "Can you tell the difference between my reading and the poet's own recitation?"

Then I would begin the students' readings of the material. I would provide students with a handout containing the reading material. In order to have more volunteers to read aloud, I would ask each student to read only one stanza at a time. Then after individual students, the class along with the teacher read the entire poem together. I would end the activity with some praise such as "What a great job!" and encourage students to "Keep your handout as a part of your collection of RAWU activities. Every time you feel like it, just pull it out and read it aloud to yourself." I wanted to encourage students to read aloud even when not in class. I did this by asking them to read aloud to others. For example, I would often encourage them by saying, "You can read aloud to your niece or nephew or anyone else that would like to listen to you!" Lastly, I would suggest them to memorize parts of poems or other excerpts that they felt were especially meaningful to them.

4.0 Results

4.1 Willingness to Listen Questionnaire

A total of 39 questionnaires were administered in the freshmen listening and speaking class. Only those that were filled out in both the beginning and at the mid-term were considered valid. I found 37 out of 39 subjects' questionnaires were valid. The response rate is 95%. Results of the willingness to listen questionnaire showed a reliability rating above .85. The result show that students had a moderate willingness to listen at the beginning of the semester (M = 70.838) which improved by the mid-term (M = 74.541), yet still considered as being a moderate willingness to listen (see Table 1). A pairwise sample t test was performed to investigate whether students' improvement in their willingness to listen was statistically significant; results indicate that the improvement was significant (see Table 2). This means that in about 10 weeks, the RAWU activities did make a difference and significantly increased students' willingness to listen to English.

Table 1

Descriptive Statistics of Students' Willingness to Listen

	M	SD
Beginning	70.838	9.720
Mid-Term	74.541	8.761

Table 2

Students' Improvement in Terms of Their Willingness to Listen

Mean difference	t value	df	p value
-3.703	-2.497	36	.017*

Note. *Difference is significant at the 0.05 level (2-tailed)

4.2 Open Response Questionnaire

The qualitative feedback I have received from students is rather positive; more than 97% of the feedback was positive. I received qualitative feedback from 39 students. The qualitative data is discussed further in the sections that follow. The following quotes are only a few of their comments concerning RAWU activities:

"I ...learned to appreciate a poem."

"I enjoy reading poems and story books because they are very interesting."

"The most important thing is I started to read sentences loudly. I never thought it can help me learn English well..."

"RAWU not only [helps] me warm up, but also [introduces] me [to] many poems and songs. And the most important thing is it [allows]...me [to have] fun."

5.0 Reflections

From my class observations, students seemed to like this warm-up activity very much. I found that the class that participated in the RAWU activities no longer appeared drowsy or uninterested in Freshman English, as in previous classes taught. The qualitative data collected from the end of term questionnaire also points towards this conclusion as well. I felt reassured when

I read their responses. It was good to know that the RAWU activities were not only receiving their attention during class but that they were also enjoying themselves. Compared with previous Freshman English classes I have taught, this class seemed to be more focused and more alert during a mid-term three-minute show-and-tell type presentation I ask all my Freshman English classes to give. In fact, almost everyone in the class selected one of the RAWU materials to read aloud during their presentation. Students became more creative during their presentations than in previous taught classes; they, for example, recited poetry in interesting and unusual ways.

RAWU activities also allowed me to provide students with opportunities to express their opinions about topics that seldom appear in the textbooks that teachers are often required to teach from. For example, *An Awesome Book of Thanks* by Dallas Clayton encourages students to reflect on what they are thankful for. After reading, I began a reflective discussion with the question "What are you thankful for?" For another example, when I read-aloud Barrack Obama's *Of Thee I Sing: A Letter to My Daughters*, my students were introduced to thirteen outstanding people in all walks of life within a few minutes. This reading was able to succinctly express to students the potentiality that exists in us all.

Although the result of using RAWU was positive, I must caution any teachers that wish to incorporate RAWU activities in their classroom to clearly explain to students the benefits of reading aloud. In the beginning of the semester, the majority of my materials were selected from children's literature. Some students mistakenly interpreted this as my looking down on them. In fact, one student expressed: "Although we are a basic level class, we are not that low of a class. Teacher, those children's songs and rhymes are good, yet I wish I will learn something at a higher level." As a teacher, the negative comment was hard to take but this shows the importance of allowing students the opportunity to provide feedback regarding the activities we select and incorporate into our classroom regimes. This then allowed me the opportunity to discuss the purpose of the RAWU activity with students and the benefits of "children's literature" as well as begin to be more flexible in my selection of reading materials.

I incorporated the RAWU activities in my class in hopes students would become highly motivated to come to English class. Another hope was that students would not only be willing to listen to English, but they would also become confident enough to speak or read aloud in class. Quite a few of my students expressed that they are now more confident and better presenters than before. This activity has brought a lot of pleasure, and added something to my classes. Many students expressed a change of attitude toward learning English because of the RAWU activity. The following are some responses from the students:

"Now, English is my favorite subject, and I [anticipate] every Wednesday and Friday."

"I have never met [a] teacher like you. I really like this way [of learning]."

"How happ[y] I [am to] learn English. I feel that my teacher teaches very well."

"This class is so good and interesting. I am *more confident.* I really like this."

"This course encourages me to *decide to take the Open Course* on the net. The course is awesome, I have nothing to add. Thank you, professor."

"I am happy because I am in this class [and can] learn a lot of things from Kao teacher."

"Before this course, I don't have courage to speak. But I have more courage to speak English now. I'm very happy I could meet this teacher."

"I found there is *so much fun* in [learning] English! I really like it. Thank you, Teacher."

"*Please don't change the mode of teaching in the future.* I think this is an interesting class, and I hope that students in the future could be happy and learn useful English in the class."

The feedback from students provides a motivating force that encourages me to continue working on the RAWU activity. Every semester the content may not be the same, but this activity will stay in my Freshmen English classes. I will always remember to be flexible; I will constantly be looking for more interesting and timely materials that fit my students' needs. By carefully choosing some interesting materials, teachers are not only introducing students to the wonderful English world of literature, but also the cultures around the world. This is indeed a fun way to learn English!

This read out loud activity is a good approach in training listening skills as well as their reading and pronunciation skills. This being said, this investigation aimed to first initiate an interesting activity for college English language learners and once they are motivated and willing to participate in the class because of the RAWU activity, all the above-mentioned skills are likely to improve at a reasonable pace. Future additional assessments taken during a longitudinal study could help to add empirical data to further support this assumption.

5.1 Extending RAWU Beyond the Classroom

The successful results up to the mid-term encouraged me to extend the RAWU activities outside my classroom by inviting the Freshman English students to join one of the three activities held by the NCU LC Reading

Corner. The Reading Corner at NCU is a very special place; it is located on the second floor of the school library. In this area there are quite a few specially selected books for those who are interested in self-learning of the English language. I have been in charge of the Reading Corner events for the past three years. Besides being a special place designed for reading, the Reading Corner is responsible for the following read-aloud events held every semester.

The first event that's held every semester is the "RAP" (Read Aloud Program) Kindergarten Program. At the beginning of each semester, we would call for NCU students to participate in this program. Each semester there are more students applying; however, it is limited to 20 participants. There is five hours of required training before a student can go out to the neighborhood kindergartens. After successfully completing the training, students are given a schedule to read a picture book to an assigned neighborhood kindergarten once a week for five consecutive weeks. Students are also asked to keep a journal to reflect on all the books they have read to those kindergarteners. At the end of the program, they need to fill out a feedback form to aid the LC in improving this program. Students who have participated in this program report that the experience is great. Through their interaction with the children, they feel a sense of accomplishment.

The second event is the English Poetry Recitation Competition held every fall semester and the third event is the English Picture Books Read-Aloud Competition held every spring semester. Students are encouraged to join these competitions to showcase their English pronunciation and articulation skills.

6.0 Conclusion

Reading aloud to students can be beneficial to students' language skills. Students that are exposed to reading materials, especially literature, tend to read more and have better writing skills (Pitts, 1986; Krashen, 2004). Results have shown that reading aloud is extremely rewarding not only for students, but also for myself. My students are more focused in class and more interested in learning English. I will continue to incorporate RAWU activities in my Freshman English classes and be flexible in my selection of reading materials. I encourage teachers to experiment and see what works best for their classes.

References

Bloom, H. (2000). *How to Read and Why*. New York: Simon and Schuster.

Brown, M. W. (1947). *Goodnight Moon*. New York: Scholastic

Burton, V. L. (1939). *Mike Mulligan and His Steam Shovel*. Boston: Houghton Mifflin.

Burton, V. L. (1942). *The Little House*. Boston: Houghton Mifflin.

Carroll, L. (1865). *Alice's Adventures in Wonderland*. London: Penguin Books.

Clayton, D. (2010). *An Awesome Book of Thanks*. New York: AmazonEncore.

D'Aulaire, I., & Parin, E. (1962). *D'Aulaires' Book of Greek Myths*. New York: Dell Publishing.

Duncan, A. (2012, April 30). Jeremy Lin: The dreamers' Most Valuable Player. *Time*, 22.

Ferris, H. (Ed.) (1957). *Favorite Poems: Old and New*. New York: Random House

Fox, M. (2008). *Reading Magic: Why Reading Aloud to Our Children Will Change Their Lives Forever*. Orlando: Harcourt.

Fox, M. (1993). *Radical Reflections: Passionate Opinions on Teaching, Learning, and Living*. San Diego: Harcourt.

Frost, R. (1969). *The Poetry of Robert Frost*. New York: Holt, Rinehart and Winston.

Geisel, T. S. (1940). *Horton Hatches the Egg*. New York: Random House.

Geisel, T. S. (1997). *Seuss-isms: Wise and Witty Prescriptions for Living from the Good Doctor*. New York: Random House.

Hesse, K. (1997). *Out of the Dust*. New York: Scholastic Inc.

Krashen, S. D. (2004). *The Power of Reading: Insights from the Research*. Portsmouth: Heinemann.

London, J. (1903). *The Call of the Wild*. New York: The Macmillan Company.

Nodelman, P. (2008). *The Hidden Adult: Defining Children's Literature*. Baltimore: The Johns Hopkins University Press.

Nodelman, P. (1996). *The Pleasures of Children's Literature,* Second Edition. New York: Longman.

Obama, B. (2010). *Of Thee I Sing*. New York: Alfred A. Knopf.

Pene du Bois, W. (1947). *The Twenty-One Balloons*. New York: Viking Penguin.

Pitts, S. D. (1986). Read Aloud to Adult Learners? Of Course! *Reading Psychology, 7* (1), 35-42.

Prelutsky, J. (2008). *Be Glad Your Nose is on Your Face and Other Poems.* New York: Harper Collins.

Prelutsky, J. (2000). *It's Raining Pigs & Noodles.* New York: Scholastic.

Richmond, V. P., & Hickson, M. III. (2001). *Going public: A practical guide to public talk.* Boston: Allyn & Bacon.

Rowling, J. K. (1997). *Harry Potter and the Sorcerer's Stone.* New York: Scholastic.

Rowling, J. K. (1998). *Harry Potter and the Chamber of Secrets.* New York: Scholastic.

Rowling, J. K. (1999). *Harry Potter and the Prisoner of Azkaban.* New York: Scholastic.

Rowling, J. K. (2000). *Harry Potter and the Goblet of Fire.* New York: Scholastic.

Rowling, J. K. (2003). *Harry Potter and the Order of the Phoenix.* New York: Scholastic.

Rowling, J. K. (2005). *Harry Potter and the Half-Blood Prince.* New York: Scholastic.

Rowling, J. K. (2007). *Harry Potter and the Deathly Hallows.* New York: Scholastic.

Russell, W. F. (1984). *Classics to Read Aloud to Your Children.* New York: Crown Publishers, Inc.

Schier, J. (2012, May). Another Taiwanese Star on the Rise. *ALL+, 90* (5), 34-37.

Short, R. L. (2008). *The Parables of Dr. Seuss.* Louisville: WJK Press.

Schulman, J. (Ed.) (1998). *The 20th Century Children's Book Treasury: Celebrated Picture Books and Stories to Read Aloud.* New York: Alfred A. Knopf.

Sierra, J. (2004). *Wild About Books.* New York: Alfred A. Knopf.

Silverman, R., Crandell, J., & Carlis, L. (2013). Read Alouds and Beyond: The Effects of Read Aloud Extension Activities on Vocabulary in Head Start Classrooms. *Early Education and Development, 24* (2), 98-122.

Silverstein, S. (1981). *A Light in the Attic.* New York: Harper & Row.

Silverstein, S. (1996). *Falling Up.* New York: Harper Collins.

Silverstein, S (1974). *Where the Sidewalk Ends.* New York: Harper Collins.

Silvey, A. (2004). *100 Best Books for Children: A Parent's Guide to Making the Right Choices for your Young Reader, Toddler to Preteen.* Boston: Houghton Mifflin.

Silvey, A. (Ed.) (2002). *The Essential Guide to Children's Books and Their Creators.* Boston: Houghton Mifflin.

Silvey, A. (Ed.) (2009). *Everything I Need to Know I Learned from a Children's Book: Life Lessons from Notable People from All Walks of Life.* New York: Roaring Brook Press.

Spinelli, J. (2010). *I Can Be Anything.* New York: Little, Brown and Company.

Spinelli, J. (1999). *Maniac Magee.* New York: Little, Brown and Company.

Tomlinson, C. M., & Lynch-Brown, C. (1996). *Essentials of Children's Literature,* Second Edition. Boston: Allyn and Bacon.

Trelease, J. (2006). *The Read-Aloud Handbook,* Sixth Edition. New York: Penguin.

Tunnell, M. O., Jacobs, J. S., & Young, Terrell A., & Bryan, Gregory W. (2012). *Children's Literature, Briefly,* Fifth Edition. Boston: Pearson.

Twain, M. (1959). *The Adventures of Huckleberry Finn.* New York: The New American Library.

Appendix A

A List of Some Materials Used in a RAWU Activity

1. "Why English is sometimes called a 'stupid' or nonsensical language"
2. "It Couldn't Be Done" by Edgar A. Guest
3. "The Windmill" by Henry Wadsworth Longfellow
4. Quotations from *Life of Pi* by Yan Martel
5. "Sick" and "Ickle Me, Pickle Me, Tickle Me Too" From *Where the Sidewalk Ends* by Shel Silverstein
6. "Stopping by Woods on a Snowy Evening" by Robert Frost
7. "El Condor Pasa" by Paul Simon
8. "The Sound of Silence" by Paul Simon
9. "Letter to Bee" by Emily Dickinson
10. "Hurt No Living Thing" by Christina Rossetti
11. "The Dentist and the Crocodile" by Roald Dahl
12. "Jeremy Lin: The dreamers' Most Valuable Player" by Arne Duncan
13. "Another Taiwanese Star on the Rise?" by Joseph Schier
14. "Edelweiss" by Richard Rodgers/Oscar Hammerstein II
15. "The Lake Isle of Innisfree" by William Butler Yeats
16. "To a Squirrel at Kyle-Na-No" by W. B. Yeaats
17. "The Squirrel" (Anonymous)
18. *Wild About Books* by Judy Sierra
19. "The Chicken And The Princess: A fairy tale" and "No More Woxes: A short Tall Tale" from *I'll be You and You be Me* by Ruth Krauss
20. *Alexander and the Terrible, Horrible, No Good, Very Bad Day* by Judith Viorst
21. *I Can Be Anything* by Jerry Spinelli *There's No Place Like Home* by Marc Brown

22. *In a People House* by Theo LeSieg.

23. *Different Homes Around the World* by Pamela Rushby

24. *Of Thee I Sing* by Barack Obama

25. *Classics to Read Aloud to Your Children* (1984) edited by William F. Russell

26. *Oh, the Thinks you Can Think!* by Dr. Seuss

27. *Seuss-isms: Wise and Witty Prescriptions for Living from the Good Doctor* by Dr. Seuss

28. *The Enormous Crocodile* by Roald Dahl

29. *Anatole* by Eve Titus

30. Poems from *It's Raining Pigs & Noodles* by Jack Prelutsky

31. Poems from *I Like It Here At School: 26 Poems Collected and Introduced by Jack Prelutsky*

32. *Fancy Nancy's Favorite Fancy Words: From Accessories to Zany* by Jane O'Commor & Robin Glasser

33. *An Awesome Book of Thanks!* by Dallas Clayton

34. *Oh, Baby, the Places You'll Go!: A Book to be Read in Utero* adapted by Tish Rabe

35. *A Light in the Attic* (1981) by Shel Silverstein

36. *Falling Up* by Shel Silverstein

37. *"A Visit from St. Nicholas"* by Clement Clarke Moore

38. *"The Fly is In"*, *"Strange Wind"* by Shel Silverstein

39. *An Awesome Book of Thanks* by Dallas Clayton

40. "How to Boost Your Brain Power" an article from Unit 9 of *Hemispheres 3*

41. "I'm Caught Up in Infinity" by Jack Prelutsky

42. "My Sister Shrieked, Astonished" by Jack Prelutsky

43. "No" by Shel Silverstein

44. "Strange Wind" by Shel Silverstein

45. "One Out of Sixteen" by Shel Silverstein

46. "The Monkey" by Shel Silverstein

47. "It Was a Sound" by Jack Prelutsky

48. "I Am Inside a Seashell" by Jack Prelutsky

49. "I like to see it lap the miles" by Emily Dickinson

50. "The Road Not Taken" by Robert Frost

51. "Life is Fine" by Langston Hughes

52. "A Psalm of Life" by Henry Wadsworth Longfellow

53. "All the World's a Stage" by William Shakespeare

54. "The Raven" by Edgar Allan Poe

55. "Father William" by Lewis Carroll

56. "The Tyger" by William Blake

57. "A Wise Old Owl" by Edward Hersey Richards

58. "Dreams" by Langston Hughes

59. "The Raven" by Edgar Allen Poe

60. "The Eagle" by Alfred Lord Tennyson

Appendix B
Willingness to Listen Questionnaire

填答注意事項：以下有24個與聽故事相關的敘述；提醒您注意的是，在問題裡只提到「說／念／朗誦 故事」，實際上在課堂裡老師會挑各種不同的材料或文本念給大家聽。請根據自己的狀況寫下符合自己意願的數字：

非常不同意 = 1；不同意 = 2；沒有意見 = 3；同意 = 4；非常同意 = 5

Directions: The following twenty-four statements refer to listening to a narrator (someone who reads aloud to you). Although the questions mention 'storyteller', keep in mind the materials read to you are not limited to stories only. Please indicate the degree to which each statement applies to you by marking whether you:

Strongly Disagree = 1; Disagree = 2; are Neutral =3; Agree = 4; Strongly Agree = 5

_____1. I dislike listening to a boring storyteller.
　　　　我不喜歡聽無聊的人說故事。

_____2. Generally, I can listen to a boring storyteller.
　　　　大體來說，我可以聽無聊的人說故事。

_____3. I am bored and tired while listening to a storyteller.
　　　　當我聽人說故事時，我感到無聊和疲倦。

_____4. I will listen when the content of a story is boring.
　　　　當故事內容無聊時，我還是會聽。

_____5. Listening to a boring storyteller about boring content makes me tired, sleepy, and bored.
　　　　聽無聊的人說無聊的故事內容令我疲倦、想睡及無聊。

_____6. I am willing to listen to a boring storyteller about boring content.
　　　　我願意聆聽無聊的人說無聊的故事內容。

_____7. Generally, I am unwilling to listen when there is noise during a storyteller's reading.

大體來說，當說故事的人朗誦時有噪音，我不願意聽下去。

_____8. Usually, I am willing to listen when there is noise during a storyteller's reading.

通常來說，當說故事的人朗誦時有噪音，我會願意聽下去。

_____9. I am accepting and willing to listen to storytellers who do not adapt to me.

我願意聆聽，也可以接受我不適應的人說故事。

_____10. I am unwilling to listen to storytellers who do not adapt for me.

我不願意聆聽我不適應的人說故事。

_____11. Being preoccupied with other things makes me less willing to listen to a storyteller.

當我心不在焉時，我較不願意聽故事。

_____12. I am willing to listen to a storyteller even if I have other things on my mind.

即使是我心裡想著其他事時，我還是願意聽故事。

_____13. While being occupied with other things on my mind, I am unwilling to listen to a storyteller.

當我心裡想著其他事時，我不願意聽故事。

_____14. I have a willingness to listen to a storyteller, even if other important things are on my mind.

即使我心裡想著其他重要的事情，我還是願意聽故事。

_____15. Generally, I will not listen to a storyteller who is disorganized.

大體來說，我不願意聆聽說話沒組織的人說故事。

_____16. Generally, I will try to listen to a storyteller who is disorganized.

大體來說，我還是會試著聆聽說話沒組織的人說故事。

_____17. While listening to a non-responsive storyteller, I feel relaxed with the storyteller.

當我聆聽沒有情緒反應的人說故事，我對這個人感到比較輕鬆。

_____18. While listening to a non-responsive storyteller, I feel distant and cold toward that storyteller.

當我聆聽沒有情緒反應的人說故事，我會覺得和這個冷漠的人有距離。

_____19. I can listen to non-responsive storyteller.

我可以聆聽沒有情緒反應的人說故事。

_____20. I am unwilling to listen to a non-responsive storyteller.

我不願聽沒有情緒反應的人說故事。

_____21. I am willing to listen to a storyteller with views different from mine.

我願意聆聽和我有不同觀點的人說故事。

_____22. I am unwilling to listen to a storyteller with views different from mine.

我不願意聆聽和我有不同觀點的人說故事。

_____23. I am willing to listen to a storyteller who is not clear about what he or she wants to say.

即使說故事的人不清楚自己在說什麼，我還是願意聽。

_____24. I am unwilling to listen to a storyteller who is not clear, not credible, and abstract.

我不願意聆聽說話不清楚、不可靠、及很難讓人了解的人說故事。

移民數位華語讀寫課程模式與特色探究

黃湘玲、林青蓉 、許秀娟、鄭淑眞
社團法人台灣來去華語協會、社團法人嘉義縣扶緣服務協會
nnerse@gmail.com、applegirlhaho@gmail.com、 rlfrance0430@gmail.com、
jet3456@gmail.com

摘要

數位化世代裡，移民華語學習隨之有了漸次性的改變。過去，數位華語學習教材多所著重口語表達能力的訓練，然「來去華語100句」數位學習平台為能符應在台移民對於讀寫需求的集體文化特性，將漢字納入學習（鍾鎮城，2012）。究此，本研究目的為：探討移民華語教師使用「來去華語100句」平台發展數位讀寫課程模式與特色。研究問題有二：第一，移民華語教師如何使用此平台進行讀寫課程規劃？第二，此移民數位華語讀寫課程所呈現的特色為何？

本研究以2011年9月迄2012年8月，社團法人台灣來去華語協會所開設之10個班別為主要研究對象，研究參與者計有9位教師，118位學習者，採用問卷調查及課堂觀察等方法搜集資料，以利分析論述。研究結果顯示，移民華語教師在規劃數位讀寫課程時，除因考量數位落差因素，佐以資訊素養教學外，並發展了數位教材紙本化，紙本資源數位化雙向度課程。另從課程實踐歷程可看出，教師多採功能性觀點來設計數位讀寫教材，此回應了「來去華語100句」教材編輯初衷：提升在台移民職場競爭力與公民意識，這也成為了移民數位華語讀寫課程之最大特色。

關鍵詞：數位華語、移民華語、讀寫課程、來去華語100句

The Inquiry of Immigrants E-Learning Literacy Program and Features

Xiang-Ling Huang, Qing-Rong Lin, Hsiu-Chuan Hsu, Shu-Chen Cheng
nnerse@gmail.com, applegirlhaho@gmail.com, rlfrance0430@gmail.com,
jet3456@gmail.com

In this digital age, teaching Chinese to immigrants has gradually changed directions. In the past, digital teaching material for teaching Chinese primarily focused on training speaking abilities, but the digital learning platform "Lai-Qu Huayu 100 Sentences" incorporates Chinese characters into the learning process to satisfy the collective reading and writing requirements of immigrants in Taiwan (Chun, 2012). The purpose of this study is to discuss how Chinese teachers of immigrants utilize the platform "Lai-Qu Huayu 100 Sentences" to design curriculum models and features for reading and writing classes. There are two research questions guiding this study: Firstly, how do Chinese teachers of immigrants utilize this platform for the curriculum design of reading and writing classes? Secondly, what are the special characteristics of these digital reading and writing classes aimed at immigrants?

This research took place from September 2011 to August 2012, and the main research subjects were the 10 classes taught by the Association of Taiwan Lai-Qu Huayu. Research participants included 9 teachers and 118 students. Information was collected via questionnaires and class observations for better analysis and discussions. The research findings show that when Chinese teachers of immigrants design the curriculum for reading and writing classes, in addition to information literacy teaching due to the digital divide, the teachers also created hard copies of digital material as well as digitalized paper resources. In addition, as can be seen from the implemen-tation of the curriculum, the teachers designed the digital reading/writing material mainly based on functionality. This fulfills the original purpose of the teaching material editor at "Lai-Qu Huayu 100 Sentences," which is to increase the competitiveness of immigrants in Taiwan and raise public awareness.

Keywords: Digital Chinese, Chinese for immigrants, reading/writing classes,
Lai-Qu Huayu 100 Sentences

研究背景與目的

所謂數位學習（e-learning）即是透過網際網路或各式數位載具進行學習，對於語言學習來說，數位科技可免除紙本教材地域性的限制，並藉由影音媒材提供多樣化的學習模式，也因而數位教材往往可在口語表達能力的提升上，達到立竿見影的效益。

華語數位學習隨著這波浪潮，因應遠距及自學等需求，而漸次發展出各類數位華語學習平台。社團法人台灣來去華語協會（以下簡稱本會）於2010年與經濟部資訊工業策進會合作，研製台灣第一套針對在移民的數位華語平台「來去華語100句」（附錄一），開創移民數位華語學習之先鋒。該平台設計概念雖是以口語表達能力為主要的學習目標，但為能符應在台移民對於讀寫需求的集體文化特性，因而，加入了漢字練習，此一殊性也讓原本以口語表達為主的課程，自然融入了讀寫學習元素，終致呈現了截然不同的數位華語讀寫課程樣貌。本研究目的即是，探討移民華語教師使用「來去華語100句」平台後，所發展的數位讀寫課程模式與特色。研究問題有二：

移民華語教師如何使用此平台進行讀寫課程規劃？

此移民數位華語讀寫課程所呈現的特色為何？

文獻探討

（一）移民華語讀寫發展

目前，華語讀寫研究領域，關於移民華語讀寫的探究主要集中於識字和閱讀兩個區塊，前者有各類型成人教育班，強調透過識字能力的重要性，但識字是否能夠延續到讀寫能力有待商榷。後者，則如透過閱讀差異分析（Reading Miscue Analysis），來探討學習者在進行華語閱讀時所採行的策略（孫劍秋、林文韵，2010）。或是同樣以閱讀差異分析為基礎，所設計的多媒體閱讀課程（吳靜芬，2011）。另外，也有彭妮絲（2011）著眼於系統功能語言學，融合雙語合作統整閱讀理解模式進行閱讀教學。然而上列研究對象均為各大專院校語文中心的外籍學生，與本研究所聚焦的移民學習者並不相同，而談及移民華語讀寫，鍾鎮城、黃湘玲（2009）曾指出移民在進行口語、書面語的個別或跨層面語言轉換時，均會使用多種語言來幫助其華語的讀寫習得。綜合上列文獻，可得知當前針對移民華語讀寫課程所進行的研究為數有限。

（二）移民數位華語學習歷程

數位式語言學習因為不受時間、空間限制，亦可反覆操作或旁及其他資源進行擴充，近年來成為廣泛使用的學習媒介，林麗娟（2011）指出學生學習華語的數位資源多元，因為使用頻繁，所以熟悉以拼音方式進行文書輸入，也偏好透過網路等各種數位媒介取得文化相關之資訊。張于忻（2010）認為高學習成效的數位化教材需具模組化特性，將主題切割成彼此有相互關聯的小單位，並用有意義的彈性結構，如學習認知、內容、情境、過程技能等要素串起，教師可引導學員反覆操作使用。不過，這類數位資源的使用和操作方式多是針對因課業、商業需求、語言進修的學習者設立，並無法完全貼合移民學習者的學習特性與需求。

在移民數位華語學習方面，除了語言學習，有時還得同步處理學習者資訊素養（Information Literacy）和數位落差（Digital Divide）的問題。例如，黃湘玲（2012）便曾指出基本資訊設備、數位華語平台內容、學習者資訊素養及教師數位華語教學專業知能四者，造成數位落差，也是教師要實行數位華語課程所要面對的挑戰。因應這樣的挑戰，許雅雯、周怡均（2012）則探討數位與紙本教學並存之模式，發現當學習者對於數位操作不夠熟悉或是不習慣長時間使用數位設備時，容易產生疲憊和焦慮感，但搭配紙本教材的混合使用，可降低學習上的不安情緒。

（三）來去華語100句

　　因本研究旨在探討移民華語教師使用「來去華語100句」平台發展數位讀寫課程模式與特色，故針對「來去華語100句」數位華語學習平台作一簡單說明，此數位華語學習平台在學習目標上設定為提升口語表達能力，同時為了讓「主題句」與移民生活經驗相聯結，將「情境動畫」置首，也就是提供語言情境來促成實用性，而後，依序透過詞語、漢字及語音辨別來進行學習（附錄一）。

研究方法

（一）研究期程及參與者資料分析

　　本研究資料搜集期程自2011年9月迄2012年8月，以本會於台灣各地所推動之10個數位華語課程為主，包含9位授課教師，以及118人次學習者。10個移民數位華語課程分別與不同的在地組織或學校單位合作，相關資料請見下頁表1。

　　參與本研究教師共計9位，其中半數左右同時橫跨兩個場域之教學或管理職責：教師AT1同時負責BS課程總體規劃與評估，並身兼AS課程規劃與授課教師；教師CT同時擔任CS與FS授課教師；教師DT1除了是DS授課教師外，亦為BS輔導員；教師AT2同時身兼AS與ES助理教師。表2是9位教師的基本資料介紹，以及編碼形式。

　　至於參與本研究之118位學習者，僅27位未曾有過華語學習經驗，代表三分之二以上的學習者瞭解華語課程，至於數位華語課程參與經驗僅有5位勾選，特別說明的是，本研究並未採計學習者參與一般電腦班資料，因考量電腦班多以資訊技能操作教學為主，與本研究所欲探討：以華語為學習媒介的數位學習內容，在概念上並不相符。表3與表4為根據學習者基本統計表中，提列出華語能力自評與學習主題調查前五項，兩相對比可論證：移民學習者對於讀寫的渴望性，而學習主題中以電腦科技居冠，更可為數位華語讀寫課程的必要性立

表1 數位華語課程場域資料表

課程場域代號	課程場域（合作單位）	學習者／教師人數	課程期別與時數
AS	嘉義縣扶緣服務協會，開設移民華語課程5年以上	學習者人次（註1）：AS1-AS41，共計41位	第一期：2011/10-12 共計30小時 第二期：2012/03-06 共計48小時
AS		教師人數（註2）：教師計有2位	
BS	高雄市三民區愛國國小，開設成人教育班10年以上	學習者人次：BS1-BS22，共計22位	第一期：2011/10-12 共計24小時 第二期：2012/03-06 共計24小時
BS		教師人數：教師計有4位	
CS	高雄市鳳山區忠孝國小，中斷成人教育班約10年	學習者人次：CS1-CS5，共計5位	2011/09-11，共計72小時
CS		教師人數：教師計有3位	
DS	高雄市新移民家庭教育中心，未曾開設移民華語班	學習者人次：DS1-DS15，共計15位	第一期：2011/11-12 共計24小時 第二期：2012/07-08 共計24小時
DS		教師人數：教師計有2位	
ES	台中市西區忠信國小，開設成人教育班10年以上	學習者人次：ES1-ES29，共計29位	第一期：2011/10-12 共計20小時 第二期：2012/03-06，共計30小時
ES		教師人數：教師計有1位	
FS	台南市疼厝邊協會，5年以上未開設移民華語課程	學習者人次：FS1-FS6，共計6位	2012/03-06，共計36小時
FS		教師人數：教師計有1位	

註1：學習者人次含連續兩期上課之學習者
註2：教師人數總計13位，但當中有4位橫跨兩個服務場域，因此總人次應為9位
資料來源：研究者根據課程計畫整理而成

表2 移民華語教師基本背景表

教師代號	服務地點（合作單位）	最高學歷	可使用語言	移民華語教學年資	移民數位華語教學資歷
AT1	嘉義縣扶緣服務協會	華語教學碩士	華語、英語、閩南語	4年	數位華語教師，以及「來去華語100句」教材編輯
AT2	嘉義縣扶緣服務協會	中文系學士	華語、英語、閩南語	1年	無
BT1	高雄市愛國國小	企管系學士	華語、英語、閩南語	0.5年	無
BT2	高雄市愛國國小	教育所博士	華語、英語、閩南語	0.5年	無
BT3	高雄市愛國國小	俄文所博士	華語、英語、閩南語、俄語	0.5年	無
CT	高雄市鳳山區忠孝國小暨台南疼厝邊協會	華語所在學中	華語、英語、閩南語、法語	1.5年	曾擔任數位華語教學實證點教師
DT1	高雄新移民家庭服務中心暨高雄市愛國國小	華語所在學中	華語、英語、閩南語、西班牙語	3年	「來去華語100句」教材編輯與錄音
DT2	高雄新移民家庭服務中心暨高雄市愛國國小	華語所在學中	華語、英語、閩南語、西班牙語	0.5年	無
ET	台中市西區忠信國小	華語所在學中	華語、英語、閩南語	2年	「來去華語100句」教材編輯

資料來源：研究者根據教師基本資料表整理而成

表3 學習者自評學習華語最感困難的一部分統計表

	聽	說	讀	寫	其他
人數	10	15	10	80	3（注音）
比例	8.5%	12.7%	8.5%	67.8%	0.2%

資料來源：研究者根據學習者基本資料表整理而成

表4 學習主題需求統計表

排序	一	二	三	四	五
主題	電腦科技	中文閱讀	中文寫作	家庭教育	法律規定／口語表達
人數	78	74	69	61	55
比例	66.1%	62.7%	58.5%	51.7%	46.6%

資料來源：研究者根據學習者基本資料表整理而成

基。

（二）研究資料分析與編碼

　　本研究均已取得所有研究參與者之同意函，為能確實瞭解各地數位華語讀寫課程建構歷程，本研究採問卷調查、正式與非正式訪談及文件分析三種方法來蒐集研究資料，繼而進行編碼分析與主題彙整。以下分項說明：

1. 問卷調查與分析

　　本研究於各地課程結束前針對移民華語教師及學習者進行問卷調查，總計教師問卷為9份，學習者方面的有效問卷為118份，問卷調查內容包含基本背景資料、學習主題、華語能力自評以及參與本數位華語課程之使用回饋。

2. 正式與非正式訪談與分析

　　為能更深入地瞭解教師如何處理數位學習落差，本研究採取正式與非正式訪談以收集資料，分別與每位教師進行一次半結構式訪談，與數次非正式訪談。訪談題目以教師如何以「來去華語100句」來建構學習者數位讀寫能力。訪談內容先以逐字稿形式譯出，再編碼統整，以利主題分析。學習者部分則採非正式訪談，至於訪談內容則融入研究者課堂觀察日誌裡。

3. 文件收集與分析

　　除了問卷調查及訪談外，本研究亦透過文件收集來完備研究資料，其來源包含移民華語教師日誌、研究者觀察日誌、以及學生數位學華語學習作品等等，以便有系統的深究數位華語讀寫課程脈絡。以下將針對研究調查成果，進行系統性的分析與探究。

研究結果

　　本研究旨在探討與分析影響移民華語教師建構數位讀寫課程運作之因素，及其課程之特性。據此發現，教師之華語讀寫教學知能、學習者之資訊素養二者，深深影響數位華語讀寫課程的內涵。以下分就數位華語閱讀與數位華語寫作兩部分逐次討論，最後歸納移民數位華語讀寫教學模式之特性。

（一）數位華語閱讀

　　網際網路及各式數位載具作為學習素材，無論居主副位，往往在課程初期就能誘發極高的學習動機，這點與本會過去所調查的學習主題需求，「電腦科技」始終高踞榜首不謀而合（鍾鳳嬌、林苑平、趙善如，2008）。究其緣由，學習者身處數位學習世代浪潮，無論於職場或家庭裡，數位工具比比皆是。然而，學習者資訊近用能力與素養，卻是直接與間接的影響數位華語讀寫課程發展樣貌。例如，當課程進入第四週，多數學生已經習慣使用「來去華語100句」的操作介面，但仍經常可聽到教室裡傳來：「老師！我要怎麼回去？」，此句意指如何操作滑鼠回到上一個頁面，或是當課程進入自學階段，由學習者操作平台時，幾個學生看似有興趣，但仍沒太多的行動，細問之下，得到的回應是：「老師！我沒辦法一直看電腦，很累！」這類回應充分顯示如學習者過去接觸數位學習課程經驗有限，加諸資訊素養不足，首當其衝就是教師必得權衡以調整數位課程模式。

綜觀10個班別，皆可看到教師透過各式各樣的方法，促使學習者逐步由紙本學習進入數位學習，包括融入部分時數的數位資訊技能教學、或讓學習者藉由打字練習來熟悉鍵盤位置。此一措舉，可謂先滿足學習者對於接觸數位資訊的渴望，進而加深數位讀寫內涵。以教師DT1為例，她結合舊版「來去華語100句」[1]帳號申請需要電子信箱一事，發展成數位讀寫小活動，同時促成同儕相互砥礪學習。

> 在完成email申請後，我要學生們先寫信給對方，然後再寄一封信給我，學得比較快的人，馬上還開始使用了email上面的文字編輯功能（我們上週教了一些WORD的簡單編輯功能）。DS3和DS9還馬上使用起Google talk對話，而且相約回家後還可以這樣練習，她們都相當興奮。教過幾次這樣的數位學習後，我已經相當熟悉這種「從零開始」的電腦學習，對於我們平常已經使用得很熟悉且習慣的工具，在進行教學時，著實要花更多的心思，將自己置於學生的角度去思考。
>
> （20111124，教師DT1，教師日誌）

此外，所有教師皆在課程開始時，先透過統一投影方式，讓全班共同學習主要句子，再以小組或個別的方式學習。以「請你到老闆的辦公室」這句為例，教師提供幾個討論句，以此探討該句所蘊含的職場相關資訊。在此同時，教師則把討論過程中的關鍵詞彙、生難字詞寫在黑板上，進行細部的詞彙或語法釐清。在這過程中，可看到數位華語教室內，閱讀包含了兩個介面，一個是螢幕，一個是黑板。而螢幕多以橫向書寫，黑板則採直書呈現，對學習者來說已無閱讀轉換的

---

1 「來去華語100句」甫推出時需要下載軟體方能使用，而申請帳號流程與一般網站相同，需要提供個人資料和電子信箱，多數移民學習者並無電子信箱，因此教師必須將此放入教學內。爾後，「來去華語100句」於2012年7月改版，可直接線上操作，帳號申請流程也簡化許多。

圖1 統一投影，共同討論。　　　圖2 螢幕與黑板雙閱讀。

資料來源：皆為教師AT2提供

困難。相反的，由於教師同始採用兩種工具，反而能讓學生不必時時緊盯螢幕，達到紓緩視力的效果。

　　而中央廣播這樣的小舉動，除了幫助學生快速掌握今日學習重點外，更能透過教師點擊與移動滑鼠，來協助學習者跟著滑鼠，搭配教師或平台語音，讓閱讀與詞組概念、語音知覺及漢字辨知三項能力同時並存發展。而在全班討論後，每個場域的教師都會保留30分鐘以上的自學時間，讓學習者或獨立或小組操作平台，教師則在此時間進行個別學習進度確認。就數位閱讀模式與成效來分析，學習者可從示範中做效，在華語語言知識提升的同時，資訊素養也跟著啟動。

　　上述數位閱讀課程內容呈現的是以「句子」為本的閱讀，意即著重在詞組與語法構成的句式，也是「來去華語100句」最為根本的學習目標。惟放入一個有系統的讀寫課程中，就能看到教師會針對學習者程度發展出篇章閱讀，以及進行閱讀理解教學。從教師CT的日誌中，也可看出教師之讀寫教學專業知能，促其在使用以「句子」為本的數位教材的同時，不斷思考如何透過課程建構歷程，讓句式學習得以發展至篇章閱讀，此乃提升學習者讀寫能力重要的關鍵。

　　CS4寫練習單時，要是我給的任務是寫下一個字，她會自動擴充成一個詞，要是給的任務是寫下一個詞，她就會自動擴充成一個句子，總是不斷地在給自己挑戰……。不過這些句子都是「來去華語100句」裡出來的單句，看到這樣的狀況，讓我思考是否應該帶領他們學習成篇的能力？

（20111022，教師CT，教師日誌）

承上概念再探，教師AT1以「那個人是網路賣家嗎？」一句為本，在第一堂課讓全班理解此句的用法後，掙脫常見的造句練習，而自編短文進行簡單的閱讀理解策略教學，當中可看出文章融合移民生活經驗，而由其題型設計則可見主要的閱讀理解在於直接訊息提取，以及間接資訊整合能力，例如排列事件順序（圖3）。儘管這是一堂數位學習課程，合該讀、寫兩者皆數位化，但誠如前列所言，對第二語言學習者來說，輸出（寫作）數位化，比起輸入（閱讀）更為艱巨，這部分會在下一小節有更深入的討論，因此，這篇購物小祕訣篇章學習，融合了數位與紙本方式呈現，照樣先透過中控系統全班共讀

購物小秘訣

姓名:__________

那個人是網路賣家嗎?

美華來自越南，她的皮膚白白嫩嫩的，很多朋友都稱讚她有很棒的膚質。最近，美華因為參加了電腦班，想要透過電腦增加收入。所以，她決定在網路上販賣美容用品。她先在奇摩拍賣註冊帳號，再將越南保養品拍照，最後將照片上傳到網路上。果然，一下子就吸引許多買家來詢問，其中，讓美華很驚訝的是有許多越南姐妹也來購買，包括彩晶和阿黎。因為美華的網路生意做得非常好，最後，她還為了買家設計貴賓卡，可以說是一位非常有生意頭腦的賣家。

※**選擇題**

1.(　)請問美華是網路賣家嗎? (1)是(2)不是。

2.(　)請問彩晶是網路賣家嗎? (1)是(2)不是。

3.(　)「很多朋友都稱讚她有很棒的膚質。」請問「稱讚」可以用哪個詞語替代?
(1)稱呼(2)讚賞(3)贊成(4)批評

4.(　)請依據文章，排列事件順序:
甲、美華設計貴賓卡。

圖3 數位閱讀篇章學習——那個人是網路賣家嗎？

資料來源：教師AT1提供

並討論，而後再發下紙本篇章，讓學習者書寫。

（二）數位華語寫作

　　觸及數位寫作，若論第一語言研究，普遍強調透過一個數位寫作教學平台，讓學習者的寫作歷程數位化，並藉由電腦的佈大記憶空間來換取人腦的短暫記憶。換句話說，學習者的認知歷程可外化到螢幕來呈現，如此可降低寫作負擔（廖本裕，2010）。至於第二語言寫作，則因考慮學習者的華語能力，因此多採寫作為主，多媒體教材為輔的概念來進行教學設計。

　　將焦點置放於移民數位讀寫課程，則仍須回歸到移民資訊素養與華語能力兩大判準，教師在進行課程規劃時，勢必得考慮上述兩點，以及因移民在台生活而產生的公民讀寫素養需求（鍾鎮城，2012），也就是說移民數位華語寫作歷程有了階段性與強烈的特殊性。先論數位華語寫作階段性，在以「來去華語100句」為主要教材的前提下，師生所建構的寫作內容必定以此為範疇，也因為透過句子來建構篇章，因而能滿足初學者以及進階學習等混能需求，從句子理解到仿寫這階段，教師往往讓學習者選擇寫在「來去華語100句」學習手冊[2]或結合WORD教學。前者，是因為能避免數位操作所帶來的干擾，讓學習者專注在句子仿寫與做練習，但後者的學習模式，則使數位資訊轉變成助力，其可提供學習者電腦檢索同音字的功能，再次辨認字型，但無論教師採用何者轉換形式，都無損以學習者為中心的句子創寫課程設計。

　　無獨有偶，與上述相同的數位寫作創作是結合母親節，教師BT2連結「來去華語100句」的親子教養議題，在教授過「我好喜歡女兒

---

2 「來去華語100句」於2010年建置完畢時只有數位平台，但在實證教學之後，發現移民學習者無法全時使用數位平台，仍需要紙本教材來輔助自學，因而於2011年7月正式製作紙本化學習手冊，內容編排與平台內容一致，但增加了索引及「短語仿作書寫」兩部分。

圖4 學習者同步使用網路及學習手冊。　　圖5 教師自行設計的手冊。

資料來源：教師AT1提供

的作品」後設計一個書寫母親卡的活動，意欲讓學習者的「兒女」角色得到情感抒發，因而讓他們試著寫母親卡，當然，正式書寫前也進行一番信件格式教學。同一場域的教師DT2於日誌中所言「BS14與其他人的書寫順序不同，她選擇先在電腦上打字，確定自己寫的字對不對，然後才寫在卡片上。」（20120509，DT2，教師日誌）

　　再進一層分析探究移民華語教師所設計的數位寫作類型，則可發現與第一語言寫作教學，在文體的選擇上有著極大的差異性，慣常在第一語言寫作中順位在前的記敘文，在移民華語寫作課程裡卻非如此；反之，應用文的寫作素材設計與應用處處可見。以場域CT為例，由於學習者資訊素養較佳，因此，無論讀與寫、教與學，幾乎可百分百數位化，從教師日誌記錄可清楚勾勒出現場的數位寫作樣貌：「接著是判別找工作時應答之間的禮貌對話，這個部分也與先前引起動機時那三句關於禮貌的句子環環相扣。在對於求職時該說的話有了一些基本概念後，學生們就開始在電腦上打出自己的求職信，最後並以一段專家對於找工作時容易犯的錯的影片作結束。」（20120521，教師CT，教師日誌）而談及多元文化主題下的「我昨天和同事一起去媽祖廟了」一句，教師AT1便設計了簡易的許願卡，讓學生選擇打字或直接手寫的方式（圖6）。或如教師AT2設計了簡訊發送活動，讓學生試著透過簡訊書寫傳達感謝或致歉，圖7則是學生將手機簡訊紙本化的成品，上述種種皆能看出教師因應數位落差現象，所調整後的數位讀寫課程進行方式與成果（黃湘玲，2012）。

　　除了各式應用書寫練習外，也有教師採用多元智能觀，讓數位讀寫與表演藝術相結合。教師 ET 便是如此，她將句子與劇本結合，讓單一句子以會話創作的方式呈現，輔以角色扮演，加上剪貼圖畫，變成了兼具各項能力發展的寫作活動。進而言之，析論移民華語教師所設計的數位寫作活動理念，可見教師經常有意及無意地凸顯功能性書寫的重要性，也就是促使學習者藉由此寫作歷程，達成個人發展或參與社會的目的。換句話說，移民華語教師在規劃寫作課程時，考量的不僅是單純的語言學習，而是透過寫作來帶動培力（empowerment），涵養其公民讀寫素養。誠如教師 ET 結合時下流行的「減肥議題」，以「我是愛運動的媽媽」為發展核心，進而提供與評論相關的表達句式，讓學習者明瞭如何以「華語」為媒介，適切的表達個人贊成或反對的意見。此寫作活動所欲達成的能力目標即是，無論移民在

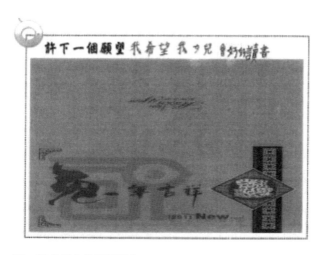

圖6 數位紙本化應用寫作。
資料來源：教師 AT1提供

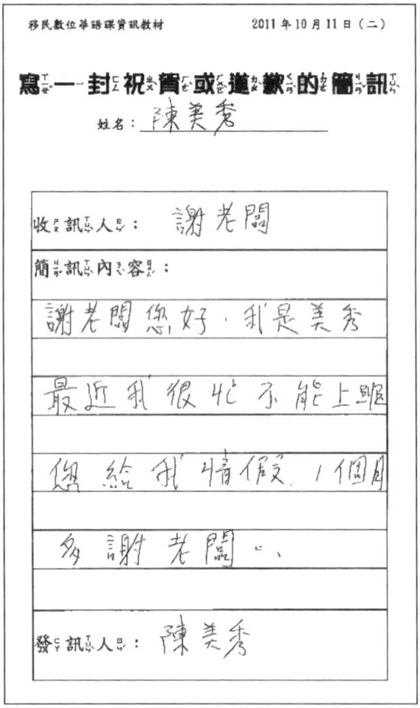

移民數位華語課資訊教材　2011年10月11日（二）

寫一封祝賀或道歉的簡訊

姓名：陳美秀

收訊人：謝老闆

簡訊內容：

謝老闆您好，我是美秀

最近我很忙不能上班

您給我情假1個月

多謝老闆。

發訊人：陳美秀

圖7 手機簡訊紙本化。

資料來源：教師AT2提供

一、　你贊成小孩子減肥嗎？為什麼

□贊成，因為我覺得____________________

____

□反對，因為我覺得____________________

____

二、　你覺得哪些方法可以順利減肥？

□控制飲食

□中醫針灸

□吃減肥藥

□運動

□其他______________________________

圖8 「減肥與健康」寫作任務單。

資料來源：教師ET提供

生活或職場上，均可運用此能力來執行以完成基本任務。

研究結論與建議

　　經由上一節的分析與論述，研究者認為移民華語教師以「來去華語100句」數位平台所發展的數位書寫模式，可謂結合紙本教學所發展的數位學習。其肇因於場域內的各式數位落差因素，像是資訊設備良莠不齊，或網際網路速度非時時順暢，再加上學習者資訊素養仍須搭配課程來涵養，因而，教師發展出「數位教材紙本化，紙本資源數位化」的雙向度課程。此又因應混能班級的需求，以及考量第二語言學習者情意因素，讓學習者有更多的選擇空間，可逐步從紙本學習進入數位學習。有趣的是，數位平台能解決紙本學習所無法創造的趣味，例如影音播放，反過來看，紙本素材則降低了時時刻刻都要數位書寫焦慮。因而，研究者確信這樣的讀寫課程模式，就是提供了最大的學習彈性。

　　另外，由數位讀寫課程實踐歷程則可看出，教師多採功能性觀點來設計數位讀寫教材，此回應了「來去華語100句」教材編輯初衷：提升在台移民職場競爭力與公民意識，這也成為了移民數位華語讀寫課程之最大特色。然而誠如鍾鎮城（2012）所拋出的省思：究竟功能性的華語讀寫，以及數位素養養成之必要性為何？研究者試圖回答這樣的問題，立基於學習者對於數位科技的好奇，以及數位學習時代浪潮難以阻擋，透過數位資訊來學習，以建構語言能力，就目前而言確屬熱潮，也正因為處於發展階段，所以，教師必須在實踐中摸索與嘗試，透過學習者的反饋來調整課程內容，再進而析論出數位華語讀寫的具體目標。至於功能性的讀寫則可視為「學習者中心」的具體展現，以本研究為例，參與的9位教師中，只有1位具備「來去華語100句」編輯者身份，其餘皆是為一般教師，故研究者將其課程所呈現的功能性讀寫觀之特性，歸因於教師考量移民學習特性後，以其為本所設計的數位華語讀寫課程。但這樣的課程對於其在職場與生活上的實用度為何，仍有待後續追蹤研究。

參考文獻

吳靜芬（2011）。〈東南亞學生之華文閱讀困難及其對應策略〉，第四屆華語文教學國際研討會暨工作坊發表之論文，銘傳大學。

林麗娟（2011）。〈台灣國際學生學習華語數位資源之使用分析〉。《圖書與資訊學刊》，78，頁1-22。

張于忻（2010）。〈華語文數位教材之模組設計探討〉。《中原華語文學報》，5，179-198。

許雅雯、周怡均（2012）。〈移民華語課程的數位與紙本教材混搭模式探究〉。面向跨文化學習者的中文學與教：挑戰與突破研討會發表之論文，香港大學。

彭妮絲（2011）。〈以雙語合作統整閱讀理解模式為基礎之華語讀寫教學研究〉。《台北市立教育大學學報》，42，189-218。

黃湘玲（2012）。〈城鄉與其他因素影響下的數位華語學習落差研究〉。2012華語文教學與創意表達學術研討會暨工作坊發表之論文，僑光科技大學。

廖本裕（2010）。〈寫作歷程模式數位教學平台之設計與實施成效之研究〉。《教育學刊》（TSSCI），34，109-142。國科會計畫編號：NSC 98-2511-S-143-001。

鍾鳳嬌、林苑平、趙善如（2008）。〈電腦學習歷程：新移民女性增能經驗分析〉。《社區發展季刊》，127，336-355。

鍾鎮城（2012）。《移民華語教學：全球在地化的語言民族誌研究》。台北：新學林。

附錄一：來去華語100句數位華語學習平台
研發與推廣單位：社團法人台灣來去華語協會

在外籍配偶已成為台灣第五大族群之際，當前台灣學術與實務教育領域對於移民華語教材之開發卻面臨教材質量與教材合適性不足的窘境；尤其是透過數位平台資源以進行外籍配偶華語的學習與教學模式，更是鮮少在以往教學現場中出現。為促進外籍配偶華語之有效學習，以及豐富第一線移民華語教師之華語教材使用資源，社團法人台灣來去華語協會研發本套數位華語學習平台——**來去華語100句**（教材下載網址如下：http://atlh.ideas.iii.org.tw/ChineseblvdDownLoad/），以期豐潤外籍配偶之華語與數位學習需求及職場識寫能力，以提升其就業機會。

一、來去華語100句之設計架構

此套數位學習教材在華語能力的培養上極重視實用概念，強調華語在各類場合的常用性（frequency）與熟練精確（proficiency and accuracy），以提升外籍配偶之就業機會及職場識讀能力。此教材以100句主題句，400句主題延展擴句為主要課程架構，各主題句之練

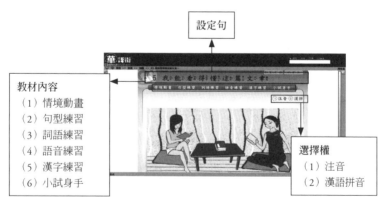

圖A1　來去華語100句操作頁面。

習項目可分為：情境動畫、句型練習、詞語練習、語音練習、漢字練習，以及小試身手，圖A1擷取此平台內第五句主題句說明內容架構。

表A1為各練習項目所欲培養學生之對應能力說明。

表A1　來去華語100句練習項目與對應能力指標說明

練習項目	對應之能力指標	圖　示
情境動畫	語言在各類場合的常用性（frequency and accuracy）能力：設定句之主題情境連結	
句型練習	常用語言的擴充與延伸能力：設定句句類、語法與擴句	
詞語練習	語言的熟練精確（proficiency and accuracy）能力：詞彙的應用與練習	

練習項目	對應之能力指標	圖　示
語音練習	語言的熟練精確（proficiency and accuracy）能力： 聲調及相似音的比較與覺識	
漢字練習	語言的熟練精確（proficiency and accuracy）能力： 漢字部件與筆畫覺識的學習	
小試身手	語言在各類場合的常用性（frequency）與熟練精確（proficiency and accuracy）能力： 句中發音及詞語辨別	

二、 來去華語100句之學習內容

　　來去華語100句之編輯內容統計「移民最想學習主題」及「教材最常出現之句型」，經過縝密的計算後，以此為依據進行教材內容編輯。來去華語100句以下述17個主題為主要教學內容：

　　（1-1）就業說明
　　（1-2）就業環境
　　（1-3）自主學習
　　（1-4）權利義務
　　（1-5）人際互動
　　（1-6）申辦證件
　　（1-7）飲食健康
　　（1-8）多元社會
　　（1-9）親子教養
　　（1-10）民間習俗
　　（1-11）購物方法
　　（1-12）就醫知識
　　（1-13）學校系統
　　（1-14）生活禮儀
　　（1-15）觀光景點
　　（1-16）文學閱讀
　　（1-17）購買活動

論對外漢字教學的策略與課程規劃

賴秋桂

東海大學華語中心 / 中文系 助理教授

julie_lailaoshi@thu.edu.tw

摘要

　　對外漢字教學策略不外是筆畫教學、隨文識字、部首教學、部件教學、字源教學、字族教學等。這些教學策略都各具優、缺點，或說各有適用的時機，因此很難採用單一的方式達到預期的效果。本文將以各項策略的切入時間點作為關注對象，期望能觀察出對外漢字教學策略在學生習字過程中應如何調整與配合。

關鍵詞：對外漢語教學、漢字、漢字教學、課堂經營、策略

How to Set Up a Curriculum for Teaching Chinese Characters to Non-native Speakers?

Julie Lai
Tunghai University
julie_lailaoshi@thu.edu.tw

The strategies for teaching Chinese characters as a second language are none other than the teaching of character strokes, character radicals, character components, character etymology, radical groups, and recognizing words when reading. These teaching strategies each have their own strengths and flaws. In other words, these strategies can and should be implemented at the right time during the learning process. Therefore, it is difficult to apply only one strategy to achieve the intended effect. This chapter discusses the correct time periods for applying these strategies and hopes to inform readers how to adjust and use these strategies when teaching Chinese characters to second learners.

Keywords: Teaching Chinese as a foreign language, Chinese characters, teaching Chinese characters, classroom management, strategies

前言

在對外華語教學這個區塊中，漢字教學一般被認為最具難度。

除了日本籍學生，漢字的學習對只有以拼字母為主要學習經驗，而且至多只有二、三年學習機會的學生而言，是一條似乎找不到科學路徑的坎坷路。在教學上，通常老師們各有主張，因此採用的策略也不同，但一般不外是筆畫教學、隨文識字、部首教學、部件教學、字源教學、字族教學等。這些教學策略各具優、缺點，或說各有適用的時機，因此很難採用單一的方式達到預期的效果。

基於教學法應用的彈性需求，本文將以各項策略的切入時間點作為關注對象，期望能觀察出對外漢字教學策略在學生習字過程中應如何調整與配合。論文的撰寫首先以針對師、生所設計的問卷之調查結果出發，[1] 據以汲取教師的心得與經驗、關注學生的難題與期望。最後，根據文字的適用學理，設計教學內容，並以為學生找到習字的科學途徑為最終目標。

課堂經營

根據調查表，教師的教學回饋可歸納為以下幾點：

1. 漢字教學需漸進：對西方學生，剛剛開始學習時不要求一定要寫字。隨著學生程度的提高，漸進式地要求學生寫字。

2. 混和式教學：各種教學法經常需彈性應用。

3. 學習動機的激發：漢字在初學時難度太高，有些學生很快放棄，甚至只用拼音學習。激發學生的興趣是解決學生抗拒寫字最重要的方式。

4. 教師的專業學習：使用華語的華人，包含中國人、台灣人，本

---

1 調查表參附錄一、二。

身對漢字的認知並不完全正確，有許多將錯就錯的例子，因此教師對漢字學理應有一定程度的認識。

5. 學生認為漢字沒有書寫系統，很難記住。故教學應強調部首、反覆練習、引起興趣。

而，針對「認識漢字時，您最常碰到的問題」，學生認為是字形類似的字太多及整字忘記；「寫漢字時，您最常碰到的問題」，學生認為是整字忘記及筆畫記不住。

顯然，對於漢字的學習，教師與學生各有心得。值得關注的是雖然漢字很難，而且有各種電子工具可以顯示出漢字，然而，本文所做的問卷調查顯示仍有70%的學生認為學寫字是需要的。這麼高的比率是一種鼓勵與責任，從事對外漢字教學的教師應持續關注並設計出更多策略以幫助學生。於此，將參酌師生各自的表述並以之為依據設計課堂的教學策略。

（一）教學法的彈性應用

本文調查顯示，超過八成五的教師教授漢字的時機是「隨文識字、寫字」與「隨文識字、選擇性寫字」；在初級班，認字的要求與說、聽同步，而超過一半教師對寫字的要求是與說、聽、讀同步進行，因此，如果可能，初級班的漢字教學最宜採用隨文識字。當然，雖然語言學習的最佳狀況是說、聽、讀、寫同步進行，[2] 但由於漢字本身的複雜性，在實際教學時，四者很難腳步一致，故根據狀況予以「選擇性寫字」的彈性是合理的。

而根據教師與學生提供的經驗及意見可看出教師的教法與學生的學法都會隨著學生程度的改變而改變。學生程度高低差異不只來自學習時間的長短，學生本身資質與用功程度亦是重要因素。因此，教師實際教學時，通常會根據學生狀況而調整；綜觀之，各種策略其實是

---

2 寫，在初級班指寫字，非撰文。

交叉的，亦即是彈性的。

（二）習字的基礎工作

學生在正式課程進行前，最好有基本的習字訓練及簡單的字構說明，使學生清楚知道漢字的學習是怎麼回事。這種基礎工作主要是練習筆法、筆順，讓學生學會運筆，進而讓筆韻呈現。

中國人習書法有所謂永字八法，其實並非只有書法，硬筆字同樣有橫、豎、提、撇、捺、點、勾、折的筆法；要把字寫得對味又美觀，筆畫的掌握絕對需要。對於基礎訓練，有以下策略：

1. 部首、筆法、筆順三合一練習

根據部首的使用頻率，並考慮書寫的不複雜性，本文從正中書局2011年2版5刷的新版《實用視聽華語1》找出人、女、木、心、貝、氵、言、子、見、扌、彳、辶、麻、雨、儿、月、小、夕、弓、宀、糸、气、刀、犭、毋、阝、氺等27個部首作為筆法、筆順練習的發端。這些部首跟筆法的關係如表1。

這27個部首囊括了絕大部分的筆法，而且筆畫不多，對於剛入門的學生是很好的練習材料。這個練習可以搭配部首的學習，讓學生知道部首的發音、意義及筆順，讓練習獲得較大的效能。[3] 練習設計如表2。

表格應事先預備，在學生開始學習漢語拼音時，即可開始練習。一旦學生發音規則掌握好，將開始進入單元學習時，學生運筆亦已成熟。

---

3 很多教師認為國語注音符號是學習漢字很好的入門材料。國語注音符號只在台灣使用，若要求學生學習無疑是增加學生負擔，而且國語注音符號的筆畫過簡，故此作法的效用存疑。

表1 筆法與相關部首

筆法	筆法類型	字例
橫	橫	木（1）、貝（3、4）、言（2、3、4、7）、子（3）、見（3、4、5）、扌（1）、毌（4）、雨（1）、月（3、4）、弓（2）、气（2、3）[4]
豎	豎	木（2）、貝（1）、言（5）、見（1）、扌（2）、彳（3）、麻（5、9）、雨（4）
提	上提	氵（3）、雨（6）
	橫提	扌（3）
撇	長撇	犭（2、3）
	短撇	貝（6）、宀（2）、見（6）、雨（7）、小（2）、夕（1）、糸（5）、灬（3、4）、气（1）
	直撇	麻（3、6、10）、儿（1）、月（1）、毌（3）
捺	長捺	人（2）、木（4）、灬（5）
	短捺	貝（7）、糸（6）
	平捺	辶（4）
點	左點	心（1）
	右點	氵（1、2）、宀（1）、心（3、4）、言（1）、辶（1）、麻（1）、雨（5、8）、灬（2）、糸（3）
	右長點（點捺）	小（3）、夕（3）
勾	豎彎勾	子（2）
	豎左勾	小（1）、糸（4）
	彎豎左勾	犭（2）
	彎短豎左勾	阝（3）
	豎右橫折勾	見（7）
	豎右彎折勾	心（2）
	豎右橫折勾	儿（2）
	橫豎折左勾	雨（3）、月（2）
	橫彎豎折左勾	刀（1）、毌（2）

---

4 部首旁數字乃筆畫序。

筆法	筆法類型	字例
勾	橫彎豎折右勾	气（4）
	左斜豎橫折彎豎折勾	弓（3）
折	橫豎折	貝（2）、言（6）、見（2）
	橫短豎折	弓（1）
	橫撇折	辶（2）、乑（1）
	橫短撇折	辶（1）、阝（2）
	橫左彎折	夕（2）
	豎右折	麻（7）、毋（1）
	撇捺折	糸（1）、女（1）
	撇平提折	糸（12）

表2 部首筆順練習

部首 （發音）	意義	筆順	寫寫看				
人（rén）	human	ノ 人					
女（nǚ）	female	く 女 女					
木（mù）	wood	一 十 才 木					
心（xīn）	heart	、 心 心 心					
貝（bèi）	shell	丨 冂 冃 月 目 貝 貝					

2. 簡介漢字結構

　　漢字教學入門階段除了簡單運筆練習之外，漢字構造亦應該簡介。畢竟學生將面臨很大的挑戰，因此以字構的理由與趣味來加強學生的信心與學習意願是值得嘗試的。入門以圖畫性強或表義明顯的字開始。字例介紹應由字源開始，除了趣味外，讓學生了解漢字歷史對學習的深度有助益。字例如下：

表3 漢字字源表

甲骨文	金文	楚文	小篆	楷書
（字形）	（字形）	（字形）	日	日
（字形）	（字形）	（字形）	車	車
（字形）	（字形）	（字形）	天	天
（字形）	二、上	上、上、上	上	上
—	—	—	看	看
（字形）	（字形）	林、林、林	林	林

　　日、車可看漢字字形的改變；天、上、看、林等字可看漢字如何立意，教師應為學生解釋這些字的字形與字義的關連性。這些字，同時可作為一般人認為漢字沒有科學性的一種反證。

　　形聲字佔漢字的大宗，形符與聲符的組合不但有表義功能，而且有標聲的作用。然而形符的意義一般是泛化的，[6]聲符也因古今音變的因素無法真正作為發音依據，因此在做漢字結構簡介時宜慎選字例，形義變化較複雜的形聲字可待日後適當時機再教授。字例如表4。

　　表4所列形聲字的聲符與本字的發音有不同程度的關連，這些字例不僅利於介紹字構類型，對於聲、韻概念的強化及古今音變的認知亦有幫助，同時對字音教學也有輔助的功能。漢字不像拼音文字有很強的表音條件，但認為漢字一定沒有發音的人，其觀念也有一些修正的空間。

---

5 說文篆文。

6 「泛化」一詞，沿用黃德寬之說：泛化指把概念相近或可相比擬的字歸在同一部首，藉以簡化部首的分類。參黃德寬撰，〈漢字構形方式：一個歷時態演進的系統〉，《安徽大學學報——哲學社會科學版》第3期，1994年。

表4 形聲字表

懂（dǒng）	忄+董（dǒng）
汽（qì）	氵+气（qì）
啊（a）	口+阿（à）
們（men）	亻+門（mén）
姐（jiě）	女+且（qiě）
謝（xiè）	言+射（shè）
客（kè）	宀+各（gè）
忙（máng）	忄+亡（wáng）
影（yǐng）	景（jǐng）+彡

（三）正式習字——混合式教學

學語言如能說、聽、讀、寫同步進行是最佳狀況，因此如能隨文識字及寫字是最好的。然而漢字筆畫太繁複，在學生剛開始寫字時會有非常多書寫的問題，因此教師在教學上的收放需有相當技巧。一般來說，漢字量隨學生聽說能力的增強而大量出現，一旦放任學生的學習意願或速度不管，學生很快就因為新字的大量出現而失去方向；而要求太嚴，又怕學生因壓力太大而不知所措甚至失去信心。這些可能性，教師不可掉以輕心。漢字大多是部件的組合，無論從何時開始都可以是新的開始，因此彈性給予學生選擇性識字是可行的方式。只要字量增加，學生部件量亦跟著增加，其組字能力會因此越來越好，這種概念對開始時對書寫漢字感到畏難的學生應特別給予建立，並督促其不間斷練習，則能較早度過陣痛期。

學生開始學字即開始接觸筆畫、部首、部件，而這些都包括在字構中，因此混合而漸進式的教學除了是呼應教師教法及學生希望外，應是最值得採行與研究的方式。各項策略應用如下。

1. 筆畫教學

基礎筆畫練習之後，學生正式進入課程。學習開始漢字即出現，單元所列生字筆畫繁複程度不一，譬如初級用語「你好」、「謝謝」

、「再見」、「對不起」、「沒關係」等字的難易就相差很多，學生一開始要寫這樣的字一般非常具挑戰性。在這個階段，記住筆畫不是最重要的，將筆畫放在對的地方，寫出結構合宜的字才是最重要的。教師應利用有筆順的寫字本督促學生做模寫練習，並細心批改每個字，檢視筆法、筆畫及結構是否有失誤。通常兩、三週後，學生就可寫出看起來尚稱自然的字來。下列二實例乃相隔三週、同一位學生的習字實例：

實例一：第一週習字實例

1. How are you, Mr. Li?
   nǐ hǎo ma, lǐ xiānshēng? 你好嗎，李先生？
2. I'm David, not Michael.
   wǒ jiào David, bù jiào Michael: 我叫David，不叫Michael，
3. I'm Chinese, and you?
   wǒ shì zhōngguó rén, nǐ ne? 我是中國人，你呢？
4. Are you English?
   nǐ shì yīngguó rén ma?
   你是英國人嗎？

實例二：第四週習字實例

1. 我媽媽做飯，做得好吃　　。
2. 老師說話，說得好聽　。
3. 他妹妹唱歌兒，唱得好聽．
4. 我的字，寫得好看　　．
5. 王先生做事，做得都很好

　　例一的漢字筆畫不流暢，結構大小不一；例二的筆畫已經流暢許多，且每個字大小幾乎一致。可見書寫很容易習慣。在學生能控制自己筆勢很自然寫出字後，教師即可開始評量學生寫漢字的情況。此時，學生一般完全靠記憶寫出一個字，因此錯誤發生率一般不低，這

不值得大驚小怪。再過些時候,學生會開始發現漢字不僅僅是線條,而常常是部件組成的。當然,無論部首或是部件都是筆畫串成的,在漢字當中,這三者無法完全分野。

2. 部首教學

關於部首教學,本文問卷調查顯示,主張「獨立教學」與「隨生字教學」的教師是46.88%及50%,可見教師各有主張。這兩個主張各有優點;若將部首獨立教學,可較全面地作部首介紹,而隨生字教學則可逐步學習,學生可以較從容不迫。

現今通行楷書部首多達240個,各個部首的使用頻率不一,而且有些部首不成文,有些與部中字的關係不具體,因此即使「獨立教學」,教師亦無須全面性介紹。特別「隨生字教學」是以生字部首的出現先後為教學依據,這些部首不一定是常用的部首,如:而、厶、己;有的部首本身意義不明,如:乙、風;有些部首與部中字的關係極不密切,如:再與冂、去與厶。此類部首點到即可,其學習最大目的及效能就是當檢索工具。而若部首本義與部中字有意義關連,或其形體與部中字有所連結,則應多費心教授。

用「獨立教學」策略,對於預定要教授的部首,可嘗試作認識部首與書寫部首分流的方式;除了配合正規課程的生字外,對於使用頻率高的部首可先介紹並要求學生書寫,其他則可先行認字再根據進度寫字。[7] 若是「隨生字教學」,則按課程進度,將有必要講解的部首逐一介紹。[8]

若將部首教學的重要性歸納,有如下三點提供給教師們參考:

(1)部首具領字作用,將漢字分門別類做歸納,有利於字的檢

---

7 常見部首根據台灣中央研究院史語所《現代漢語語料庫詞頻統計》中8,100組詞中的2,159字歸納。部首見附錄三。

8 若以正中本《實用視聽華語》第一、二冊為例,此二書已帶出149個部首。見附錄四。

（2）由於部首大量表義，亦有少數表音，對漢字構造的了解極
為重要。

（3）部首字常作為字中部件，因此學會部首有利於漢字的書寫
及字構的了解。

至於教法與注意事項說明如下：

（1）講解部首字源

現代漢字 240 個部首中，有眾多找得到完整的字源。字源的追
溯，對學習而言，不僅提供了趣味性，而且對本義的了解極為重要。
部首學習表製作如下：

楷書	甲骨文	金文	楚文	小篆	英文	筆順
忄（心）（xīn）					heart	㇐ 忄 忄
貝（bèi）					shell	丨 冂 冂 目 目 貝 貝
女（nǚ）					femal	㇇ 女 女
木（mù）					wood	一 十 才 木
戈（gē）					dagger-axe	一 弋 弋 戈

舉女、木二字說明。

女字初形象女跪踞自守之狀而強調其胸，此字在周器已見「ㇺ」
形，跪姿失。隸書作女、女，此形構造已異於小篆，然而女子胸形仍
在。[9] 到了楷書，字形變作「女」。在初級本中，以女作為部首的字
有姓、好、她、姐、媽、女、妹、妝、始、如等，使用頻率不低。
木，象樹木之形，楷書第一筆橫畫乃是象樹枝的筆畫拉平形成的。在
初級本中，以木作為部首的字有李、本、東、枝、杯、機、校、樓、

___
9 參陳煒湛，〈甲骨文異字同形例〉，《古文字研究》第六輯。

桌、椅、樣、末、條、果、概、極、林、枱、櫃、架、板、楚、橘、樂、業、等字，使用頻率非常高。[10]

　　從上舉字例可見部首原始狀態非常象形，後隨時間推移形體做有跡可尋的改變，這種軌跡對部首字義的了解極有幫助，更促進記憶的速度與準確度。

（2）說明部首在字中扮演的角色

　　如：麼的部首「麻」標音，姐的部首「女」表義，南的部首「十」為南字的小部件。

（3）認字與寫字分流

　　適度要求學生背寫或單純認字，並作檢試。

（4）部首寫法差異的說明

　　相同部首有寫法上的差異，在初級班時應該說明。一般有兩大類：

　　a. 立於左偏旁時，最後一筆橫畫一般上提，如：土與 𡈼、金與 釒、工與 工、立與 立、止與 止、子與 孑、牛與 牜等。

　　b. 寫法不同，如：手（扌）、水（氵）、人（亻）、糸（糹）、辵（辶）、心（忄）、艸（⺿）、肉（月）、阜（阝）、刀（刂）、竹（⺮）、玉（王）、足（⻊）、衣（衤）、犬（犭）、火（灬）、示（礻）、邑（阝）、食（飠）、羊（⺶）、攵（夂）、爪（爫）。下列小篆、隸書、楷書字形以檢視部首變形軌跡：[11]

---

10 東，甲骨文作「𣛀」，象囊形；參《甲骨文字詁林》第四冊（北京：中華書局，1996年），頁3010。另《說文・丵部》：「業，大版也。所以飾縣鍾鼓。捷業如鋸齒，以白畫之。象其鉏鋙相承也。从丵从巾。巾象版。」東、業二字與部首木之義無關。

11 隸書字形皆擷取自《隸辨》。顧藹吉，《隸辨》（北京：中華書局，1986年）。

屮→手→手	水→水→水	尺→人→人	糸→糸→糸	辵→⻌→辵
擤→捼→接 枝→技→技	没→沒→沒 酒→酒→酒	伯→伯→伯 候→候→候	給→給→給 紹→紹→紹	近→近→近 迎→迎→迎
肉→肉→肉	邑→邑→邑	阜→阜→阜	刀→刀→刀	竹→竹→竹
育→育→育 肝→肝→肝	鄰→鄰→鄰 郊→郊→郊	阿→阿→阿 附→附→附	剛→剛→剛 刻→刻→刻	篇→篇→篇 筆→筆→筆
衣→衣→衣	犬→犬→犬	爪→爪→爪	火→火→火	示→示→示
補→補→補 被→被→被	狗→狗→狗 獄→獄→獄	爭→爭→爭 采→采→采	烈→烈→烈 然→然→然	社→社→社 神→神→神
羊→羊→羊	艸→艸→艸	足→足→足	夊→夊→夊	玉→玉→玉
美→美→美 善[12]→善→善	華→華→華 草→草→草	距→距→距 路→路→路	冰→冰→冰 冬→冬→冬	玩→玩[13]→玩 班→班→班
心→心→心	食→食→食			
惜→惜→惜 慕→慕→慕	飢→飢→飢 飯→飯→飯			

上舉字例可見隸變是部首寫法改變最大的原因。而心、刀、示、衣四字的隸書仍見小篆形體，到了楷書則已變形。於此，教師可說明隸書與現代楷書字形的關係，為學生灌輸漢字演變的一些知識，並加強不同形體之間的聯繫。

3. 部件教學

部件教學在初級時甚常為教師及學生所用。學生習字一開始強調筆畫是無法避免的基礎訓練，一旦筆畫書寫漸漸習慣，漢字量逐步增加時，教師可以開始將可獨立出的構字部件作提醒，而其實一般來說，學生自己也很快會發現不同的字有時會有相同或相近的部件。

---

12 䰍，說文篆文「署」。
13 亦見从「玉」作「玩」。

如：「汽車」的「汽」是很快出現的字，當天氣的「氣」出現時，學生很容易在老師提醒前就已發現「气」這個部件曾記憶過；[14] 若部首隨生字教學則學生進一步可很快獲知「气」這個部首。部件觀念的建立使學生在記憶生字時開始塊狀化，這對能否記住或寫出一個漢字深具意義。適度提醒或等學生去發現是一種彈性。慢慢地，學生開始會用部件去記憶漢字。關於部件，若要合理化，應該注意兩個問題，第一是部件如何劃分，第二是如何讓部件意義呈現。

首先，部件的拆解若是學生學字手段，而手段一般巧妙不同，則可想見學生拆解方式會五花八門，因此若要合理化應把握一些原則。下舉數例說明：

德	彳、十、罒、一、心（彳、悳）	視	礻、見
喜	十、豆、口（壴、口）	都	耂、日、阝（者、阝）
歡	艹、口口、隹、欠（雚、欠）	我	我
會	亼、罒、曰	報	土、丷、干、卩、又（土、羊、𠬛）（幸、𠬛）
最	冂、二、耳、又（冃、取）	賣	士、罒、貝（士、買）

（1）部首不拆解。如：欠為部首，故不拆解為「𠂉、人」。不拆解的理由是部首的功用原本作為領字，在字中應該有完整性，不適合拆開。

（2）部首字不拆解。見、豆二字分別是視、喜的部件，但此二字本身是部首，應該被完整保留，不作拆解。

（3）拆解單位大小應有一致原則；先出者求小，後出者可求完整。如：若「德」字出現早於「聽」，則前者部件記憶的內容應包含：「彳、十、罒、一、心」，後者則可作「耳、壬、悳」；若「買」已經先出現，則「賣」的部件可為「士、買」。

---

14 敏感度更高的學生或可發現連聲音都有關係。

（4）結構緊緻的字考慮用筆畫策略。如：「我」雖列入「戈」部，然而戈與其他筆畫密切地交錯，故很難作合理的部件劃分，因此可考慮用筆畫策略即可。

（5）常用二層部件可獨立。如：「亼」、「羊」雖可再分成更小單位，但由於被使用的頻率高，因此可獨立。

（6）造字學理優先。如：「最」雖入「曰」部，然而其上半部件是「冃」，因此可考慮作「冂、二、耳、又」或「冃、取」。

（7）部件筆順依整字考量。如：「園」可獨立出「囗、袁」部件，但「囗」部件的第三畫仍是「園」的最後一畫。

　　拆解的呈現在初期可以列表讓學生背記，學生慢慢地即能習慣拆字原則。拆字表除了有記憶部件的功能外，也可觸及部首及表聲、表義偏旁的認知。

　　此外，雖然部件教學策略原來只是拆解和記憶，但有太多部件重複，因此對可以具體註解意義或說明功能的部件應嘗試講述。如書、畫、筆都有「聿」部件，這個部件古文字作「𦘒」、「𦘕」、「肅」，是手握一枝筆，而「筆」的意涵與這三字關係是密切的。「手」是拜和看的部件，這個部件看似不成文，但其實是「手」的變形，而手在看與拜二字中，都有很強的構意功能。[15] 將部件做說明並不違背部件教學的精神，而是將此種策略科學化。當然，相同部件不一定來源相同，而不同部件也可能有相同來源，此種觀念應先為學生建立。

　　部件教學另一個需要執行的是與部件組合相反路徑的部件解構。有時候，先學字的成文部件是後學字，如：「念」先學，而其部件

---

15 《說文・目部》：「看，睎也。从手下目。」又《說文・手部》：「𢫦，揚雄說拜从兩手下。」

「今」後學，因此當今字出現時，一般學生很快可以記住。[16] 此時，是告訴他們中文其實不真的很難且很有科學性的時機，亦是鼓勵他們士氣的適當時候。整字解構後產生很多新字的例子比比皆是，教師應該耐心觀察。

至於部件形似如日、曰，或有共用部件如氣、汽等情況，教師應該適時提醒與複習。而有教師提出「學生對部件與文字整體的認知混淆」的疑慮，此當會隨字量的增加而形成判斷能力。

4. 字族策略

在初級課堂進行到一半或結束時，教師可作字族的整理。初級程度由於字量不是很大，可作字族整理的字尚不多，但觀與歡、喝與渴都有重疊部件，而且有聲音關係，這是值得歸納分析的。當然，在此時將有相同部首的字歸類是很好的複習。

5. 字源、字構教學

根據調查，一般教師在初級班時較少利用字構學理，可是學生卻在初級班時已非常關注字的構造。由於坊間有不少解釋字構的書籍或多媒體，因此即使教師不教，學生亦會想辦法得到這方面的資訊，這是值得關心的狀況。

字構教學對漢字能有較深刻的了解應是無庸置疑的。上下合成卡，不用是甬，手目合成看；這些字都是由常用字結合而成的字。然而楷書字形已經過分記號化，漢字部件拆解後，經常會發現已失去原形之部件的功用很難了解，因此字構講解經常需要用到字源才能詳盡；能將字源與字構二者配合才是較理想的教學方式。字構教學應該有幾個原則：

16在初級班時，一般情況是，當教念字時，為了不增加學生負擔，不會告訴他們今字的含義與用法。

·不要每個字作結構分析

有的漢字記號化後變形嚴重，作字構分析牽涉太多過程，因此除非有關文化意義，否則無需強調。如「疑」，甲、金文時作「疑」、「疑」，象拄杖者張口作疑惑狀。字到了小篆作「疑」，張口人形不復見，代之的是子、止，而且加了聲符「矢」。楷書子形失。這樣的字特別在初級班太複雜，不適合拆解。另外，若漢字的構字本義不明，則拆解無由，如「黃」，在甲、金文時作「黃」、「黃」，而究竟如何解字，至今不明。

漢字結構取義的不規則性應提醒。由於造字取義的主觀性，因此部件結合後如何表義是需要學習的。如：日、月表光明義，穴、犬結合取突襲義。

·以有趣、有文化意義的字為講解對象

字例如下：

甲骨文	金文	楚文	小篆	楷書
—	—	—	睡	睡
天	天	天	天	天
—	電	電	電	電
祭	祭	祭	祭	祭

眼睛下垂就是睡覺；正面人形之上有大首代表天；電字下半部件是申，代表閃電；

以手持肉塊以祭祀。這類字不但立意明顯、有趣，如天、祭二字且有文化含義，是非常值得介紹給學生的。

6. 遊戲設計

漢字教學的過程應配合遊戲，寓教於樂。設計表格見下頁。

另外，在漢字與文化的連結方面，除非有獨立的課，且無語言障礙，在初級班時宜隨生字教學。如：出現貝字，可談貝在古代曾作為

遊戲考題	
1. 以部首為中心的練習 （1）寫出有心部首的字：應、愛、息 （2）寫出這些字的部首：男、思、畫	3. 拆字 （1）「念」可拆成什麼字？ （2）「相」可拆成什麼字？
2. 以部件為中心的練習 （1）口、夕、卜可拼出哪些字？ （2）有「見」的字有哪些？ （3）用「艹、吅、佳、欠」構造一個字	4. 猜字（圖畫聯想） （1）𦫼是什麼？ （2）𦫺是什麼？
	5. 猜字義（部首、部件聯想） （1）慶是什麼意思？ （2）鮮是什麼意思？

錢幣，而男的構字跟農業生活有關。在學生自我學習方面，除了教師設計的作業之外，亦可充分利用網路資源，如：教育部的筆順學習網站。[17]

（四）進階程度之後的習字

部首教學在初級時所費功夫非常大，到中高級時主要在複習與應用。有時久久未被使用的部首其實早早已經學過，如「馬」部雖很晚出現，但很早出現的「嗎」字已經讓學生認識馬部件。因此，中高級班不需再特別強調部首的認與寫，主要談的是部首如何幫助字構與字義。在部件教學方面，初級班部件的記憶較零碎，到了中高級班，學生一般已經越來越能將部件結合成二層甚至三層部件，因此習字更加快速與容易。通常學生在此時也很容易創造出自己的心得及成就感。

一般來說，進階程度的學生習字經常是課後作業，教師教授漢字的時機也變得不固定。對於有趣、有文化意義的漢字可主動講解，其餘不妨在作業繳交或測驗之後針對錯誤做講解。筆畫增減在中級程度

---

17 其他如：translate.google.com、www.nciku.com、www.yellowbridge.com、www.mdbg.net、zhongwen.com/zi.htm、www.chineseetymology.org。iPhone, Android 手機的 www.pleco.com、memeo。

仍常出現；高級班常見的問題是同音或音近字誤植。[18] 由聲音誤導的字可以用字構分析來講解字義及字用，使學生知道各字的差異為何。將字由單純字形牽涉到字用對於寫別字的問題來說是必要的。

字族教學在進階班的使用價值比在初級班高出許多。譬如字族構、溝、講、購的聲音與意義關係為何；字族場（chǎng）、暢（chàng）、湯（tāng）、傷（shāng）、揚（yáng）、楊（yáng）、瘍（yáng）、陽（yáng）、腸（cháng）與古（gǔ）、估（gū）、故（gù）、姑（gū）、固（gù）、胡（hú）、苦（kǔ）的關連是什麼。而將各（gè）、格（gé）、閣（gé）、客（kè）、絡（luò）、駱（luò）、洛（luò）、略（lüè）、路（lù）集合成字族的意義存在否。這些都是教師可思考的。

此外，進階班學生的中文已愈具能力，對於字形的理解越來越不成問題，因此字構策略的應用應不致太難。由於字構經常牽涉造字當時的文化及思想，對教學的深度而言是不可或缺的。茲以正中書局2011年2版的新版《實用視聽華語5》的城邦、遺棄、種族、節育四詞中的四個漢字為例作說明：

甲骨文	金文	楚文	小篆	楷書
峀	𢾇	𢼵	𨝋	邦
㐃	𢷎	—	𣾀	棄
㫃	𣃚	㫃	㫃	族
—	節	𥰠	節	節

邦，金文作「𢾇」，左邊部件「丰」是封的古字。《說文·邑部》：「封，爵諸侯之土也。从之从土从寸，守其制度也。公侯，百里；伯，七十里；子男，五十里。」甲骨文的封有𡉚、丰、𡉖等形，郭

---

18 參賴秋桂，〈外籍生漢字錯誤書寫研究〉，第五屆古典與現代國際學術研討會，高雄文藻外語學院，2011年5月。

96　大學語言課程教研薈萃

沫若曰：「♦即以林木為界之象。」[19] 李孝定同郭說曰：「字象植樹土上以明經界，爵諸侯必有封疆，乃其引申義。」[20] 知「♦」與劃定疆域有關。甲骨文的邦作「♠」，上半部件即象插林木為界，到了金文為加強表義而加了偏旁邑，其邦域義亦顯。而小篆從「丰」聲；《說文·生部》：「♦，艸盛♦♦也。从生，上下達也。」此「丰」與甲、金文的♠、♦恐不同。邦字在漢字教學上的價值是古人劃定疆界的方式，這當然是文化教學的一環。

棄，《說文·華部》：「捐也。从廾推華棄之，从㐆。㐆，逆子也。」甲骨文有♠字，象棄子之形，而金文、小篆更見雙手捧器，其捐棄童子之象更顯。棄子本天道不容，因此棄的本誼當然非簡單數語可說清的。《史記·三代世表》：「文王之先為后稷，后稷亦無父而生。后稷母為姜嫄，出見大人蹟而履踐之，知於身，則生后稷。姜嫄以為無父，賤而弃之道中，牛羊避不踐也。抱之山中，山者養之。又捐之大澤，鳥覆席食之。姜嫄怪之，於是知其天子，乃取長之。」這個故事，《烈女傳·母儀》亦有「以為不祥而棄之」的記載。根據文獻，周先人感天而生，其母因其無父棄之。這種故事牽涉中國遠古政權的宗教性及穩固性。[21]

族，甲骨文作♠、♦、♦，丁山：「族字，从㫃，从矢，矢所以殺敵，㫃所以標眾，其本誼應是軍旅的組織。」[22]《說文·㫃部》：「旗，熊旗五游，以象罰星，士卒以為期。从㫃其聲。《周禮》曰：『率都建旗。』」古人有以旗聚眾、領眾的傳統。族字作為種族，從字形上可探討其所从㫃的意義，而這種傳統亦見於其他國家，是很好

---

19 參于省吾，《甲骨文字詁林》第二冊（北京：中華書局，1996年），頁1327-1328。
20 李孝定，《甲骨文字集釋》（台灣：中央研究院歷史語言研究所印行，1965年），頁3997。
21 魯瑞菁，〈兩漢「三代始祖感生說」論述〉，《學燈》第十期（北京：國學時代，2009年4月）。
22 《甲骨文所見氏族及其制度》（北京：中華書局，1988年），頁33-34。

的教材。

節，《說文・竹部》：「竹約也。从竹即聲。」根據《說文》，節的本義是竹節；竹節一截一截，約而不亂，故除常作為段落單位外，亦引申有節制之義。中國傳統的修養講分寸、節操，這是非常特別的文化內涵。

學習中文者除本身興趣外，對中國文化亦應有一定程度的了解，畢竟語言牽涉的層面很廣。文化可從多方面了解，而漢字是理解中華文化的極重要途徑。

結語

針對「漢字學習經驗」，學生的表述歸納如下：

1. 容易忘記。

2. 需每天練習。

3. 寫字很難，可是很有趣。

4. 老師應解釋字的構造。

5. 寫字練習本幫助很大。圖畫、故事、字源幫助很大。

學生對漢字似乎又愛又怕，因此幫助學生的漢字學習可以作為從事對外華語教學教師們的挑戰和職志。本文以漢字教學與漢字習得皆難的現況為關注對象，利用問卷讓問題具體化，期望進一步了解師生雙方的問題。

根據問卷的回饋所設計的教學法是交叉的，任何一種教學法不可能獨立存在。部首書寫不可能脫離筆畫，筆畫極易牽涉部件；部首、部件是字構的要素，彼此相依存；字構離不開字源，字源可看出部件變化軌跡。漢字經常由如此多概念形成，教學工作如何養成是很大的課題。

附錄一：漢字教學問卷（教師版）

1. 您認為對外漢字教學的困難度 □（1）極高 □（2）高 □（3）還好 □（4）不高 □（5）低

2. 您認為學生識字的困難度為 □（1）極高 □（2）高 □（3）還好 □（4）不高 □（5）低

3. 您認為學生寫字的困難度為 □（1）極高 □（2）高 □（3）還好 □（4）不高 □（5）低

4. 您認為漢字學習應該 □（1）隨文識字、寫字 □（2）選擇性識字、寫字 □（3）隨文識字、選擇性寫字 □（4）只識字，不寫字 □（5）其他：＿＿＿＿＿＿＿

5. 您認為筆法、筆順教學最佳時間點為 □（1）獨立教學 □（2）隨生字教學 □（3）其他：＿＿＿＿＿＿＿

6. 您認為部首應該 □（1）獨立教學 □（2）隨生字教學 □（3）其他：＿＿＿＿＿

7. 請問初級班您最常使用的漢字教學法為（可複選）□（1）筆畫教學 □（2）部首教學 □（3）部件教學 □（4）六書字構 □（5）字源教學（6）字族教學（如：種腫懂；諸豬暑）□（7）其他：＿＿＿＿＿＿＿

8. 請問中級班您最常使用的漢字教學法為（可複選）□（1）筆畫教學 □（2）部首教學 □（3）部件教學 □（4）六書字構 □（5）字源教學 □（6）字族教學 □（7）其他：＿＿＿＿＿＿＿

9. 請問高級班您最常使用的漢字教學法為（可複選）□（1）筆畫教學 □（2）部首教學 □（3）部件教學 □（4）六書字構 □（5）字源教學 □（6）字族教學 □（7）其他：＿＿＿＿＿＿＿

10. 請問您認為「筆畫教學」策略的困難為（可複選）□（1）筆法多樣 □（2）筆畫複雜 □（3）沒有科學性 □（4）沒意見 □（5）其他：＿＿＿＿＿＿＿

11. 請問您認為「部首教學」策略的困難為（可複選）□（1）部首太多 □（2）部首意義不清楚 □（3）部首來源不明 □（4）部首與領字關係不密切 □（5）沒意見 □（6）其他：＿＿＿＿＿＿＿

12. 請問您認為「部件教學」策略的困難為（可複選）□（1）部件太多 □（2）部件多形似 □（3）部件意義不明 □（4）沒有科學性 □（5）沒意見 □（6）其他：＿＿＿＿＿＿＿

13. 請問您認為「六書字構、字源教學」策略的困難為（可複選）□（1）字構不明 □（2）字源不明 □（3）講解困難 □（4）沒意見 □（5）其他：＿＿＿＿＿＿
14. 請問您認為「字族教學」策略的困難為（可複選）□（1）字族的發音不完全相同 □（2）字族的意義的關連性不明 □（3）字族的普遍性不夠 □（4）沒意見 □（5）其他：＿＿＿＿＿＿＿＿
15. 整體而言，您對漢字教學的成就感為 □（1）完全沒有 □（2）不多 □（3）還好 □（4）不錯 □（5）其他：＿＿＿＿＿＿＿＿＿＿
16. 請問您是否發現有其他更需關注的問題？（請敘述）
17. 如果可以，請說說您的漢字教學流程。（請敘述）
18. 如果可以，請說說您漢字教學的絕招。（請敘述）

附錄二：漢字教學問卷（學生版）

---

1 *How difficult is it to learn to read Chinese characters?*
☐ (1) Extremely ☐ (2) Very ☐ (3) Moderately ☐ (4) Slightly ☐ (5) Not difficult at all

2 *How difficult is it to write Chinese characters?*
☐ (1) Extremely ☐ (2) Very ☐ (3) Moderately ☐ (4) Slightly ☐ (5) Not difficult at all

3 *When you began studying Chinese, how did you learn to recognize characters (select all that apply)?*
☐ (1) Memorize strokes ☐ (2) Memorize characteristics ☐ (3) Memorize the structure
☐ (4) Make up a story to help you remember ☐ (5) Other: _____

3-1 *When you began learning to read Chinese characters, speaking and listening...*
☐ (1) Improved as your reading improved ☐ (2) You only learned speaking and listening, not reading ☐ (3) You only learned a few characters at that time ☐ (4) Other: _____

4 *When you first began writing Chinese, how did you learn (select all that apply)?*
☐ (1) Memorize strokes ☐ (2) Study the radicals ☐ (3) Memorize the component ☐ (4) Memorize the structure ☐ (5) Other: _____

4-1 *When you began writing Chinese characters, speaking and listening...*
☐ (1) Improved as your writing improved ☐ (2) You learned to write later, you didn't write at this time ☐ (3) You only learned to write a few characters at that time ☐ (4) Other: _____
(BEGINNERS CAN GO TO QUESTION #9)

5 *After a year of studying Chinese, how did you learn to recognize characters (select all that apply)?*
☐ (1) Memorize strokes ☐ (2) Memorize characteristics ☐ (3) Memorize the structure
☐ (4) Make up a story to help you remember ☐ (5) Other: _____

5-1 *After a year of learning to read Chinese characters, speaking and listening...*
☐ (1) Improved as your reading improved ☐ (2) You only learned speaking and listening, not reading ☐ (3) You only learned a few characters at that time ☐ (4) Other: _____

6 *After a year of writing Chinese, how did you practice your writing of characters (select all that apply)?*
☐ (1) Memorize strokes ☐ (2) Study the radicals ☐ (3) Memorize the component ☐ (4) Memorize the structure ☐ (5) Other: _____

6-1 *After a year of writing Chinese characters, speaking and listening...*
☐ (1) Improved as your writing improved ☐ (2) You learned to write later, you didn't write at this time ☐ (3) You only learned to write a few characters at that time ☐ (4) Other: _____
(STUDENTS WHO HAVE STUDIED LESS THAN TWO YEARS CAN GO TO QUESTION #9)

7 *After two years of studying Chinese, how did you learn to recognize characters (select all that apply)?*
☐ (1) Memorize strokes ☐ (2) Memorize characteristics ☐ (3) Memorize the structure
☐ (4) Make up a story to help you remember ☐ (5) Other: _____
(Beginners don't fill)

7-1 *After two years of learning to read Chinese characters, speaking and listening...*
☐ (1) Improved as your reading improved ☐ (2) You only learned speaking and listening, not reading ☐ (3) You only learned a few characters at that time ☐ (4) Other: _____

8 *After two years of writing Chinese, how did you practice your writing of characters (select all that apply)?*
☐ (1) Memorize strokes ☐ (2) Study the radicals ☐ (3) Memorize the component ☐ (4) Memorize the structure ☐ (5) Other: _____

8-1 *After two years of writing Chinese characters, speaking and listening...*
☐ (1) Improved as your writing improved ☐ (2) You learned to write later, you didn't write at this time ☐ (3) You only learned to write a few characters at that time ☐ (4) Other: _____

9 *When you are reading Chinese characters, some common problems you have are (select all that apply):*
☐ (1) Many characters look similar ☐ (2) Many characters have similar characteristics
☐ (3) There are many homonyms ☐ (4) You forget the whole character ☐ (5) Other: _____

10 *When you are writing Chinese characters, some common problems you have are (select all that apply):*
☐ (1) You can't remember the strokes ☐ (2) You remember the strokes incorrectly
☐ (3) You write the radicals in the wrong place ☐ (4) You forget the whole character
☐ (5) You write a homonym ☐ (6) Other: _____

11 *Because typing is so common, how important is it to learn to write Chinese characters by hand?*
☐ (1) Absolutely necessary ☐ (2) Necessary ☐ (3) A little important ☐ (4) Not necessary at all

12 *What is the best way to learn to write characters, in your opinion?*
☐ (1) Practice constantly ☐ (2) Research the character's structure ☐ (3) Make up stories about the characters ☐ (4) Other: _____

13 *Please describe your own experience of learning about Chinese characters:*

附錄三：高頻使用部首

手（扌）、水（氵）、人（亻）、口、木、糸（糹）、辵（辶）、心
（忄）、艸（艹）、土、肉（月）、宀、日、女、言、貝、阜
（阝）、刀（刂）、金、目、竹（𥫗）、彳、广、玉、頁、禾、足
（𧾷）、車、攵、力、虫、衣（衤）、田、犬（犭）、石、火
（灬）、巾、尸、馬、一、示（礻）、疒、隹、邑（阝）、隹、子、
欠、走、鬥、雨、食（飠）、囗、門、寸、皿、米、网、儿、十、
八、又、大、山、戈、止、牛、方、月、見、曰、酉、行、羽、穴、
弓、夕、二、丿、亠、羊、乙、仌（冫）、卩、工、干、彡、斤、
歹、殳、白、矢、立、虍、豕、里、高、鬼、魚、鳥、黑

附錄四：按課程進度部首

心（忄）、貝、女、木、儿、生、玉、戈、口、日、羊、門、人（亻）、一、艸（艹）、麻、子、丨、言、水（氵）、土、走、小、弓、丿、見、彳、乙、辵（辶）、大、气、火（灬）、厶、攵（夂）、欠、目、雨、彡、邑（阝）、月、車、襾、曰、竹（𥫗）、文、二、八、十、夕、金、禾、毛、刀（刂）、幺、入、糸（糹）、手（扌）、宀、父、白、片、老、巾、寸、豸、田、犬（犭）、斤、臼、亅、矢、耳、黑、隹、夊、肉（月）、食（飠）、足（𧾷）、舛、穴、衣（衤）、尢、爪（爫）、戶、毋、面、阝（阜）、广、方、門、尸、亠、飛、舟、示（礻）、己、頁、馬、工、立、行、父、辛、風、虍、疒、舌、酉、山、牛（牜）、匕、高、魚、非、青、自、石、用、丶、止、力、長、里、凵、匚、皿、臣、骨、黃、色、皮、革、厂、香、麥、缶、音、米、身、羽、瓦、虫、甘、鹵、瓜、鼻、廾、癶、鬥

Lexical Richness and Syntactic Complexity Analysis — From an Online Genre to Academic Discourse

Hsiao-Ping Wu
Texas A&M University-San Antonio
hwu@tamusa.edu
Koying Sung
Utah State University-Logan
Koyin.Sung@usu.edu

Written communication in instant messaging (IM) appears to have generated a "new language" of abbreviations, acronyms, symbols and word combinations, and mixed use of punctuation. This study investigates whether the informal interactive written discourse in IM is permeating the more formal writing found in school writing. This naturalistic study analyzes English as a Foreign Language (EFL) college students' IM chat scripts and academic essays for six months. Computer-mediated discourse analysis is used to determine the positive and negative relationships between IM features in school writing. The findings confirm that literacy is contextual because participants are able to distinguish IM language and academic language use. Online literacy practices also develop students' multiliteracies while developing fluency in the English language. On the other hand, the frequent use of IM is consistently associated with the use of particular informal written communication techniques. Specifically, problems with syntactic complexity as well as the inclusion of a nonstandard orthography are related to frequent use of socially interactive technologies among the students in the current investigation. The study results suggest that further attention from linguistics and communication researchers regarding possible relationships between IM use and formal written discourse is warranted. Possibilities for future research examining school and IM contexts are given in hopes of providing teachers with information on IM use and explore the potential for incorporating its use into a required college-level English curriculum.

Keywords: Lexical richness; syntactic complexity; instant messaging; school writing

線上及學術寫作字彙密度及文法複雜度分析

吳曉萍
德克薩斯州農工大學聖安東尼奧校區
hwu@tamusa.edu

宋可音
猶他州立大學（羅根）
Koyin.Sung@usu.edu

　　即時通訊的書面溝通模式看似能促進「新語言」的生成，包含縮寫、頭字縮略、符號、字詞組合與標點符號的混用。本文探究即時通訊中的非正式書面互動語篇是否能一窺學校場域的正式寫作表現。本文採用自然研究法，分析以英語為二語的大學生，他們的即時通訊聊天文本及其所寫的學術短文六個月。本研究運用電腦中介語篇章分析來決定即時通訊的語言特色與學校正式寫作之間的正向與負向關聯。研究結果證實讀寫能力是具有語境的，因為受試者能夠區分即時通訊與校內寫作在語言使用的差異。線上的讀寫練習能發展學生的多元識讀，同時增進英語流利度。另一方面，即時通訊的頻繁使用與特定的非正式書面溝通技巧有關。具體而言，句法複雜度的問題以及使用非正規的拼字法在本研究中也與學生經常使用社會互動傳播科技有關。本文結果顯示語言學與傳播學研究者應持續關注即時通訊的語言使用與正規寫作之間的可能關聯，後續的相關研究可望給予教師對於即時通訊語言使用的資訊，並探究將即時通訊融入大學英語必修課程的可能性。

關鍵詞：詞彙豐富性、句法複雜度、即時通訊、校內寫作

Introduction

New technologies and the Internet have shifted literacy practices and created new contexts for developing new literacies. New literacies are diverse, dynamic, immediate, interactional, multimodal, rapidly evolving, and requisite for living and learning in the age of information and communication technologies (ICTs). Thus, literacy practices, through computer-mediated communication (CMC), lead to new stylistic forms and increase the expressive range of a language. In particular, young adults have embraced new information technologies in large numbers, as they were born in the digital world and grew up with technology naturally. These young adults are what we have termed "digital natives" (Prensky, 2001). Meanwhile, the change of literacy practices has raised many a researchers' attention. For example, Kress (2003) claims new literacy practices have challenged the traditional view of literacy in reading, writing, speaking, and listening. With the increasing dominance of visual images and technology in everyday life, people should consider that there is no single literacy, but rather "multiliteracies" (New London Group, 1996). Similarly, Lankshear and Knobel (2003) stated that we can no longer interpret, understand and respond to the world in traditional verbocentric terms alone, but must make connections to everyday literacy practices, presented in different forms. However, online literacy practices have provoked a very strong, negative response from teachers, parents and language experts. For example, studies have found that the surrounding of the use of text speak, the process of shortening and adding numbers to a text message such as shorthand abbreviations or emoticons, is potentially detrimental to literacy development (Androutsopoulos & Schmidt, 2002, cited in Thurlow & Poff, 2009; Crystal, 2001). Based on this criticism, this study will examine how online written literacy practices affect standard academic English literacy practices in school.

College Students and Instant Messaging (IM)

The rationale of selecting college students' instant messaging (IM) is because IM has rapidly grown in college students' academic and social life both in the United States (Flanagin, 2005; Madden & Jones, 2002; Rainie, 2005) and in Taiwan (Insight Xplorer Ltd, 2005; 2006). Studies have shown that college students are the main population using IM in the U.S. For example, Madden and Jones (2002) reported that college students aged 17-25 are early adopters and heavy users of the Internet. Flanagin (2005) also found that 85% of college students use the Internet for networking. Similarly, college students are the main users of IM in Taiwan (Insight Xplorer Ltd, 2005; 2006). Studies indicate the use of the Internet by Taiwanese college students has increased dramatically in recent years because it is entertaining, interesting, interactive, and satisfactory (Chou & Hsiao, 2000). Wang (2009) also noted that college students in Taiwan spend about five hours everyday surfing on the Internet, particularly focusing on IM and blogging. Therefore, due to their focused interest on IM and the Internet, Taiwanese college students are selected for this study.

Theoretical Framework

Different researchers have contributed to the New Literacy Studies (NLS) framework (Baron, 2008; Gee, 1996; Street, 1995). This framework examines literacies in everyday social practice, understands the literacy practices embedded in different forms of activities and claims that literacy cannot be defined or used in a vacuum. Drawing on the NLS framework, the researchers discuss literacy as social practice and contextually bound, literacy as multiple literacies, and literacy as multimodal, to guide this study.

Literacy as Social Practice and Contextually Bound

NLS maintains that the meaning of language and literacy are embedded in the particular cultural contexts in which it is used (Bazerman, 1989; Gee, 1996, 2001, Street, 1995). Previous researchers (Gee, 2001; Street, 1993) have agreed that literacy is a social practice. Larson and Marsh (2005) stated "literacy is not simply an individual cognitive activity, but is a communicative tool for different social groups with social rules about who can produce and use particular literacies for particular social purposes" (p. 25). Barton and Hamilton (2000) claimed that there are different literacies associated with different domains of life. Thus, it is significant to understand how the sociocultural context influences literacy practices.

Literacy as Multiple Literacies

The next compelling notion within the NLS is multiliteracies developed by the New London Group (1996). In September 1994, a group of researchers from the United States, England, and Australia had a dialogue to discuss the future of literacy teaching and developed a new way of talking about social context and literacy (Cope & Kalantzis, 2000; New London Group, 1996). They attempted to broaden the understanding of literacy and literacy teaching and learning to include negotiating a multiplicity of discourses. The multiplicity includes two principal aspects. First, they wanted to "extend the idea and scope of literacy pedagogy to account for the context of our culturally and linguistically diverse and increasingly globalized societies" (New London Group, 2000, p. 9). Second, they argued, "literacy pedagogy now must account for the burgeoning variety of text forms associated with information and multimedia technologies" (New London Group, 2000, p. 9). Based on the notion of multiliteracies, literacies encompass more than traditional reading and writing skills. The concept emphasizing the integration of school learning and extra-school communities is important because these contexts exemplify multiliteracies. Students employ their understandings of different literacy practices in different domains.

Literacy as Multimodal

The traditional conceptualization of literacy is that of a set of skills in reading and writing; however, NLS claims literacy practice has moved "from linguistics to semiotics" (Kress, 2003, p. 35). Gee (2003) argues that there are reasons why we should conceptualize literacy more broadly than reading and writing. First, language is not the only tool we use for communication. Other forms of literacy, such as visuals, symbols, and images, used in advertisements, magazines, or books are also tools for communication. The reading of hypertexts, linked text displayed on computer, is completely different because hypertexts are composed of images, sounds, animation, or video clips. Second, Gee states that images are often combined with text; therefore, people have to understand the meaning of images in order to comprehend the text.

Literature Review

What is computer-mediated communication (CMC)?

A working definition of computer-mediated communication (CMC) that, pragmatically and in light of the rapidly changing nature of communication technologies, does not specify forms, instead is described as "the process by which people create, exchange, and perceive information using networked telecommunications systems that facilitate encoding, transmitting, and decoding messages" (December, 1996). CMC can be divided into synchronous and asynchronous modes. For example, in synchronous communication, all participants are online at the same time (e.g. IM), while asynchronous communications occurs at different times (e.g. email). Researchers (Baron, 2005, 2009; Craig, 2003; Herring, 2001; Murray, 1991; Plester, Wood, & Bell, 2008) have documented that languages used in the different forms of CMC have positive influences on language learning and literacy in different ways.

Murray (1991) conducted an ethnographic study for eight months through observations, interviews, discussions, and fieldnotes on an adult language user. Data included 78 conversational partners and 442 written conversations (1,302 messages). The main analysis focused on the composing process of CMC from the lens of the cognitive process model in order to explicate "the cognitive effects of a changing sociocultural environment for the writing task" (Murray, 1991, p. 38). Findings showed that the CMC writing required multiple writing processes, i.e., drafting, editing, and publishing, rather than one writing process. During the writing process, participants employed cognitive and contextual strategies, such as planning, translating, and reviewing, in order to maximize the communicative effectiveness of their interaction based on their knowledge of different audiences. Based on Murray's finding, CMC context provides a cognitive and social learning environment for writing. Murray further observed that online conversationalists create a new mode of discourse and appropriate language for particular tasks and topics. Although Murray found that computer conversations often display speech-like interpersonal involvement using active voice, personal pronouns, emotive diction, hedging, vagueness, and paralinguistic cues, participants still have opportunities to employ different language functions. Through language play, students are able to improve their writing. Namely, Murray noted that the language use in the CMC provides a positive influence on students' writing.

Many studies found that the language use in the CMC is more spoken-based; however, online users adopt these language patterns for different reasons. Herring (2001, p. 5) mentioned online linguistic structure is "less correct, complex and coherent than standard written languages" but there is "only a relatively small percentage of such features appear to be errors caused by inattention or lack of knowledge of the standard language forms" (Herring, 2001, p. 617). Similarly, Baron (2004) examined corpus data collected from American undergraduates through IM on America Online Instant Messenger (AIM). The study suggested that the IM context serves pragmatic information sharing and social-communication functions. Although the data contained few abbreviations or acronyms, participants still spell out the full words. This study only discovered a mere 0.3% of the words had typical IM abbreviations, (e.g., *hrs, cuz*), less than 0.8% acronyms (e.g., *lol, brb*) and 0.4% emoticons (e.g., :)). Herring (2001) further stated the use of these simplified linguistic features and patterns is to economize on typing effort, and the deliberate practice of textual representation or non-language forms, such as graphics or icons are to "adapt the computer medium to their expressive needs" (p. 617).

Craig (2003) discussed the role of IM and youth literacy. He pointed out that IM is a beneficial force in the development of youth literacy, because the context promotes "regular contact with words, the use of a written medium for communication, the learning of an alternative literacy, and a greater level of comfort with phonetics and the overall structure of language" (p. 119). Craig (2003) analyzed 11,341 lines of text from IM conversations between youths in the United States. Young children in this study were able to employ phonetic replacement (e.g. "everyone" become "every1") to learn how words string together to express ideas. Craig (2003) found that students use different varieties or hybrid vernacular varieties as part of language development. For example, participants learned about phonetic replacement and were able to learn alternative literacies, thus becoming comfortable with phonetics and the overall structure of language. Craig suggested that "language play through the Internet should be practiced in schools and these literacy practices will help students to have a better command of language" (p. 124).

Craig (2003) further examined a standardized language assessment scores, particularly the verbal section of the College Board's SATs. The data show that the average verbal score dropped in the students' seven-year path. Possible factors that affect the decline of scores vary, such as television or IM, were identified. However, the reason causing the low verbal scores was likely due to the "insufficient enrollment in English composition and grammar classes" (p. 131), and there is no evidence showing online literacy practices affects academic language learning at school. Similarly, Drouin and Davis (2009) surveyed 80 college students (24 males and 56 females) studying in a Midwestern four-year commuter university. Students were enrolled in an introductory psychology class and participated in this study to fulfill a research requirement. In order to explore the usage of text speak and the relationship between its use and literacy, participants were required to complete e-mail, translation, reading fluency, spelling and survey tasks. Findings showed that there were no significant differences in either GPA or standardized literacy. The study found that text speak users were more proficient with vocabulary. More importantly, there were no significant differences between the two groups (text speak users and non text speak users) in standardized literacy scores or misspellings of common text speak words.

The study supports that engaging in text speak is not related to low literacy performance. In addition, findings also showed that students could differentiate between the two registers and students thought it was inappropriate to use text speak in formal communication. The only influence of engaging in abbreviated use of language is the possibility of hindering their ability to remember Standard English.

Plester, Wood, and Bell (2008) conducted a study of 65 11- and 12-year-old children in the Midlands of England in order to explore whether high and low text speak users differ in the academic outcomes on verbal, reasoning and translation exercises on standardized tests. High text speak users use many online linguistic features; on the other hand, low text speak users do not adopt the online linguistic features in different literacy practices. Their results showed that those who had the highest ratio of text speak when translating from English to textisms and fewer errors in translating from text speak to English had higher verbal reasoning scores but there was no relationship between verbal reasoning and text speak translation errors. Furthermore, Plester, Wood, and Bell (2008) examined more specifically the association between text speak use and children's (26 girls and 9 boys) performance on spelling and writing tasks. Their results found that there was a strong relationship between their use of text speak and level of ability in spelling and writing. The study suggested that the enthusiasm of text speak and ability of engaging in playful use of language are highly related to the skills that enable scoring well on Standard English learning at school. The reason is that students engaged the frequent use of spelling.

Baron (2005) examined the IM usage patterns among American college students from a corpus in order to explore the overall linguistic characteristics of IM conversation and discourse conditions in different domains. Findings showed that students use abbreviations (e.g., k for okay), acronyms (e.g., brb for "be right back"), and emoticons (e.g., ☺ to represent a smiling face). Although students made some spelling errors, there were relatively few CMC abbreviations found in the students' IM corpus. There were only 31 abbreviations, 90 acronyms, and 49 emoticons out of 11,718 words. Although students made spelling errors (171 words), they were able to self-correct themselves during the conversation. Regarding discourses in different domains, the language used in college IM conversation is more spoken-based than written-based. IM language uses include one-word or chunking utterances. Baron's study showed that students understand what kind of language is appropriate in what context; therefore, students tended not to use online language in the school-related literacy activities. Besides, Baron found punctuation in IM conversation remarkably good. Jacobs (2008) conducted a qualitative case study for two years through observing, videotaping, and interviewing a teen girl's use of IM at home. Jacobs (2008) collected over 100 online status postings (away messages) and 7 biographical sketches (profiles) for comparisons of IM features and school writing. Findings showed that none of the conventions of IM appeared in any of the writing because the participant was aware of the differences between writing for friends and for school.

In this section, the researchers reviewed studies on the overall linguistic features found in the IM context from various perspectives from different populations. These studies do not support the negative influence of language use of CMC on academic English, but it is important to continue to test the framework in different contexts; therefore, the following research questions are proposed to investigate the possible relationship between text speak and school writing with Taiwanese college students.

Research Questions

The NLS framework allows the researchers to conceptualize IM as a literacy event in which literacy practices or particular ways of thinking about and doing reading and writing take place. The following research questions are proposed:

1. What linguistic features in English do EFL college students generate in both IM and school writing?
2. How do linguistic features in IM and school writing compare with one another?

Method

Research Design

This study adopted a qualitative case study research approach. Writing from participants was examined from two contexts: IM – Windows Live Messenger 8.5 and school writing. A case study is appropriate because it presents "the depth of instances of a phenomenon in its natural context and from the perspective of the participants involved in the phenomenon" (Gall, Gall, & Borg, 2003, p. 436).

Participants

The participants are 20 English-major junior undergraduate students categorized as either High, Mid-high, and Low IM users enrolled in classes at two different private Taiwanese universities (ten students were recruited from each university). The high, mid-high, and low IM users were categorized based on few criteria designed in this study. 1. Self-report on length of using IM daily; 2. Numbers of friends on IM; 3, Years of using IM. In addition, as

Table 1

Participants' Profiles

#	Name	Gender	Age	English Proficiency	Major	IM Group	Years of Learning English
1	Nathan	M	21	Intermediate	Department of English	High	9
2	Victoria	F	22	Intermediate	Department of English	High	9
3	Bob	M	21	Intermediate	Department of English	High	10
4	Shirley	F	22	Intermediate	Department of English	High	11
5	Henry	M	21	Intermediate	Department of English	High	9
6	Emily	F	21	Intermediate	Department of AFL	Mid-high	9
7	Olivia	F	21	Intermediate	Department of AFL	Mid-high	9
8	Emma	F	21	Intermediate	Department of AFL	Mid-high	9
9	Chanel	F	22	Intermediate	Department of AFL	Mid-high	9
10	Arianna	F	21	Intermediate	Department of AFL	Mid-high	13
11	Lari	F	21	Intermediate	Department of English	Mid-high	12
12	Samuel	M	21	Intermediate	Department of English	Mid-high	9
13	Irene	F	21	Intermediate	Department of English	Low	9
14	Taffy	F	21	Intermediate	Department of English	Low	11
15	Kathy	F	21	Intermediate	Department of English	Low	11
16	George	M	21	Intermediate	Department of AFL	Low	9
17	Tiffany	F	21	Intermediate	Department of AFL	Low	9
18	Lori	F	21	Intermediate	Department of AFL	Low	9
19	Faith	F	22	Intermediate	Department of AFL	Low	9
20	Ashley	F	21	Intermediate	Department of AFL	Low	9

Note. AFL stands for Applied Foreign Language

a research, We also analyzed their IM chat to examine if they are using more IM-related languages.

These participants are divided into three different IM groups (High, Mid-high, and Low IM users) based on the use of IM linguistic features found in their chatting scripts. The participants majored in the Department of English (n = 10) and Applied Foreign Languages[1] (n = 10), and their English proficiency level was assessed based on the Test of English as a Foreign Language (TOEFL) test. The students with intermediate level were selected because it might predict that they were capable of using English in various domains. Table 1 lists each participant's profile.

The participants were from diverse ethnic backgrounds including Chinese, Taiwanese, Hakkanese, and Aboriginals. Participants' ages range from 20 to 21 years old, which falls within the range of between 17 and 25 based on the concept of "early adopter of technology" discussed by Jones (p. 35, 2002). The researchers adopt purposive sampling according to the needs of the study, but the researchers selected all participants on the basis of criteria selected to align with the research purpose. The researchers hypothesized students who have an intermediate proficiency would generate richer content in essays.

Source of Data Collection

Data were collected from a number of sources to address the research questions. The researchers used different methods of data collection because multiple sources enabled the researchers to increase the strength and validity of the study. Sources of data include: 1) a background questionnaire; 2) the IM chat scripts generated by participants; 3) participants' English school writing assignments; and 4) a series of qualitative interviews conducted through IM. In the following sections more details regarding each source of data is given.

---

1 In Taiwan "Applied Foreign Language" majors study English as a foreign language along with a third language that is most commonly Japanese, although other foreign languages may also be available.

Background Questionnaire

The background questionnaire (see Appendix A) was written in English and translated into Mandarin Chinese in order to ensure participants involved in this study fully understood the questions being asked of them. The background questionnaire requested biographical information, IM experience and willingness to participate in the study. In addition, this information allowed the researchers to contact participants through IM and e-mail.

IM Chat Scripts

The purpose of collecting online scripts is to identify the linguistic or paralinguistic features that appeared in the online context. For this study IM communication is considered to be naturally occurring if it would have occurred whether or not it was observed or recorded by a researcher. Naturally occurring data help researchers to capture subtle details of interaction. The researchers asked the participants to collect the data. The researchers requested the participants to save their IM chat scripts and forward them on regularly. The IM chat data was collected during the Spring semester of the 2009-2010 academic year. The researchers collected 1,500-2,000 lines of chat from each participant. The researchers felt that this amount of data would be adequate to allow for generalizability of IM language use without overburdening the participants.

School Writing Assignments

In order to compare the relationship between IM literacy practices and school writing, students from school A (Department of English) and school B (Department of AFL) shared their descriptive essays for analysis. In this assignment, students were assigned the topic on "description of a space". For example, students can describe their rooms, visit of museum, a restaurant. A total of 6,225 words were collected from the twenty participants.

IM One-On-One Semi-structured Interview

IM one-on-one interview data were collected through MSN IM software. Researchers (Kivitis, 2005; Rennecker, 2005) have discussed the advantages of online interviews. First, the medium of IM supports near synchronous communication among two or more parties. Second, online interviewing enables access to participants who cannot be interviewed face-to-face or who are uncomfortable discussing topics face-to-face (Bampton & Cowton, 2002; Chaney & Dew, 2003). Third, interviewing through IM also empowers participants in that they will not be judged by the researcher through non-verbal reactions (i.e. facial expressions). The online interview process followed Seidman's (1991) three-part interview structure. First, participants were interviewed through IM in Chinese regarding their language learning and perceptions of language use in the IM context. Second, the researchers encouraged participants to provide concrete details about those experiences by explaining and elaborating on why they use different linguistic features through IM in certain ways. For example, participants would provide further explanation of how they use smilie faces. Third, participants were asked to describe their literacy practices and told to collect their interview chat scripts in order for the researchers to be able to examine what reasons they change or do not change their language use and learning during chat. During the months of April 2010 through June 2010 each student participated in at least one online interview that lasted a minimum of 30 minutes.

Data Analysis

This section describes the approach taken for data analysis – Computer-Mediated Discourse Analysis (CMDA) (Herring, 2001). CMDA encompasses all kinds of interpersonal communication carried out on the Internet. CMDA is also an approach of "counting and coding"; therefore, the researchers will calculate tokens by numbers and percentages to examine the amount of CMC linguistic features shown in both contexts: school writing and IM. The researchers also borrowed counting approaches used in previous studies (Warschauer, 1996; Abrams, 2003) to count lexical density, lexical richness, and syntactic complexity. The counting processes allow the researchers to examine whether there is a transition of online linguistic features to school writing. The researchers adopted Warschauer's (1996) and Abrams's (2003) formula to define positive language characteristics. If students had higher lexical richness, higher lexical density, and higher syntactic complexity, these would be considered as a positive transition from the IM context to the school context.

Traditionally, type-token ratio (TTR) has been used to analyze spoken and written discourse; however, Daller, Van Hout and Treffers-Daller (2003) stated that there is "a problem with this measure because longer texts automatically obtain lower TTRs because the change of a new word occurring gets lower text length increases since the speaker/writer has only a limited number of different words at his/her disposal" (p. 199). The use of TTR to compare spoken and written language will yield problems because spoken discourse is usually longer than written discourse. Therefore, Foster, Tonkyn and Wigglesworth's (2000) approach provided a new way of defining a token or sentence that will be calculated in order to calculate lexical richness, lexical density, and syntactic complexity. Foster, Tonkyn, and Wigglesworth's (2000) stated that "the analysis speech unit (AS-Unit) is a single speaker's utterance consisting of an independent clause, or sub clausal unit, together with any subordinate clauses(s) associated with either" (p. 365). They proposed use of the AS-Unit because they have found that "sentences are paused at syntactic unit boundaries, especially clause boundaries" (p. 365). In addition, Foster, Tonkyn and Wigglesworth's definition of sentence allows for analyzing multi-clause units produced in the IM context. Thus, the AS-Unit is suitable for measuring IM chat scripts. In order to compare language use in both contexts, the descriptive essays are also analyzed using the same procedure. The next section provides our definition of sentences and tokens, including examples from IM chat scripts from Taiwanese EFL college students.

Lexical Richness, Density, and Syntactic Complexity in Essays

The researchers analyzed students' school writing and IM chat scripts by following two steps. First, the total number of words in the school writings and IM chat scripts were calculated by using online text analysis (Textalyser, n.d.). This online tool, designed by Bernhard Huber Internet Engineering Company, can provide the analysis of word groups, the frequency of words in a text, and the detailed statistics of your text. Second, the researchers entered data generated from online text analysis to Excel in order to manual code the IM features and rank different features. One of the researchers and two other TESOL trained teachers independently searched for and categorized the IM features in the school writings while the two researchers independently searched for and categorized the IM features found in the IM chat scripts. Any inconsistencies in the coding were discussed in order to ensure reliability of the coding.

Lexical Richness

To measure lexical richness (the number of different words), one may choose to adopt Warschauer's (1996) formula of "the total number of different words divided by the total number of words a learner uttered" (p. 13). Warschauer implied that the higher the value of lexical richness students displayed the greater the complexity of their language. However, we adopted Daller, Van Hout and Treffers-Daller's (2003) index of Guiraud to calculate lexical richness. Daller, Van Hout and Treffers-Daller (2003) stated that "the square root in the denominator leads to a higher value of lexical richness for a longer text within the same TTR as a shorter one" (p. 200). Therefore, the number of words will be the square root of total number of tokens in the denominator (see Figure 1). The measure combines characters of type/token measures with the notion of different layers of frequency/productivity in the lexicon. It will provide more accurate calculation of lexical richness.

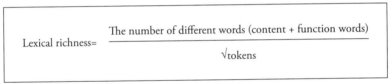

$$\text{Lexical richness} = \frac{\text{The number of different words (content + function words)}}{\sqrt{\text{tokens}}}$$

Figure 1. Lexcial richess formula

Lexical Density

Abrams (2003) stated that lexical density could indicate students' competence in using a varied lexicon. She analyzed students' content words for their complexity. In other words, the higher the lexical density, the greater the complexity. The researchers adopt Abrams's formula for calculating lexical density (see Figure 2).

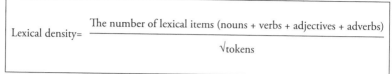

$$\text{Lexical density} = \frac{\text{The number of lexical items (nouns + verbs + adjectives + adverbs)}}{\sqrt{\text{tokens}}}$$

Figure 2. Lexical density formula

Syntactic Complexity

To determine syntactic complexity, the researchers adopt Warschauer's (1996) formula. Warschauer claimed that this index was "considered to be inversely proportional to complexity, since more advanced writers of language generally use proportionally more subordination than do beginners" (p. 14). Warschauer's coordination index is the number of independent clauses divided by the total number of independent and dependent clauses. The smaller the value, the more dependent clauses a writer uses, meaning the greater the complexity of the writing. However, the definition of independent clauses, dependent subordination will be drawn from Foster, Tonkyn, and Wigglesworth (2000) (see Figure 3). The use of TTR of comparisons between spoken and written language will yield problems because spoken discourse is usually longer than written discourse. Therefore, Foster, Tonkyn and Wigglesworth's (2000) approach provided a new way of defining token or sentence that will be used to calculate lexical richness, lexical density, and syntactic complexity.

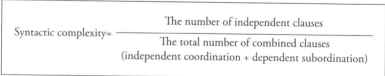

$$\text{Syntactic complexity} = \frac{\text{The number of independent clauses}}{\substack{\text{The total number of combined clauses} \\ \text{(independent coordination + dependent subordination)}}}$$

Figure 3. Syntactic complexity formula

Trustworthiness of the Study

In order to establish the trustworthiness of the study, several other strategies, such as "triangulation of data, prolonged time in the field, persistent observation, and transferability" suggested by Lincoln and Guba (1985, p.328) were used. The researchers adopted triangulation of data, prolonged time in the field, and reassurance of the students' confidentiality to share their opinions.

First, in this study, triangulation of data and sources was performed. The researchers employed various data collection methods such as open-ended questionnaires, actual written data, virtual observation, research log, and a series of online interviews. These various data enabled the researchers to not only have a deeper understanding of the phenomenon but also corroborated the findings for validity. The researchers also employed a quantitative strategy of supporting the credibility of qualitative analyses. For example, students' writing will be measured through qualitative coding and quantitative analyses for comparisons. Second, spending a prolonged time at the research site is another strategy for gaining credibility. Lincoln and Guba (1985) stated that "prolonged engagement provided the scope, and persistent observation provided depth" (p. 304). In this study, the researchers spent approximately two months building up a relationship and rapport with the participants before starting to collect data. In the beginning of our research, the researchers visited two different classes in two different universities twice a week during the stay in Taiwan. The researchers had formal and informal conversations through chatting and Facebook with the participants. After visiting the participants, the researchers spent almost two months interacting with them through instant messaging or email before they started to be interviewed. During the preparation stage, the researchers had informal chatting with the participants about different topics, such as school life, travel experience, or experience sharing. The researchers stayed online at least four hours a day to maintain interaction with participants at all times. The researchers also continued to engage in persistent observation of their behavior when they were online. The researchers conducted all the individual interviews before asking their availability of being online, so they would be able to reveal their true feelings about the interview questions. For example, the researchers checked their availability to stay online and compared this to their self-reported IM use behavior on the questionnaires. This virtual observation allowed assurance that the analysis is accurate.

Besides the above-mentioned methodological procedures to ensure the trustworthiness of the study, the researchers reassured the students that their writings and interviews were anonymous and would not affect their grades, and their teachers would not have access to the collected data. Moreover, participants were completely empowered in the interview process because they were interviewed through IM. They were able to provide their responses without worrying about being judged by other non-verbal interaction. They were able to terminate the interview by logging off or they could send a text stating they did not wish to continue without worrying about the awkward situation that could happen in face-to-face interaction.

Findings

Number of Linguistic Features in Essays and IM Chat Scripts

In the next two sections, the researchers present data related to research questions one and two. Specifically: 1) What linguistic features in English do EFL college students generate in both IM and school writing? 2) How do linguistic features in IM and school writing compare with one another?

Scope of Data – Number of Words

This section presents the scope of data collected from participants' school writing and IM chat scripts. Table 2 presents the total number of words in school writing and IM chat scripts, participants' IM usage ranking, IM or IM-like features found in both contexts, and percentage of IM features out of total words.

Table 2 shows that there are a total of 16,255 words from twenty students' school writing and 9,857 words from English IM chat scripts available for analysis. There are 81 IM or IM-like features found in students' school writing, and a total of 2,055 IM or IM-like features found in IM chat scripts. While all participants have IM or IM-like features in their school writing, the overall percentage is low (<1%).

The use of IM features or IM-like features during IM is very common, accounting for approximately 21% of the total data. IM or IM-like features range from 16% to 51% for the Mid-high and High IM groups. For example, participant #1 (Nathan) had five IM-like features in his school writing; however, IM linguistic features are mostly found in his IM chat scripts. Slightly more than half (51%) of his chat scripts are comprised of IM features. When comparing the number of IM features in school writing with those found in IM chat scripts, there is a clear difference in the distribution between IM scripts and school writings. The range from 23% to 51% of IM features in IM chat scripts suggests that the students in the high IM group used IM features in their IM chats, but not in their school writings.

The result is not surprising, indicating that these twenty participants used many IM features during their conversations online because in this context informal language and Internet English is expected to be used. Topics in IM conversation vary, and few topics are related to academics. They discuss non-academic events and track friends' real lives. Topics found in IM chatting

Table 2

Number of Words in Essays and English IM Chatting scripts

	Participants	Essays (words)	IM (like) Feature in Essays	%	English IM Chat scripts (words)	IM Features in IM Chat Scripts	%
			High IM Group				
1	Nathan	397	5	1%	1111	567	51%
2	Victoria	432	1	0%	299	122	41%
3	Bob	1001	11	1%	130	51	39%
4	Shirley	498	0	0%	80	31	39%
5	Henry	995	6	1%	291	67	23%
			Mid-high IM Group				
6	Emily	1461	5	0%	384	85	22%
7	Olivia	945	4	0%	566	145	26%
8	Emma	700	2	0%	118	26	22%
9	Chanel	612	0	0%	1486	277	19%
10	Adriana	952	5	1%	408	71	17%
11	Lari	1071	7	1%	258	40	16%
12	Samuel	1190	4	0%	111	18	16%
			Low IM Group				
13	Irene	423	1	0%	2766	377	14%
14	Taffy	1759	14	1%	407	49	12%
15	Kathy	497	3	1%	159	19	12%
16	George	440	0	0%	137	17	12%
17	Tiffany	255	2	1%	91	9	10%
18	Lori	232	0	0%	225	20	9%
19	Faith	1429	8	1%	335	28	8%
20	Ashley	966	3	0%	495	36	7%
	Total	16,255	81	<1%	9,857	2,055	21%

scripts were informal, mostly to do with students' everyday lives or MSN IM was used as a cell phone replacement to communicate with friends. Participants considered IM context as less formal when compared to other literacy contexts, such as school. Data from the online interviews showed that participants usually used IM to chat and share information with their friends.

School writing requires a different style. Namely, students have to write in a "Standard English" and the language usage has to be grammatically correct. Thus, students followed their instructors' requirements when writing essays. For example, data from the online interviews noted that the instructors taught students how to draft a descriptive essay and what format should be followed. Namely, students were aware of using a certain format in school writing.

In the case of all participants, the presence of IM features is higher in the IM scripts than in the school writing. The finding is what was expected. One explanation for this is that students might be required to write in a certain genre at school. These results showed that language use is contextually embedded, and participants were able to differentiate between appropriate and inappropriate language use for different literacy events. The next section will present specific types of linguistic features found in the two contexts analyzed.

Types of IM Features in Two Contexts – School Writing and IM Chat Scripts

The analysis of IM features was based on Crystal (2001). Crystal describes Internet English as including specific graphic, orthographic, grammatical, lexical, and discourse features. Moreover, phonetic features, and phonological features are found online because Internet English is written based on play with pronunciation and imitation of sounds.

Table 3

Types and Numbers of IM Features in School Writing and IM Chat Scripts

Features	Types	IM Chat Scripts	%	Top 5 Rank in IM	IM Features in Essays	%	Top 5 Rank in Essay
Graphic Features	Uses of computer keyboard symbols	47	2%		-		
	Emoticon	9	-		-		
	Font	3	-		-		
	Missing capital letters	583	28%	2	3	<1%	
	Spelling mistakes	67	3%		9	<1%	3
	Use of abbreviations and acronyms	72	4%		9	<1%	3
OrthographicFeatures	Use of capital letters	142	7%	3	4	<1%	5
	Use of punctuation for emphasis	48	2%		1	<1%	
	Use of non-standard punctuation	119	6%	5	-		
Grammatical Features	The use of non-sentence fragments (run-ons sentences)	141	7%	4	24	<1%	2
Lexical Features	Lexical vagueness	13	1%		3	<1%	
Discourse Features	Discourse markers	68	3%		-		
	Hesitation features	-	-		-		
	Connection by coordination	99	5%		25	<1%	1
	Comma use, quotation mark use & no period at the end	595	29%	1	3	<1%	
Phonetic Features	Vowels and consonants: emotional expressions	49	2%		-		
Phonological Features	Non-standard spelling reflects pronunciation	0	-		-		
Total		2055	99%		81	1%	

Note. - No IM features found.

Table 3 presents an overview of IM and IM-like features based on Crystal (2003), including the five most frequent IM or IM-like features found in school writing and IM chat scripts. Under each feature, different types of features are also listed. In school writing, participants used the following IM or IM-like features most frequently: (1) connection by coordination; (2) the use of non-sentence fragments or run-on sentences; (3) spelling mistakes; (4) use of abbreviation and acronyms; and (5) use of capital letters. In contrast, in the IM chat scripts, students used the following five IM or IM-like features most frequently: (1) comma use, quotation mark use, and no period at the end; (2) missing capital letters; (3) use of capital letters; (4) the use of non-sentence fragments or run-on sentences; and (5) use of non-standard punctuation.

The most frequent type of IM feature found in both school writing and IM chat scripts is the use of capital letters and non-sentence fragments or run-on sentences. Thus, in the following the researchers highlight these two features and provide examples found in the students' writing. The researchers present specific examples under each category found in IM chat scripts and school essays. First, participants sometimes used all capitals while chatting. For example, her homestay family in Australia told participant Irene that they met a new international student (see Excerpt 1). Her homestay would like to confirm whether Irene came from the same country (line 3). Irene replied by saying no repetitively (line 4). Irene switched to all capitals to explain where she is from (line 3 – line 8). The use of all capitals in this case is to show emphasis because Irene's homestay family was confused about her nationality, and Irene wanted to clarify that Taiwan and Thailand are two different countries. These linguistic features in IM context are appropriate and acceptable because they did not negatively affect the conversation since IM genre has been identified as spoken-based genre.

Excerpt 1

Example of the use of capitals in IM chat (Irene)

Homestay: the student come from Taiwan? really!!

Irene: you sure?

Homestay: *ARE YOU FREOM THAILAND OR THAI*

Irene: no no no no !!!!!! it's TAIWAN NOT TAILAND!!!
TAIPEI IS OUR CAPITAL CITY! GOT IT?
YOU CAN CHECK IT OUT ON THE INTERNET
AND FIGURE IT OUT!!! DO NOT BE CONFUSED
ABOUT THE TWO COUNTRY AGAIN
PLEASE!!!!!!!!!!!

The use of all capitals was found in students' essays (see Excerpt 2). Nathan, in his descriptive essay, was introducing the image of Buddha, Jackie; however, he capitalized Jackie every time he mentioned this name in his essay. In this case, it is unknown why Nathan capitalized all letters of the name Jackie, which made his use of capitalization unconventional for the academic genre.

Excerpt 2

Example of the use of capitals in school writing (Nathan)

"The right side is for JACKIE the Living Buddha; the middle side, for Guanyin"

The next example is the use of a non-sentence fragment in the IM chat scripts and in the school writing. The use of a non-sentence fragments means that a participant produced part of sentence rather than a complete sentence. On the other hand, a run-on sentence means that multiple sentences were used without conventional, academic conjunctions to link the two main clauses. In the example below, line 1 of Nathan's IM chat contains a run-on sentence without a conjunction linking the two ideas (see Excerpt 3). Line 4 contains an example of a non-sentence fragment. Similarly, a run-on sentence is also found in Emily's school writing shown in Excerpt 4 below. Her sentence is written without a conjunction.

Excerpt 3

Example of the use of a non-sentence fragment and run-on sentence in IM chat highlighted in bold (Nathan)

Nathan: It was a beautiful day there was not a cloud in the sky. (Run-on sentence)

Nathan: Do you wanna go out?

Kim: I am sorry I just prefer staying home LOL

Nathan: cuz I am checking the frech books

Kim: hey if you find out that book remember to let me chick it out (Sentence fragment)

Excerpt 4

Example of the use of non-sentence fragment or run-on sentence in school writing highlighted in bold (Emily)

"Many **people usually are the poor labor were captured by the other tribe's people** and forced to mine the diamond." **(Run-on sentence)**

There are a number of possible explanations for these features found in school writings and IM chat scripts. In IM chat, first, participants would like to economize typing speed; so abbreviation, punctuations and missing capitalization were used. Second, IM chat focuses on ideas more than the accuracy of language use. Third, IM chat is viewed as a conversational genre; thus, language use is relatively short and less complex. For example, 7% of fragment sentence structures were used in IM chat, so it is acceptable to have non-sentence fragments in the IM chat. On the other hand, only 1% non-sentence fragments were found in school writings. A likely explanation for the presence of the IM-like features in the school writing rests with editing or proofreading skills of the English/Applied Languages majors. First, the use of all capitalization in a student's essay might need to be addressed by an editor before submission since students may be more focused on the content of the school writing rather than the format of the text. Second, the use of run-on sentences found in their school writing might be due to a need for sentences to be longer and more complex to discuss topics assigned by teachers. The use of run-on sentences would be from students' misuse of sentence structures. In the following sections, the researchers discuss lexical richness, lexical density, and syntactic complexity in both contexts.

Lexical Richness, Lexical Density, and Syntactic Complexity in School Writing

School writings from both universities were collected from February to March 2010. Warschauer (1996) implied that the higher the value students displayed in lexical richness and lexical density, the greater the complexity of their language use in vocabulary. On the other hand, the lower the value students displayed in syntactic complexity, the greater the complexity of their sentence structures. First, participants were divided into either High, Mid-high or Low IM groups depending on the amount of text speak found in their chat scripts. Second, the researchers calculated the value of lexical richness, lexical density, and syntactic complexity across participants and contexts.

Table 4 presents the ranked and actual results of lexical richness and lexical density of students' school writing. The lexical richness ranges from

Table 4

Lexical Richness and Lexical Density of School Writing

	High IM to Low IM	Lexical Richness Rank	Lexical Richness	Lexical Density Rank	Lexical Density
		High IM Group			
1	Nathan	13	9.34	14	6.88
2	Victoria	6	10.15	12	9.59
3	Bob	20	7.55	20	9.59
4	Shirley	9	9.77	11	7.35
5	Henry	18	8.32	10	7.55
		Mid-high IM Group			
6	Emily	4	10.56	5	8.45
7	Olivia	10	9.73	1	9.59
8	Emma	17	8.45	18	5.59
9	Chanel	1	11.96	4	9.34
10	Arianna	14	9.31	6	8.45
11	Lari	11	9.6	7	8.45
12	Samuel	12	9.59	15	6.66
		Low IM Group			
13	Irene	5	10.5	8	7.78
14	Taffy	3	10.7	3	9.59
15	Kathy	7	9.96	13	7.26
16	George	15	9.09	16	6.57
17	Tiffany	19	7.64	19	5.13
18	Lori	16	8.8	17	5.65
19	Faith	2	10.84	2	9.59
20	Ashley	8	9.79	9	8.45
	Mean		9.58		7.48

7.55 to 11.96 in school writing with a mean of 9.58. Lexical density ranges from 5.13 to 9.59 with a mean of 7.48. Higher value indicates that students have better lexical richness. In this study, if the participants' lexical richness is above 9.59, it means that students' lexical richness meets the correct and

Table 5

Syntactic Complexity of School Writing

		Rank	Raw Scores
High IM Group			
1	Nathan	19	1.17
2	Victoria	15	0.72
3	Bob	16	0.75
4	Shirley	14	0.62
5	Henry	13	0.54
Mid-high IM Group			
6	Emily	1	0.06
7	Olivia	11	0.47
8	Emma	20	1.60
9	Chanel	3	0.14
10	Arianna	5	0.25
11	Lari	2	0.13
12	Samuel	9	0.38
Low IM Group			
13	Irene	7	0.27
14	Taffy	8	0.38
15	Kathy	10	0.44
16	George	18	1.14
17	Tiffany	17	1.00
18	Lori	4	0.15
19	Faith	6	0.26
20	Ashley	12	0.50
	Mean		0.55

Note. – The higher the rank the lower the syntactic complexity.

complex language use in school writings. Similarly, if participants' lexical richness is higher than the cut-of point 7.31, the mean in the group, it means that they can use appropriate vocabulary to express their thoughts in the school writings.

Findings showed that all groups contained participants whose school writings analysis resulted in both high and low lexical richness and density. For example, participants Nathan, Victoria, and Bob are the top 3 High IMers in this study; however, their ranks of lexical richness and density do not all fail to meet the lexical richness and density thresholds set by the researchers. On the other hand, Low IMers such as Tiffany, Lori, Irene, Taffy, Faith, and Ashley also demonstrate high lexical richness and lexical density. In terms of the relationships among high IM use and school writing quality in terms of lexicon use, the perception that high IM use would result in less rich vocabulary use is not supported based on the measurement of lexical richness and density.

Table 5 presents the syntactic complexity ranks and raw scores of each participant. Syntactic complexity ranges from 0.06 to 1.60 with a mean of 0.55. Namely, a value greater than 0.54 for students' school writing was considered by the researchers as indicating more complex language use in school writing. Table 5 further shows that the students in the High IM group received a low syntactic complexity rating. The top 5 High IMers tended to generate lower syntactic complexity than the remaining students, with the exception of Nathan and Emily.

The high IM group displays a lack of syntactic complexity in their school writing. However, students in the low IM group have strengths and weaknesses in three different linguistic categories. As a result, the perception that high IM users would generate low syntactic complexity due to the high use of features such as coordination by conjunction in their IM scripts is partially born out. For example, school writing done by participant Nathan, a High IMer, did receive a high lexical richness (rank 13), lexical density (rank 14), and syntactic complexity (rank 19) ranking. On the other hand, participant Ashley, a Low IM user, also received an above average ranking for all three categories; her school writings obtained a lexical richness rank 8, lexical density rank 9, and syntactic complexity rank 12. Also, the school writings of Lori and Faith, low IM users, received syntactic complexity rankings higher than the High IM users.

Lexical Richness, Lexical Density, and Syntactic Complexity in IM Chat Scripts

This section will present the results of the analysis of the IM Chat Scripts for lexical richness, lexical density, and syntactic complexity. This section aims to use results from the data analysis to determine whether high IM use would cause a decrease of lexical richness and density in Taiwanese college students' school writings.

Table 6 presents the results of the analysis of students IM chat scripts in terms of lexical richness and lexical density. No fixed pattern can be found in lexical richness and lexical density across groups. For example, participants Nathan, Victoria, Shirley, Olivia, Chanel, Arianna, Taffy, Kathy, Faith, and Ashley's IM chat received a good lexical richness and lexical density ranking. Moreover, Nathan and Victoria are the top two IM users in this study, but their IM chat scripts received high lexical richness and density rankings. Namely, the hypothesis of being high IM user would affect their academic English language is not supported based on the measurement of lexical richness and density. The measurement of lexical richness and density shows that higher and lower IMers are able to use rich and dense words in IM genre.

Lexical Richness and Lexical Density in Both Contexts

The lexical richness ranges from 7.55 to 11.96 in school writing with a mean of 9.58, and the lexical richness in IM chat ranges from 3.45 to 11.51. Namely, the lexical richness in school writing is higher than IM chat.

Table 6

Lexical Richness and Lexical Density of IM Chat Scripts

	Names	Lexical Richness Rank	Lexical Richness	Lexical Density Rank	Lexical Density
			High IM Group		
1	Nathan	1	11.52	1	9.57
2	Victoria	5	8.50	4	7.52
3	Bob	12	6.93	13	5.18
4	Shirley	3	8.95	5	7.38
5	Henry	13	6.53	11	5.71
			Mid-high IM Group		
6	Emily	14	5.99	14	4.32
7	Olivia	2	9.63	2	8.21
8	Emma	17	5.27	16	4.28
9	Chanel	6	8.17	6	7.25
10	Arianna	8	7.71	7	6.47
11	Lari	15	5.54	18	4.05
12	Samuel	16	5.32	17	4.06
			Low IM Group		
13	Irene	18	5.13	15	4.32
14	Taffy	11	7.02	10	5.79
15	Kathy	10	7.45	9	5.95
16	George	20	3.45	20	2.80
17	Tiffany	19	4.40	19	3.56
18	Lori	7	7.73	12	5.60
19	Faith	9	7.53	9	6.16
20	Ashley	4	8.89	3	6.89

Similarly, lexical density in school writing ranges from 5.13 to 9.59 with a mean of 7.48. The range is also higher than in IM chat, ranging from 2.80 to 9.57.

Based on the raw scores of the two genres, lexical richness and density in school writing is greater than that found in IM chat, which is perhaps an indication of the time and effort placed in school writing that adhere to genre expectations with respect to lexicon. However, there was no positive transfer found between the two contexts. Namely, participants who demonstrate greater lexical richness and density in IM chat do not demonstrate higher lexical richness and density in school writing. For example, participants Nathan and Victoria generated high lexical richness and density in IM chat, but their ranking of richness and density in school writing was low.

Syntactic Complexity in IM

In the examination of syntactic complexity of IM generated by high and low IM users, it was found that they were all below the average. There are 18 participants whose syntactic complexity ranges from 0.898 to 0.988. Overall, the syntactic complexity tends to be lower in the IM chat. However, two participants, Irene and George, had a more complex syntactic complexity in their chat scripts. The syntactic complexity is 0.375. These students appeared to use their chatting to support their academic learning. For example, Irene used IM to discuss a research paper group project with group members. Thus, the syntactic complexity more closely mirrors that of an academic rather than a social interaction. An example of a more complex language use is presented in Excerpt 5. Participants adjusted their writing styles to generate more complex sentence structures and followed the conventions of punctuation expected in school writing. Due to the purposes of chatting and people they chat with, participants were able to generate more complex sentences in the IM context. The next section will compare syntactic complexity in both contexts.

Excerpt 5

The example of high syntactic complexity in IM chat

Irene: Fifty questionnaires were discarded because of incomplete data and wrong information. Therefore, data from 200 participants (100 male and 100 female) were used and processed with the statistical software, SPSS. Descriptive statistics were shown. Furthermore, make up really increase women confidence and happiness.

Ruby (Irene's group member): 喔喔 [oh oh]

Irene: ok.

Irene: Furthermore, make up really increase women confidence and happiness.
視這句要刪除嗎 [Do I have to delete this sentence?]

Ruby: Descriptive statistics were shown 是什麼意思 [What does it mean?]

Irene: 就是平均數 [It is the mean.]

Ruby: 喔喔 [oh oh]

Ruby: 了解 [understood]

Irene: The questionnaire was given to the participants in the end of the first semester in 2009. In order to have accurate answers, the participants were told to be free to answer what they think. And there have as much as they need. After participants finished the questionnaire, the follow up one to one interviews were conducted by the research with ten participants (five male and five female) who were randomly chose. And the questionnaires and interview all in Chinese to make sure all the participants understand the whole question and easy to talked about their thought.

Syntactic Complexity in Both Contexts

When comparing syntactic complexity for school writing and IM chat, it is found that half of high IM users received a low rank in both contexts.

Data analysis showed that the high IM group produced low syntactic complexity in both contexts. Namely, the hypothesis that high IM users would produce low syntactic complexity is supported. For example, participant Nathan's school writing ranked 19 and his IM chat script ranked 17. Similarly, participants Victoria, Shirley, Henry, Emma and Samuel are also high IMers who produced low syntactic complexity in the school writing. Although there was not a direct relationship between syntactic complexity in school writing and IM chat scripts, the researchers interpret this to mean that high IM users would have less contact with academic genres if they engaged in IM literacy practices.

Conclusions

This study began with the assumption that literacy use is contextual, and set out to examine the potential influences of language use in on-line contexts, specifically IMing, on the academic performance of English/Applied Foreign Language majors at two universities in Taiwan. To examine these issues, High, Mid-high, and Low IMers were compared in terms of their language use in two contexts: IM chat scripts and school writing. The study concluded that context affects literacy practice, and the digital generation is establishing a genre in this generation.

Language is Contextual

First, the researchers found language in school writing is more structurally complex than in IM chat. School writing is about specific topics resulting in more complex sentence structures. On the other hand, IM chat scripts include pictograms, logograms, initialisms, omitted letters, nonstandard spellings, shortenings, and genuine novelties. There is a low percentage of

IM or IM-like features found in students' school writings. Both high and low IM users use IM-like features in their school writing and IM chat. Although these features were used, they were acceptable forms in the written genre (i.e., acronyms). Both High and Low IMers showed a clear difference in the English used in the two contexts. That is, an examination of language use in the two contexts bears out the assumption that language use is contextual, even for intermediate English language learners such as the participants in this study. An examination of language use in the IM chat indicated a number of features that distinguish it from other varieties, in particular school writing. The impact of the IM chat on English language is seen in the areas of vocabulary, graphology, morphology, and syntax.

In addition, this study has shown that the same students are proficient, to varying degrees, in the variety of school writing in an academic context. That is, the participants are able to write academic essays that align with the instructor's expectations. Moreover, it appears that engaging in online literacy practices does not hamper writing academic English. This conclusion aligns with Warschauer (1999) comparing real time chat and traditional writing practice in an intermediate ESL class. Students involved in that study largely met the expectations set by the instructor. Specifically, the instructor demanded a product that included both sophisticated and highly professional writing. Similarly, students in this study indicated their awareness of and attempts to produce school writing in line with instructor expectations.

On the other hand, the IM genre does not require a specific writing style, and the digital generation is establishing a new IM genre. Baron (2008) stated that electronically-mediated language is very new. Users are still "in the process of settling upon conventions that ostensibly will become the new rules to be followed or broken" (p. 173). Namely, no one has established a proper IM chatting style. There are some reasons that sentence structures are broken. Through deeper examination of students' IM chat interview data it was found that participants used IM as a tool to practice their English, even though they noticed that there were many wrong usages when conversing.

Spelling mistakes and inappropriate punctuation are found in IM but students stated that there is no need to check spelling and sentence structures as long as it does not affect the conversation. IM is a genre that includes written and spoken styles. Baron (2008) states that "language users do simply not know which spoken or written pattern conforms to the rules" (p. 169). Thus, students usually expressed that they merely type whatever they want to express. Gradually, students are learning the different cultural meanings tied to colors, fonts, screen names, and profiles that are important elements of IM communication. When students understand the rules of IM, they can use their creativity to piece the elements together in order to express their ideas.

Thus, this study rejects the claim that IM is the linguistic ruin of the new generation (e.g., Axtman, 2002) or a breakdown in the English language (e.g., O'Connor, 2005). The results of this study indicate that language use depends on the context. In what follows, the researchers outline some subtle ways in which IM may be seen as both positive – particularly with respect to fluency and authenticity – and potentially negative, particularly with respect to syntactic complexity and accuracy.

Creating Authentic Contexts for Fluency and Proficient Language Users

The study confirms that IM serves as an authentic context to improve fluency and develop a proficient language user as a High IM user. The use of IM in English serves a specific function for the majority of the High IM participants. High IM participants view the IM literacy practice as a support in maintaining their fluency in using English. Prior studies suggested that real time written exchanges enable students to have meaningful and authentic conversations with others in the target language (Meskill & Anthony, 2007). Participants expressed that they seldom speak English after school. Using the Internet to communicate with different people in their buddy lists is one channel they can use to practice their English skills (Blake, 2000). Although participants expressed that they were not sure whether they had correct usage in their IM conversation, unlike in the school context, they rarely receive feedback, resulting in participants' positive response to IM as a venue for conversing in the target language.

Syntactic Complexity-Second Language Learners' Weakness

Through the comparison of lexical richness, lexical density, and syntactic complexity, no consistent pattern was found in lexical richness and density across groups. The use of vocabulary is rich and dense in both contexts because participants are able to articulate their thoughts by using a variety of words. In addition, punctuation and spelling were generally accurate for both contexts. However, there is a tendency for High IMers to have lower syntactic complexity. The low syntactic complexity could be due to several reasons including the frequent use of less complex sentences. Sentence structures in IM contexts are less complex. Namely, IM has its particular genre and school writing requires a style required by the instructor and reinforced by a textbook. In IM, sentences usually do not contain subjects but instead more phrase-like conversation. Interlocutors also read non-sentence fragments on their screens during conversations. Therefore, these literacy practices do not support the more complex sentence structures often found in school writing. The study concludes that the IM genre does not support genre students need to master at school. Namely, IM could provide fluency in language use, rather than accuracy in sentence structure.

The study found that all participants have weakness in constructing sentences. Although the study found that High IM students produced less complex sentences, High and Low IMers self-reported a weakness is syntactic complexity. Participants stated that they always received comments on sentence structure from teachers and they have difficulties using more complex sentences to deliver their ideas. The possible explanation for this is that both High and Low IM users received similar English instruction in high school and in college. For example, the traditional English instruction in Taiwan focuses on using the L1 to teach the L2, and many studies have found the problem. The studies have shown that the problem for most of these students is that they suffer from negative L1 transfer when they write in the L2 (Sasaki and Hirose, 1996; Wolfersberger, 2003). These could produce incomplete or run-on sentences if they rely on direct translation from Chinese syntax. Students usually adopt the first definition of the word when they write their essays.

Limitation of this Study

There are three research limitations and future research is needed in order to overcome these limitations. First, in order to have precise judgment of High and Low IM users, more explicit criteria for defining IM users is needed in future research to allow for a clear picture of language use across contexts. This study only focused on the interactions between the students' written literacy practices and their self-reported language use in IM. Therefore, it was challenging for researchers in this study to collect an equal amount of data from each participant. Thus, the researchers suggest follow-up studies to investigate the actual language usage across contexts through ethnographic approaches. To address the limitation of the short time spent on observations and interaction in this study, future researchers can also utilize ethnographic approaches in longitudinal studies to see how a group of or a single student's learning in one context may influence learning in another. Follow-up studies could also focus on the issue of teaching approaches; for example, teachers' attitudes, styles, and beliefs on what multiple literacies students had really learned through the language use. What affects students' group work performance? How should a school deal with innovative linguistic features used at school?

Second, this study also only focuses on one online context, IM, and its comparison to school writing. The study relied on one context to draw conclusions on students' literacy practices, so this does not reflect a whole picture of how students learn through emerging new technologies. Further research could examine language use in different online contexts in order to find whether there is a pattern of language use online. For example, different interfaces, such as blogging or Facebook, could cause different language use. Participants in this study shared their chat scripts selectively; therefore, the privacy of IM chat scripts presented a challenge in studying naturalistic language use online. Although blogs and Facebook are more public to readers, participants would be mindful when they are in a research study. Besides, some aspects of linguistic style probably depend on the specific culture and can only be generalized with caution depending on who they are interacting with. However, it is still desirable to examine participants' social relationships within their social networking in terms of language use.

Third, the research approach, online interviewing, also can be affected by external influence on the participants who take part. This may lead to dropouts or distractions and influences on the data and their quality. This is difficult for researchers to control. Technical problems in the online connection may also disturb the interviewing process. Finally, again, the application of this approach is limited to people ready and willing to use computer-mediated communication or this kind of technology and communication in general.

Pedagogical Implications

Several pedagogical implications can be drawn from the results of this study. First, the NLS claims that literacy is a social practice and contextually bound. Literacy practice is more meaningful when embedded in the particular cultural contexts in which it is used. The framework confirmed that language use is contextually bound. Participants in this study were able to distinguish the language used in the contexts of IM and school writing. Students are aware of where they use language and who they are interacting with. This study confirms that synchronous CMC, such as IM, is used by EFL students to practice oral communicative skills. As a result, teachers may be well served by employing this tool to increase authenticity in language use and learning.

Second, literacy as multiple literacies attempts to broaden the understanding of literacy teaching and learning to include negotiating a multiplicity of discourses. Students understand IM and school writing as separate modes of communication. They are able to distinguish between language use online and academic writing. The implication for teachers rests in using this knowledge in the classroom. For example, teachers can open discussion in the classroom about different genres. This discussion will raise students' awareness to use language appropriately in the different contexts. Teachers can use students' IM chat scripts in class and ask students to edit, revise, and rewrite the chat scripts by using academic language. The ultimate goal is to develop students' ability to interpret, use, and produce electronic, live, and paper texts that employ linguistic, visual, auditory, gestural, and spatial semiotic systems in diverse contexts.

Third, literacy as multimodal claims literacy practice has moved from linguistics to semiotics. Namely, multimodal texts express meaning in alternate ways. Therefore, changes in the contemporary communications environment add urgency to the call to deploy multimodality consciously in teaching and learning. Teachers can integrate computer technology into their teaching and students' learning.

The findings of this study show that students employed different forms of written language, such as texts, images, and symbols in IM. For teaching practice, teachers should prepare students to be able to read and write critically and functionally. The multimodal nature of *Englishes* in academic, conventional, and computer-based contexts should be considered in curriculum development.

References

Abrams, I. Z. (2003). The effect of synchronous and asynchronous CMC on oral performance in German. *The Modern Language Journal, 87* (2), 157-167.

Androutsopoulos, J., & Schmidt, G. (2002). SMS-Kommunikation: Etnografische Gattungsanalyse am Beispiel einer Kleingruppe. *Zeitschrift fur Angewandte Linguistik, 36*, 49-80.

Axtman, K. (2002). R u online?: The evolving lexicon of wired teens *The Christian Science Monitor, 1*. Retrieved May 1, 2012, from http://www.csmonitor.com/2002/1212/p01s01-ussc.html

Bampton, R., & Cowton, C. (2002). The teaching of ethics in management accounting: Progress and prospect. *Business Ethics: A European Review, 11* (1), 52-61.

Baron, N. (2005). Instant messaging and the future of language. *Communication and ACM, 48* (7), 29-31.

Baron, N. (2008). *Always on: Language in an online and mobile world.* New York, NY: Oxford University Press.

Baron, N. S. (2008). Adjusting the volume: Technology and multitasking in discourse control. In J. Katz (Ed.), *Handbook of mobile communication studies* (pp. 177-193). Cambridge, MA: MIT Press.

Baron, N. (2009). Are digital media changing language? *Educational Leadership, 66* (6), 42-46.

Barton, D., Ivanic, R., & Hamilton, M. (Eds.) (2000). *Situated literacieis: Reading and writing in context* London: Routledge.

Bazerman, C. (1989). *Shaping written knowledge.* Madison: University of Wisconsin Press.

Blake, R. (2000). Computer mediated communication: A window on L2 Spanish interlanguage. *Language Learning & Technology, 4* (1), 120-136. Retrieved February 11, 2010, from http://llt.msu.edu/vol4num1/blake

Chaney, M., & Dew, B. (2003). Online experiences of sexually compulsive men who have sex with men. *Sex Addiction and Compulsivity, 10*, 259-274.

Chou, C., & Hsiao, M.-C. (2000). Internet addiction, usage, gratification, and pleasure experience: The Taiwan college students' case. *Computers & Education, 35,* 65-80.

Cope, B., & Kalantzis, M. (2000). *Multiliteracies: Literacy learning and the design of social futures.* New York: Routledge.

Craig, D. (2003). Instant messaging: The language of youth literacy. *The Boothe Prize Essays,* 116-133. Retrieved August 1, 2012 from http://bootheprize.stanford.edu/0203/PWR-Boothe-Craig.pdf

Crystal, D. (2001). *Language and the Internet.* Cambridge, England: Cambridge University Press.

Daller, H., van Hout, R., & Treffers-Daller, J. (2003). Lexical richness in spontaneous speech of bilinguals. *Applied Linguistics, 24* (2), 197-222.

December, J. (1996). What is computer-mediated communication? Retrieved May 1, 2012 from http://www.december.com/john/study/cmc/what.html

Drouin, M., & Davis, C. (2009). R u txting? Is the use of text speak hurting your literacy? *Journal of Literacy Research, 41,* 46-67.

Flanagin, A. J. (2005). IM online: Instant messaging use among college students. *Communication Research Reports, 22,* 175-187.

Foster, P., Tonkyn, A., & Wigglesworth, G. (2000). Measuring spoken language: A unit for all reasons. *Applied Linguistics, 21* (3), 354-375

Gall, M., Gall, J., & Borg, W. (2003). *Educational research: An introduction* (7 ed.). White Plains: Longman Publishers.

Gee, J. P. (1996). *Social linguistics and literacies: Ideology in discourse.* Bristol, PA: Taylor & Francis.

Gee, J. P. (1996). *Social linguistics and literacies: Ideology in discourse* (2 ed.). London: Falmer Press.

Gee, J. P. (2003). What video games have to teach us about learning and literacy? New York: Palgrave/Macmillan.

Herring, S. C. (2001). Computer-mediated discourse. In D. Schiffrin & D. Tannen (Eds.), *The handbook of discourse analysis* (pp. 612-634). Malden, MA: Blackwell.

Insight Xplorer (2005). 2005 即時通訊江湖混戰篇 (i.e. The mixed use of instant messaging), Retrieved July 30, 2013 from http://www.insightxplorer.com/ specialtopic/kuso_0223_05.html

Jacobs, G. E. (2008). We learn what we do: Developing a repertoire of writing practices in instant messaging world. *Journal of Adolescent and Adult Literacy, 52* (3), 203-211

Jones, S. (2002). *The Internet goes to college: How students are living in the future with today's technology* (Pew Internet & American Life Project report). Retrieved September 15, 2013 from http://www.pewinternet.org/PPF/r/71/report_display.asp

Kivitis, J. (2005). Online interviewing and the research relationship. In C. Hine (Ed.), *Virtual methods: Issues in social research on the Internet* (pp. 35-50). Berg: Oxford.

Lankshear, C., & Knobe, M. (2003). *New literacies: Changing knowledge and classroom learning.* Buckingham: Open University Press.

Larson, J., & Marsh, J. (2005). *Making literacy real: Theories and practices for learning and teaching.* Thousand Oaks, CA: SAGE Publications Ltd.

Lincoln, Y., & Guba, E. (1985). *Naturalistic inquiry.* Newbury Park, CA: Sage.

Meskill, C., & Anthony, N. (2007). Form-focused communicative practice via CMC: What language learners say. *CALICO Journal, 25* (1), 69-90.

Murray, D. E. (1991). The composing process for computer conversation. *Written Communication, 8* (1), 35-55.

New London Group. (1996). A pedagogy of multiliteracies: Designing social futures. *Harvard Educational Review, 66* (1), 60-92.

New London Group. (2000). A pedagogy of multiliteracies. In B. Cope & M. Kalantzis (Eds.), *Multiliteracies: Literacy learning and the design of social future* (pp. 9-37). London: Routledge.

O'Connor, A. (2005). Instant messaging: Friend or foe of student writing. Retrieved July 25, 2013 from: http://education.jhu.edu/PD/newhorizons/strategies/topics/ literacy/articles/instant-messaging/

Plester B., Wood C., & Bell L. (2008) Txt msg n school literacy: does texting and knowledge of text abbrev iations adversely affect children's literacy attainment? *Literacy, 42,* 137-144. doi: 10.1111/j.1741-4369.2008. 00489.x.

Prensky, M. (2001). Digital natives, digital immigrants. *On the Horizon, 9* (5), 1-6.

Rennecker, J. (2005). Invisible whispering: Instant messaging in meetings. *Sprouts, 5,* 198-213.

Sasaki, M., & Hirose, K. (1996). Explanatory variables for EFL students' expository writing. *Language Learning,* 46, 137-174.

Seidman, I. E. (1991). Interviewing as qualitative research: A guide for researchers in education and the social science. New York: Teachers College Press.

Street, B. (1995). *Social literacies: Critical approaches to literacy in development ethnography and education.* London: Longman

Textayser. Net text analysis (2004). Textalyser. Retrieved March 15, 2012, from http:// textalyser.net/

Thurlow, C., & Poff, M. (2009). The language of text-messaging. In C. Herring, Susan, D. Stein & T. Virtanen (Eds.), *Handbook of the pragmatics of CMC.* Berlin and New York: Mouton de Gruyter.

Wang, F. (2009, April). Taiwan: Survey reveals students' web habits. Taipei Times, Retrieved July 1, 2009, from http://www.asiamedia.ucla.edu/article.asp?parentid =107371

Warschauer, M. (1996). Comparing face-to-face and electronic discussion in the second language classroom. *CALICO Journal, 13* (2&3), 7-27.

Wolfersberger, M. (2003). L1 to L2 writing process and strategy: A look at lower proficiency writers. *TESL-EJ.* Retrieved March 9, 2013 from http://www.tesl-ej. org/wordpress/issues/volume7/ej26a6/.

Appendix A
Background Questionnaire

Please check answers that meet your background
（請填寫基本個人資料且打勾選填符合你的情形）

Background Information 基本個人背景	
中文名字（Chinese name）	英文名字（English name）
學號（School ID）：	Gender性別：□ 男（Male）□ 女（Female）
MSN：	E-Mail：
Contact Phone #：聯絡電話（手機）：	Do you own a computer?：（是否有個人電腦） □ Yes □ No
Where do you have Internet access (check all that apply)：□ home □school □dormitory □Internet Café（可複選）	
English proficiency：□beginner □ intermediate □advanced	
無名小站 Wretch：	Facebook：
First Language 第一語言：□ 國語（Mandarin）□ 台語（Taiwanese）□ 客家語（Hakka）□ 原住民母語（Indigenous Language）□ 其他 Other	
Second Language 第二語言：□ 國語（Mandarin）□ 台語（Taiwanese）□ 客家語（Hakka）□ 原住民母語（Indigenous Language）□ 英語 English □ 其他 Other	
MSN use	
How many hours do you use MSN each day?（你一天上MSN幾個小時？） □ Always logged on （都是掛在線上） □ An hour （一小時） □ 2 hours （二小時） □ 3 hours （三小時） □ 4 hours or more （四小時以上）	
Do you stay logged on even when you are not chatting?（你就算沒有在聊天也會掛在線上嗎？） □ Yes □ No	
In what year did you start to use MSN?（你從哪一年開始用 MSN？） 西元：＿＿＿＿＿＿＿	
How many people are on your MSN buddy list?（你MSN朋友大約有幾人？）＿＿＿＿＿＿	

How many people from your department are on your buddy list? （你MSN裡大約有幾人是英文系的？）_____
Do you IM in English? （你用英語MSN嗎？） ☐ Yes ☐ No
Do you ever use both English and Chinese when IMing/chatting? （你夾雜英語和中文聊天嗎？） ☐ Yes ☐ No
Who do you use English with when chatting? （請寫下你都和誰用英語聊天？）
How many people do you IM with in English? （MSN裡要跟他講英文的約多少人？） _____
Do you think you are a high IM-user? （你認為你是常用MSN者？） ☐ Yes ☐ No
寫作能力自我分析（Writing Proficiency Self-Evaluation） What is your current level of writing proficiency? （你目前的寫作能力？） ☐ beginner ☐ intermediate ☐ advanced （初級　中級　高級）
Are you satisfied with your writing samples submitted previously in your writing class? （你滿意你之前交出的作文？） ☐Yes ☐No What difficulties do you have in writing? (Open-ended) （寫下你在寫作時有的困難？） _____ _____

　　填完以上基本資料，請指出你參加後續研究的意願。假使你同意參加後續研究，你的 MSN 帳號才會加到研究者的 MSN 裡。我會再進一步跟您聯絡。（After filling out the background questionnaire, please indicate your willingness to participate in a study about English language use. If you agree, your MSN account will be added to the researcher's MSN IM list and the researcher will contact you with further information.）

☐ I agree to participate in the future study 我同意參加後續研究 ☐ I decline to participate in the future study 我拒絕參加後續研究

〜Thank You〜謝謝您填寫問卷調查

華語讀寫能力對學術摘要寫作之預測作用及其教學應用[*]

謝佳玲、吳欣儒

國立台灣師範大學華語文教學研究所

clhsieh@ntnu.edu.tw、xinruwu@ntnu.edu.tw

摘要

　　西方文獻同意學習者的摘要寫作可反映閱讀與寫作能力，然而對摘要寫作與讀寫能力的相關程度仍存歧見，至今也尚未證實兩者的關連程度是否屬跨語言的現象。因此本文透過字形辨識、字義理解、理解推理、引導式短文寫作與摘要寫作的檢測，探討華語的讀寫能力是否能預測摘要寫作的表現。統計結果顯示，上述各自變項與摘要寫作成績皆高度相關，其中短文寫作關聯性最高，其次為字義理解、字形辨識與理解推理，而多項式迴歸分析指出短文寫作為預測效果最佳的參照指標。本研究突破以往以單一指標測量閱讀能力的作法，結論透露讀寫能力與摘要寫作的關連性具跨語言之普遍性，最後參考以上結論提出教學建議。

關鍵詞：學術寫作、摘要寫作、閱讀能力、寫作能力、華語教學

＊本研究感謝科技部「漢語學術社群之溝通功能與語篇機制研究」（MOST 106-2410-H-003-125-MY2）與「跨國頂尖研究中心計畫」（MOST 104-2911-I-003-301）以及教育部「邁向頂尖大學計畫」與國立臺灣師範大學「華語文與科技研究中心」的支持。

The Predictive Effects of Chinese Reading and Writing Performances on Academic Summary Writing

Chia-Ling Hsieh, Xin-Ru Wu
Naitonal Taiwan Normal University
clhsieh@ntnu.edu.tw, xinruwu@ntnu.edu.tw

Western academics agree that a student's summary writing can reflect their reading and writing skills, but scholars disagree about the degree of relevance linking summary writing with reading/writing skills. Scholars still cannot prove if the connection between the two is a cross-linguistic phenomenon. Therefore, this paper utilizes character recognition, literal comprehension, understanding and reasoning, and guided essay writing and summary writing to explore whether Chinese reading/writing skills can predict summary writing performance. The statistics show that the aforementioned variables are highly correlated to summary writing scores. Essay writing demonstrated the highest correlation, followed by literal comprehension, character recognition, and understanding and reasoning. The polynomial regression analysis results revealed that essay writing was the best indicator of predictive effects. This study made a breakthrough by not utilizing previous reading/writing evaluations that relied on a single indicator. This study showed that the link between reading/writing skills and summary writing contains a cross-linguistic universality. The paper ends with some teaching advice based on the above conclusion.

Keywords: Academic writing, summary writing, reading skills, writing skills, Chinese language instruction

引言

　　研究者從事研究之目的在於揭示新的事實與法則，而學術寫作（academic writing）是研究者展示研究歷程與成果的書面媒介，成為研究結論轉化為學理知識的必要環節。西方文獻探討二語學習者撰寫學術論文所須具備的語言知識與技能，結果指出學術寫作考驗學習者綜合運用閱讀與寫作技能呈現個人思維與分析之能力（Keck, 2006; McCulloch, 2013; Weigle, 2004），因此近年來學術英語（English for academic purpose）的研究強調整合學習者讀寫技能之重要性（Gebril, 2010; Leki & Carson, 1994, 1997; Plakans, 2008, 2009; Rosenfeld, Leung & Oltman, 2001）。

　　在眾多整合讀寫技能的教學任務中，摘要寫作（summary writing）指不加入寫作者之看法與評論，以簡明扼要的文字重述文本內容的短文，為現今培養語言學習者發展讀寫技能之常見任務（Baba, 2009; Hood, 2008; Keck, 2006）。撰寫摘要涉及閱讀理解與寫作表達之共同作用（Bracewell, Frederiksen & Frederiksen, 1982; Spivey & King, 1989），因此不僅要求寫作者具備辨識文本重要訊息的技能（Spivey & King, 1989），亦考驗寫作者將理解內容以合乎邏輯的方式轉化為文字之能力（Asención Delaney, 2008）。基於上述原因，西方文獻同意學習者的摘要寫作可反映其閱讀理解與寫作表達之能力（Spivey & King, 1989; Trites & McGroarty, 2005; Watanabe, 2001），亦有諸多研究關注讀寫能力於摘要寫作歷程的中介作用，以及這兩種能力用以預測摘要寫作表現的可行性。

　　西方學界探討學習者閱讀、寫作能力與摘要寫作能力之關聯，至今雖已累積豐碩的研究成果，然而對於摘要寫作與讀寫能力的相關程度仍存歧見（Asención Delaney, 2008; Baba, 2009; Keck, 2006; Schoonen et al., 2003; Spivey & King, 1989; Trites & McGroarty, 2005; Watanabe, 2001），至今也尚未證實兩者的關聯程度是否屬於跨語言現象，此外，過去檢測學習者閱讀能力之實驗工具亦未能反映人類閱讀階段之獨特性。有鑑於此，本研究擬以華語高級學習者為研究對象，探查華語的讀寫能力與摘要寫作表現是否具關聯性，並進一步探討讀寫能力是否能夠預測學術摘要寫作的表現。本文期能闡明語言理解與表達對摘要寫作之作用，並根據研究結論提出華語摘要寫作之教學建議，希冀能以有效方式提高華語學習者的摘要寫作能力。

閱讀、寫作與摘要寫作能力之關聯

本節將分別從閱讀能力、寫作能力與摘要寫作能力的互動表現，以及摘要寫作作為獨特個體兩個層面評述目前此領域的研究現況。

西方文獻探究學習者的閱讀能力與摘要寫作表現的關聯，主張摘要寫作能力與閱讀能力呈現高度相關性。Spivey & King（1989）調查外語學習者於英語摘要寫作中引述原文的命題數量、語篇的組織結構、語篇的銜接連貫以及摘要的整體品質，統計結果指出閱讀能力越好的學習者於上述四個層面的表現越優異，顯示學習者綜合多項文本訊息並重新合成、組織成為新語篇的能力與閱讀能力重疊，意即學習者對文本的理解能力與摘要寫作的品質呈現相關性。而 Trites & McGroarty（2005）則以 105 名英語母語者以及 145 名於美國攻讀學位之非英語母語者為研究對象，探討閱讀能力與摘要寫作表現的關聯程度，研究結果指出受試者的 Nelson-Denny 與 TOEFL 閱讀理解成績與其英語摘要寫作成績呈現高度相關，此結果亦支持學習者之閱讀能力與摘要寫作表現具有關聯。

然而，亦有實證研究結果對上述閱讀能力的高度相關性提出反證，主張學習者的摘要寫作能力與寫作能力較具關聯性。Baba（2009）探查 68 名日本大學生的多項語言能力與摘要寫作表現之關聯，研究結果顯示受測者的英語閱讀成績與英語摘要寫作成績低度相關，顯示閱讀與摘要寫作能力不具明顯關聯。而 Watanabe（2001）觀察47位即將進入夏威夷大學的研究生所進行的英語分班測驗，對比這些不同國籍的受試者在英語閱讀、寫作與摘要寫作三方面的能力，結果指出摘要寫作表現與受測者的閱讀能力並無顯著的相關性；相反地，寫作能力與摘要寫作表現的關聯程度較高。

除上述探究閱讀與寫作能力關聯程度的文獻外，亦有研究主張摘要寫作是獨立於上述兩種能力外的個體，強調其特殊性。Asención Delaney（2008）以62名英語二語學習者與27名英語外語學習者為研究對象，進行閱讀測驗、寫作測驗、摘要寫作測驗及撰寫評論短文測驗，並假設上述測驗與寫作任務分別代表摘要寫作能力之不同面向，結果指出摘要寫作表現與閱讀能力與寫作能力皆較無關聯，反駁過去高度相關之主張。結論指出教學者不應將摘要寫作視為閱讀理解或寫作表達之附屬產物，而應將摘要寫作視為獨特的讀寫構成體（reading-to-write construct），培養語言學習者對此構成體特殊性之意識，並傳授其他可能影響摘要寫作品質之要素。

綜觀上述文獻，目前學界大多同意摘要寫作能力與閱讀、寫作能力相關，差異在於不同研究對於其關聯性強弱抱持不同看法。然而，過去研究界定閱讀能力的定義過於寬鬆，導致研究之測試工具存在缺失。人的閱讀歷程分為多個階段，如Gagné, Yekovich & Yekovich（1993）主張閱讀歷程可分為四個層次，依序為解碼、字義理解、推論理解與理解監控，然而過往文獻傾向使用單一閱讀理解測驗，如Nelson-Denny或TOEFL閱讀測驗測試受測者整體之閱讀能力，因此即使文獻最後證實摘要寫作與閱讀能力呈現關聯，亦無法細緻地闡明與何種閱讀能力面向較相關或較不相關。有鑑於此，本文設計可測得閱讀能力部分面向之字形辨識、字義理解與理解推理能力之測驗，輔以可評估寫作表現之引導式短文寫作以及學術摘要寫作，期能瞭解閱讀次能力、寫作能力與摘要寫作之相關性，並探究兩者的關聯程度是否屬於跨語言的現象。最後，本文檢視華語學習者的讀寫能力作為預測學習者摘要寫作表現之成效。綜上所述，本文研究問題條列如下：

（1）閱讀能力中的字形辨識能力、字義理解能力、理解推理能
　　力，以及寫作能力與學術摘要寫作表現的關聯性為何？
（2）閱讀能力中的字形辨識能力、字義理解能力、理解推理能
　　力，以及寫作能力表現可否作為預測學術摘要寫作成績的
　　參照指標？

研究方法

（一）受試者

　　本研究受試者為25名台灣某國立大學開設的「高級華語」課程
之修課學生。受試者來自不同國籍，皆學習華語多年，華語水平達到
高級程度，符合本文之研究目的。上述受試者皆於台灣攻讀學士或碩
博士學位，其專業領域要求學生須以華語撰寫學術研究報告，因此平
時即面臨大量以華語撰寫學術寫作之壓力與挑戰。

（二）實驗設計
1. 測驗形式

　　本實驗受試者須完成五項學術性測驗，包含（1）字形辨識測
驗；（2）字義理解測驗；（3）理解推理測驗；（4）引導式短文寫
作；（5）摘要寫作。前三項測驗測試受試者的閱讀能力，第四項測
驗受試者的寫作能力，最後一項則為摘要寫作能力。每位受試者以投
幣方式決定閱讀文本A或B，文本A主題為「語言的流失與死亡」，
共652字；文本B主題為「淺談華語教學中的文化教學」，共757個
字。寫作測驗僅一版本，題目為「任務型教學法簡介」。以下分述五
種測驗之內容。

　　（1）字形辨識測驗

　　字形辨識測驗診斷受試者閱讀能力中的解碼能力，是本研究用以
判斷學習者詞彙辨識能力之評估工具。本測驗設計參考Flynt & Cooter

（2004）為記錄與歸納學生解碼的錯誤類型而發展的誤讀格（miscue grid），並以此為依據，將解碼時的錯誤類型分為發音錯誤、斷詞錯誤[1]、自行插入字、念成其他字、尋求教師協助與省略字彙六種錯誤類型。受試者於測驗前可默讀文本一至兩遍，接著研究者請受試者以正常語速讀出文本內容。受試者朗讀時，研究者根據上述歸納的六種錯誤類型記錄受試者錯誤的次數與類別。

（2）字義理解測驗

字義理解測驗測試受試者閱讀能力中的字義理解能力。研究者各從文本A與B隨機抽取20個生詞，設計10題單一選擇題與10題字義填空題，測試受試者對這20個詞之理解程度。單一選擇題的測驗方式為：受試者必須先寫出詞語的拼音，並從A、B、C、D四個選項中選出最符合該詞意義的選項。而字義填空題亦先要求受試者寫出詞語的拼音，接著以華語或英語寫出該詞詞義。

（3）理解推理測驗

理解推理能力測驗受試者對文本的理解程度，以及歸納文章主旨、擷取重要論點、辨識資訊關聯性與推論隱藏訊息的能力。研究者根據文本A與B各設計5題單一選擇題，受試者閱讀完文章後，須根據題幹之說明從四個選項中選出一個標準答案，作答時可同時翻閱文本。

（4）引導式短文寫作

本研究之寫作測驗評估受試者於學術文體運用關鍵詞組句成章之寫作能力。此項測驗選取一篇名為「任務型教學法簡介」之學術文章，此文章共分三段，第一段介紹任務型教學法的定義，第二段對比傳統型教學法與任務型教學法的差異，最後一段總結上述差異，點出

---

[1] 「斷詞錯誤」檢測學習者能否正確抽取與切分句中有意義且可獨立存在的最小語言單位，學習者必須有能力完成這種解析，才能進一步解讀句子的意義。因此，斷詞錯誤的能力測試屬於詞彙辨識能力之範圍，是字形辨識測驗的內容之一。

任務型教學法之特色。本測驗呈現文章首段與結論的寫作內容,第二段提供六個句子,每個句子給予四至六個關鍵詞語,這些關鍵詞語已涵蓋受試者完成句子所需要的專業術語,並於特定名詞後提供英文翻譯,以確保受試者理解關鍵詞語的意義,受試者必須使用各句提供的關鍵詞組合成一個合語法的句子,再將這六個句子連同文章提供的首段與結尾組織成一篇結構完整、前後連貫的語篇。

　　(5)學術摘要寫作

　　本測驗要求受試者以華語撰寫學術性摘要一篇,考驗綜合運用閱讀理解與寫作表達之能力。受試者須根據文本A或B的內容,於40分鐘內寫出一段300字以內的摘要。研究者於受試者寫作前以華語詳細告知寫作注意事項,包括摘要寫作須包含文章最重要的觀點,但不能加入個人對文章的看法與意見;寫作時可同時翻閱文本並於空白處隨意註記,但不可使用字典或參考任何書籍。研究者要求受試者於40分鐘內完成摘要寫作,每篇平均為208.2個字,標準差為22.89,最大值為290個字,最小值為167個字。

2. 施測流程

　　本實驗的25名受試者於台灣某大學的教室進行上述測驗,施測流程簡述如下。首先受試者以投擲硬幣的方式決定閱讀文本,減低因順序效應造成的研究誤差,接著由研究者陪同進行字形辨識測驗。完成第一項測驗後,研究者以華語說明接下來字義理解測驗與理解推理測驗的進行方式與限定時間。受試者可自由決定字義理解測驗與理解推理測驗的先後順序,而完成三項閱讀能力測驗後,接著進行寫作測驗,最後則為學術摘要撰寫。

3. 測驗評分

　　以下分述五項測驗之評分標準、方式與評分人員。

　　(1)字形辨識測驗

此項測驗從發音錯誤、斷詞錯誤、自行插入字、念成其他字、尋求教師協助與省略字彙六種錯誤類型之偏誤率評估受試者的解碼能力。研究者統計受試者於上述六項類型的錯誤總數，並以全部次數減去錯誤次數得到正確次數；接著以正確次數除以文本全部字數之百分比，得出受試者於此項測驗之正確率。如某受試者閱讀文本 B 共計發生 3 次錯誤，由於文本 B 共 757 字，正確率為 754 除以 757，得到 99.6 正確率。此項測驗由研究者單獨評分。

（2）字義理解測驗

字義理解測驗共計 20 題，包含 10 題單一選擇題與 10 題字義填空題，兩項題型計分方式相同。10 題單選題的拼音與選擇題配分方式為拼音 2 分，選擇題 3 分，每題合計 5 分，此單一選擇題共計 50 分。10 題字義填空題之配分方式相同，拼音 2 分，填空題 3 分，每題合計 5 分，此字義填空題共計 50 分，允許受試者以華語或英語寫出某詞彙的意義，研究者即根據受試者的回答情況酌情給分，如某位受試者於「維生」一欄填入 save one's life 的答案，即為全錯；另一受試者於「洞悉」一欄填寫 become a part of; or to reach a deep understanding of something，根據教育部國語推行委員會編纂之重編國語辭典修訂版網路版 [2]，「洞悉」一詞解釋為通曉、明白，因此前項答案 become a part of 判定為多餘訊息，此題扣一分。此項測驗由研究者單獨評分。

（3）理解推理測驗

理解推理測驗為 5 題單一選擇題，計分方式為每題 20 分，總分 100 分。研究者依據受試者答題之正確題數乘以每題配分得到受試者於此項測驗之得分。此項測驗由研究者單獨評分。

（4）引導式短文寫作

本研究之寫作能力測驗評分參照 Asención Delaney（2008）之評

---

2 網址：http://dict.revised.moe.edu.tw/。

分項目與方式，但略做修改，以符合本寫作能力測驗題型之特殊性。受試者之寫作成品分別從**詞彙**、**語法**、**結構**三個項目加以評比。首先，詞彙一項檢視受試者運用本測驗規定的各項生詞之使用率及準確度；此外，受試者亦須加入其他必要的生詞，與本測驗的生詞搭配組成完整句子，因此受試者的詞彙得分將從上述兩個層面加以衡量。第二，語法一項檢測受試者語句的正確度、完整度、複雜度、長度以及句子本身是否具有意義。最後，結構一項評估受試者六個句子與上下文銜接的正確程度、完整程度與連貫流暢程度。上述三項的評分比重依次為結構40%、詞彙30%與語法30%，總分100分。

寫作能力測驗的評分由兩名華語母語者執行，兩位皆為台灣某大學華語文教學研究所的學生，各擁有約兩年與五年之海內外華語教學經驗。研究者於閱卷者評分前以電子郵件傳送測驗題目與寫作要求，接著與閱卷者當面討論評分標準、方式與各項細節。評分過程中，研究者先解釋此寫作測驗欲檢測受試者何種寫作能力面向，並說明受試者測驗進行之流程，接著研究者再次釐清此寫作測驗評分的標準與比重，並以一篇寫作成品為樣本，請閱卷者依照詞彙、語法與結構分項練習評分，並說明給分原因。閱卷者與研究者於評分方式與分數達成共識後，閱卷者即可開始獨立評分。本研究的施測者間信度（inter-rater reliability）為0.86。[3]

（5）學術摘要寫作

本研究參考新托福-iBT的摘要評分項目，分別從**摘要內容**、**引述程度**、**組織結構**、**語言表現**四個角度評估受試者學術摘要之寫作表現。首先，摘要內容一項考察受試者是否正確且精準地呈現原文主旨與論點，以及是否於摘要中加入個人看法以致論述偏離主題；其次，引述程度指受試者是否適度、適量使用原文的語言形式，以及是否能

---

3 計算方式為：$\dfrac{2 \times \text{correlation}}{1 + \text{correlation}}$。

以個人語言重新詮釋與表述原文的意旨；第三、組織結構一項代表摘要的佈局是否嚴謹、結構是否完整、語篇是否流暢以及論述是否緊湊；最後，語言表現一項檢視受試者使用詞彙與語法的正確度。

上述四項的評分比重依次為摘要內容40%、引述程度30%、組織結構15%、語言表現15%，總分100分。如此安排的原因在於摘要的寫作目的為寫作者以較小篇幅重述文本的主要訊息（Spivey & King, 1989），但同時不可過度使用原文語言形式而導致抄襲（Keck, 2006），因此內容與引述程度為本研究評判學術性摘要品質的首要因素。而組織結構與語言表現於任何寫作文體皆為判定寫作者寫作能力的評分指標，故這兩項於本研究摘要評比中的比重相同。

學術摘要寫作的評分由負責評量寫作能力的同樣兩位華語母語者執行。兩位母語者於評分前分別與研究者溝通評分標準、方式與各項細節。評分過程為研究者先闡述摘要寫作的目的與本項測驗之進行方式，並與閱卷者溝通文本A與文本B的主要觀點。接著研究者說明此摘要測驗評分的標準與比重，並以一篇摘要成品為樣本，請閱卷者依據摘要內容、引述程度、組織結構與語言表現四個項目分項練習評分，並說明給分原因。閱卷者與研究者於評分方式與分數達成共識後，閱卷者即開始獨立評分。本研究的施測者間信度為0.72。

（三）數據分析

本研究的依變項為學術摘要寫作測驗成績，與四個自變項，分別為：（1）字形辨識測驗，（2）字義理解測驗，（3）理解推理測驗，（4）寫作能力測驗。為回答研究問題一，本研究以描述統計計算上述五項測驗之平均數與標準差，並以皮爾遜相關係數（Pearson correlation coefficient）計算四個變項與學術摘要寫作之相關係數，推論自變項與依變項的相關程度。研究問題二則以多項式迴歸分析（multiple regression analysis）探討依變項與預測變項的數值變化關係，進行方式為將閱讀能力的三項能力指標：字形辨識測驗、字義理解測驗、理解推理測驗成績，引導式短文寫作成績與學術摘要寫作成績進行相關性分析，建立四個變數間的迴歸方程式以預測讀寫能力對學術摘要寫作之作用，希冀能以自變項的表現預測依變項的可能變化和發展，探查以受試者的閱讀和寫作成績作為預測學術摘要寫作表現之成效。下一節呈現研究結果。

研究結果與討論

（一）讀寫與摘要成績之關聯性分析

本研究依序進行上述施測流程，並個別計算25位受試者於五項測驗之成績。首先以表1呈現受試者於五個變項的最小值、最大值、平均數、標準差，以及四個自變項與依變項之皮爾遜相關係數的計算結果。

如表1所示，從標準差之計算結果來看，理解推理測驗之標準差（23.58）最高，而學術摘要寫作最低（11.5），說明受試者之理解推理測驗成績差異最大，而學術摘要寫作之差異性最小，成績也最為集中。其次，表1亦顯示字形辨識、字義理解、理解推理、寫作能力的測驗成績與學術摘要寫作成績皆為正相關，且為高度相關（r>0.5），然而關聯程度有所差異，其相關性由高至低依序為：寫作能力測驗（r=.92）、字義理解測驗（r=.84）、字形辨識測驗（r=.78）與理解推理測驗（r=.68），此數值表明在眾多測驗中，寫作能力測驗與學

表1 各變項之平均數、標準差與學術摘要寫作之相關係數

變項	最小值	最大值	平均數	標準差	相關係數
學術摘要寫作	60.00	95.00	81.20	11.50	─
字形辨識測驗	53.20	99.90	84.70	14.20	0.78
字義理解測驗	42.00	96.00	81.50	14.10	0.84
理解推理測驗	20.00	100.00	70.80	23.58	0.68
寫作能力測驗	50.00	96.00	79.50	15.50	0.92

術摘要寫作之關聯性最高，而與理解推理的關聯性最低。

　　上述結果闡明華語學習者的閱讀與寫作成績皆與摘要寫作成績相關，顯示學習者的讀寫能力確實可反映摘要寫作能力。其次，此結果亦支持Watanabe（2001）針對英語得到的部分研究結果，意即學習者的摘要寫作表現與其二語的寫作能力較具關聯。本研究之華語寫作能力測驗要求受試者須將數個關鍵詞組成合乎語法的句子，並將數個句子組成一篇結構完整、前後連貫、符合題旨的語篇，而研究結果顯示學習者組詞成句與組句成章之能力與摘要寫作的表現最具關聯。最後，儘管字形辨識、字義理解與理解推理這三項閱讀次能力皆與摘要寫作的表現相關，然而當中的字義理解能力是三者中與摘要寫作最為關聯之變項。字義理解測驗測試受試者對文本詞彙之理解與掌握程度，Baba（2009）亦曾表示英語學習者的詞彙知識為影響摘要寫作品質之關鍵要素。綜上所述，本研究探查華語學習者的讀寫能力與摘要寫作品質之相關性，結果證實兩者具關聯性，而摘要寫作成績與寫作成績最為相關，其次為閱讀能力中的字義理解成績，透露讀寫能力與摘要能力之聯繫屬於跨語言現象。

（二）讀寫與摘要成績之多項式迴歸分析

　　本研究以多項式迴歸分析檢視三項閱讀能力指標：字形辨識測驗、字義理解測驗、理解推理測驗成績與學術摘要寫作成績的關聯性，統計結果如表2所示。

　　如表2所示，字形辨識測驗、字義理解測驗、理解推理測驗、寫作能力測驗之估計結果依序為-0.163、0.139、-0.027、0.736。上述四個數值中，僅字義理解成績與寫作能力成績為正值，顯示僅這兩項分數對摘要寫作能力產生正面的影響。假設這兩項指標滿分皆為100分，經統計分析後可推知，在控制其他變項情況下，字義理解測驗成績每增加1分，學術摘要寫作成績即增加0.139分；同理可推論，寫作能力測驗的分數每增加1分，學術摘要寫作亦增加0.736分，顯示

表 2 多項式迴歸分析預測閱讀能力與摘要寫作能力之關聯性

摘要寫作測驗	Coef.	Std. Err.	t	P>t	[95% Conf.	Interval]
字形辨識測驗	-0.163	0.172	-0.95	0.354	-0.523	0.196
字義理解測驗	0.139	0.193	0.72	0.480	-0.265	0.544
理解推理測驗	-0.027	0.070	-0.39	0.703	-0.174	0.120
寫作能力測驗	0.736	0.206	3.56	0.002	0.302	1.169
常數項	27.147	6.101	4.45	0	14.376	39.919

在這四項測驗中，寫作能力測驗成績的增長對學術摘要寫作的影響最為明顯，其次為字義理解測驗。

表 2 亦顯示，寫作能力測驗的數值為四項測驗中最高之一，表示寫作能力的成績高低最貼近摘要寫作之可能表現，因此相較於其他三項成績，受試者的寫作成績為預測摘要成績最具效果的參照指標。此外，四項測驗的 P 值分別為 0.354、0.480、0.703、0.002，前三項數值皆大於 0.005，表示在 95% 的信賴水準下，本研究無法拒絕估計值異於 0，顯示三項估計值在統計上皆不顯著。換言之，儘管如本研究所預期，三個自變項對學術摘要寫作能力皆產生正面效果，在統計上卻沒有顯著的解釋能力。然而，寫作能力測驗的 P 值小於 0.005，因此在 5% 的顯著水準下顯著，意即相較於其他三項變數，寫作能力測驗的成績對學術摘要寫作具有顯著影響。

本研究以多項式迴歸分析模擬四項測驗成績對摘要寫作成績之預測能力，研究結果顯示同屬於閱讀能力面向之字形辨識能力、字義理解能力、理解推理能力雖皆與摘要寫作之成績呈現高度相關，然而還不足預測摘要寫作的表現。在上述三項測驗中，僅字義理解成績可預測摘要寫作成績，然而統計檢定之不顯著結果亦說明字義理解之預測效果在統計上無解釋能力。過去文獻探討閱讀能力對摘要寫作之影響，傾向以單一測驗形式概括閱讀過程所牽涉之各種能力，而本研究針對各項閱讀能力設計單項測驗，結果指出這三項測驗對摘要寫作之效力各有不同，闡明以多元研究工具檢測閱讀與寫作能力之必要性。

另一方面，統計結果亦表明寫作能力測驗對學術摘要寫作成績最具影響力與預測力，且已達統計檢定的顯著水準。此發現呼應研究問題一的結果，證實學術摘要寫作雖為學習者閱讀理解與寫作表達能力之綜合表現，然而華語的寫作表現比閱讀表現可取得較佳的預測效果。

教學建議

根據本文的研究結果，學習者的引導式短文寫作成績與學術摘要寫作成績呈現高度相關，而且前者具有預測後者的能力，由此可見，加強學習者的短文寫作知識與技巧能有效提高其摘要寫作的能力。短文寫作的知識與技巧涉及的層面廣泛，本研究進行的引導式短文寫作測驗要求受試者將數個關鍵詞語組成合語法的句子，並將數個句子組構成一篇結構完整、前後連貫、符合題旨的語篇。因此，本研究推斷寫作者組詞成句、組句成章的能力與摘要寫作的能力較為相關，教師應掌握上述訓練重點，發展學生的語篇意識，進而提升摘要寫作的能力。本節參考以上研究成果，提出適合華語摘要寫作教學的操練模式。

首先，在組詞成句方面，教師可先設置一個語境，如陳述某種情況或前提，接著輔以圖片或影片，以口述的方式敘述文章重點。教師於每張圖片展示組成句子之數個關鍵詞語，並以口說的方式將詞語融入教師講述的主題中，使學習者於自然情境下猜測或領會詞語的意義及用法。這個過程重複數遍，直到學習者已完全理解教師講述的重點。其次，教師可讓學生以複誦或重述之方式，重現教師敘述的文章重點，並將口語的內容寫成書面文字。最後，教師可傾聽或閱讀學習者重述的內容或文字，糾正詞彙與語法偏誤，導正對敘事內容之理解，並考量哪些詞彙或片段需要再次解說。這種教法可訓練學習者將關鍵詞語組成語篇並重述理解內容之能力。

其次，在組句成章方面，教師可接續上述任務，要求學習者將口語表述寫成文字，提示學習者語篇中常見之語意連接成分，如表示時間、序列、轉折、條件、讓步或總結等語意關係的連接詞語，或要求學習者按照時間順序、空間順序、發展過程、因果關係、並列關係等邏輯關係重新安排文本架構，以上教學能引導學生瞭解華語的語段構成形式，增強學習者的語篇意識。另外，同樣可促進學習者語篇意識的訓練方法還包含語篇重組，教師可將學生寫好的句子重新打散排列順序，再提供數個連接詞語，請學生將句子重新組合成篇，亦可提供其他語篇，請學生自行組合句子順序，強化對語篇連接成分的認識。最後，教師亦可提供簡短的寫作提要，要求學生運用特定的連接成分完成教師指定的寫作任務。上述活動能協助學習者體會華語語段組成之基本規律，理解前後連貫的語篇須運用何種邏輯銜接的手法。

　　本研究僅從組詞成句與組句成章兩個方面舉例說明引導式短文寫作訓練之進行方式，未來值得進一步探索可增進學習者結合理解與表達之教學任務，同時深化學習者對摘要體裁的認識，提升學習者的摘要寫作能力。

研究結論

　　本研究突破以往以單一指標測量閱讀能力的作法，針對三項閱讀次能力設計相應的測驗形式，探討華語學習者之讀寫能力與學術摘要寫作表現之相關性，以及預測學術摘要寫作表現之成效。結論透露讀寫能力與摘要寫作的關聯具跨語言意義，且學習者的寫作能力為預測摘要寫作表現之最佳指標。後續研究可改良測試讀寫能力之試題版本，控制文本的難易度，以及考量目前主流的閱讀與寫作測驗用以預測摘要寫作能力之可行性，並將實證研究成果應用於寫作教學之課程設計。

參考文獻

Asención Delaney, Y. (2008). *Investigating the reading-to-write construct. Journal of English for Academic Purposes, 7* (3), 140-150.

Baba, K. (2009). Aspects of lexical proficiency in writing summaries in a foreign language. *Journal of Second Language Writing, 18* (3), 191-208.

Bracewell, R. J., Frederiksen, C. H., & Frederiksen, J. F. (1982). Cognitive processes in composing and comprehending discourse. *Educational Psychologist, 17* (3), 146-164.

Flynt, E. S., & Cooter, R. B. (2004). *The Flynt/Cooter reading inventory for the classroom* (5nd ed.). Upper Saddle River, NJ: Merrill/Prentice Hall.

Gagné, E. D., Yekovich, C. W., & Yekovich, F. R. (1993). *The cognitive psychology of school learning* (2nd ed.). New York, NY: HarperCollins.

Gebril, A. (2010). Bringing reading-to-write and writing-only assessment tasks together: A generalizability analysis. *Assessing Writing, 15* (2), 100-117.

Hood, S. (2008). Summary writing in academic contexts: Implicating meaning in processes of change. *Linguistics and Education, 19* (4), 351-365.

Keck, C. (2006). The use of paraphrase in summary writing: A comparison of L1 and L2 writers. *Journal of Second Language Writing, 15* (4), 261-278.

Leki, I., & Carson, J. (1994). Students' perception of EAP writing instruction and writing across the disciplines. *TESOL Quarterly, 28* (1), 81-101.

Leki, I., & Carson, J. (1997). "Completely different worlds": EAP and the writing experiences of ESL students in university courses. *TESOL Quarterly, 31* (1), 39-69.

McCulloch, S. (2013). Investigating the reading-to-write processes and source use of L2 postgraduate students in real-life academic tasks: An exploratory study. *Journal of English for Academic Purposes, 12* (2), 136-147.

Plakans, L. (2008). Comparing composing processes in writing-only and reading-to-write test tasks. *Assessing Writing, 13* (2), 111-129.

Plakans, L. (2009). The role of reading strategies in integrated L2 writing tasks. *Journal of English for Academic Purposes, 8* (4), 252-266.

Rosenfeld, M., Leung, S., & Oltman, P. K. (2001). *Identifying the reading, writing, speaking, and listening tasks important for academic success at the undergraduate and graduate level.* Princeton, NJ: Educational Testing Service.

Schoonen, R., Van Gelderen, A., De Glopper, K., Hulstijn, J., Simis, A., Snellings, P., & Stevenson, M. (2003). First language and second language writing: The role of linguistic knowledge, speed of processing, and metacognitive knowledge. *Language Learning, 53* (1), 165-202.

Spivey, N. N., & King, J. R. (1989). Readers as writers composing from sources. *Reading Research Quarterly, 24* (1), 7-26.

Trites, L., & McGroarty, M. (2005). Reading to learn and reading to integrate: New tasks for reading comprehension texts? *Language Testing, 22* (2), 174-210.

Watanabe, Y. (2001). *Read-to-write tasks for the assessment of second language academic writing skills: Investigating text features and rater reactions* (Unpublished doctoral dissertation). University of Hawaii, Honolulu.

Weigle, S. C. (2004). Integrating reading and writing in a competency test for non-native speakers of English. *Assessing Writing, 9* (1), 27-55.

平衡語料與中文閱讀詞彙習得

林慧

美國西維吉尼亞大學

hhlin@mail.wvu.edu

摘要

有關中文詞彙習得的研究在範圍和數量上都很有限，然而不論是初級或高級程度的學生都常對中文詞彙的學習感到困難，也間接使得學生中文閱讀能力的發展受到阻礙。最普遍的詞彙學習方法是利用詞彙表，但沒有語境的學習造成學生許多用詞上的錯誤，尤其是美國學生常依賴直接由英文翻譯而來的詞義和用法。本研究的目的是檢視平衡語料的使用是否能對美國學生的中文詞彙習得有所助益，研究方法是讓學生閱讀並學習兩篇課文中的生詞，其中一篇課文的生詞連結了平衡語料庫的真實語料例句。在學生研讀了兩篇課文的生詞之後，採用詞彙知識評量表 （Vocabulary Knowledge Scale） 讓學生對自己的詞彙理解度做出評量。結果顯示學生對於有平衡語料連結的課文詞彙習得效益較高。此研究也提出利用平衡語料來幫助學生理解生詞意義與用法的可行性和優點。

關鍵詞：詞彙習得，平衡語料，中文閱讀，真實語料

Concordances and the Acquisition of Lexicon in Chinese as a Foreign Language

Hannah Lin
West Virginia University
hhlin@mail.wvu.edu

Research on Chinese vocabulary acquisition is limited in size and scope. Both basic and advanced students find learning Chinese vocabulary difficult, which can indirectly hinder the development of Chinese reading skills. The most common method of learning vocabulary is by using vocabulary lists, but the lack of context can cause students to use words incorrectly. This is the case for American students who rely on English translations of words to determine their meanings and usages. The purpose of this study was to examine whether the use of a balanced corpus can be beneficial to Chinese vocabulary acquisition by American students. Students were asked to read and learn unfamiliar words from two texts, one of which linked unfamiliar words to the examples of authentic sentences in a balanced corpus. After the students studied the unfamiliar words in the two texts, they were asked to fill out a Vocabulary Knowledge Scale to evaluate their understanding of the vocabulary. Results showed that vocabulary acquisition was higher for the text that was linked to the balanced corpus. This research has demonstrated the feasibility and advantages of utilizing balanced corpora to help students understand the meaning and usage of words.

Keywords: Vocabulary acquisition, balanced corpora, Chinese reading, authentic materials

中文詞彙習得研究

以中文作為外語的研究,大約是九〇年代才開始蓬勃發展的。因此,與英文詞彙研究的廣度及深度相比,中文詞彙習得的研究在範圍和數量上都很有限。詞彙習得對學習中文的學生來說不但是困難的,而且困難度在聽、說、讀、寫各方面都存在。有關中文閱讀的研究指出,學生的漢字識字能力和閱讀能力有著密切的關係。由於中文詞彙具有挑戰性,不論是初級或高級程度的學生都對詞彙的學習感到困難,也因此使得學生中文閱讀能力的發展受到嚴重阻礙(Everson & Ke, 1997)。然而到目前為止,對中文詞彙習得的研究,多是有關識字、字形與閱讀的研究(Hayes, 1988; Everson, 1998; Ke, 1996, 1998; Lin, 2000; Yang, 2000)。內容側重於對漢字語言學的討論,比如一個單詞的定義、種類、語法功能、歷史演變過程和文字結構分析等等,很少有研究專注於學生是如何學習、記憶和運用中文詞彙。並且詞彙很少被認為是課本中的重要部分,目前在美國大部分的中文教材,只列出了中文生詞,發音與其英文翻譯。

雖然有些研究指出,在外語學習過程中,和學習者母語發音、拼寫相近的詞彙最容易被掌握,然而,母語的影響卻是大部分錯誤的來源(Jiang, 2004)。美國學生一般在學習中文生詞時最常犯的錯誤就是根據中文生詞的英文翻譯詞義來使用該生詞,也就是認為中文和英文字詞有一對一完全的對等關係。這樣的錯誤也常在其他外語學習中可見,而相關的外語詞彙習得研究也不少(Jarvis, 2000)。在高年級的中文課裡,學生寫作時,字詞的使用錯誤佔了多數,因為一般學生在學習中文三、四年後,大多數都已經能掌握常用的中文語法和句型,但是在課堂上老師卻沒有辦法花過多的時間來解釋與練習新的詞彙,大多數的教科書也缺乏幫助學生理解生詞的說明以及學習新詞彙的練習。以下例子是美國學生常犯的用詞錯誤:

(1)*我問他四點給我打電話。

（2）*這幾年摩根城的經濟<u>開滿</u>。

（3）*小雪一進門就大笑，媽媽覺得很<u>陌生</u>。

一般而言，這樣的錯誤最常發生在一個英文字，因為用法和語境的不同，有兩個以上的相對中文生詞。以上述的句子為例，"ask"的中文若當做詢問問題的動詞，是「問」的意思，但"ask"在英文中還有祈使要求別人做事的意思，在中文得用「叫」或「請」來表達。但當學生第一次學到「問」這個字的意思是"ask"時，就將兩個字詞畫上了等號，而造成如上述例句的錯誤。另外兩個字「開滿」和「陌生」在以上的句子中，應該分別用「繁榮」和「奇怪」，但是因為「開滿」和「繁榮」的英文都可用"to bloom"表達，而「陌生」和「奇怪」在英文都是"strange"，所以學生就常常有以上的使用錯誤。

這樣的情況顯示學生並不完全理解這些詞彙的意思與用法，而是完全依照該詞的英文翻譯來使用這個字詞。學生之所以無法使用正確的字詞多半是因為在課堂有限的時間內，教師沒有時間給予足夠的詞彙練習，而教科書內也很少針對這樣由母語轉移來的問題多做解釋，學生就只能完全依賴對字詞英文意思的理解來使用這些生詞。類似的錯誤在學生自行查詢字典使用生詞時最常發生，一再的使用錯誤對外語學習者的自信心和興趣也會造成負面的影響。除非學生能在一個沉浸式的環境中接觸大量的真實語料，否則這樣的錯誤對在教室裡學習中文的美國學生來說，似乎很難避免。因此，如何發展出更有效的詞彙教學方法或自學工具，實是一門關鍵而重要的課題。

平衡語料與詞彙習得

在外語教學中，最普遍的詞彙學習材料就是詞彙表，一般的詞彙表會列出漢字、拼音、英文翻譯和詞性。研究指出，利用詞彙表來學習生詞的確可以在短期內學到字詞的意思（Cobb, 1999），然而這樣的短期記憶很難保留，學生常無法成功地將這些生詞應用在新的語境中。研究指出，若是讓學生從實際的語料中學習同一個生詞在不同句子和語境中的例句，不但有助於學生對生詞意義的理解，而且對生詞的應用在短期和長期上都有助益（Cobb, 1999, 2007）。

有關詞彙習得的研究指出一般學生在閱讀課文一次之後就記住大部分生字詞的可能性很小，除非這些生詞在文中出現的頻率很高，或者讀完之後，把同樣的生詞放在其他課文或短句中使用。就理論上而言，如同學習母語一般，一個生詞的用法，其深層的意思，大多是在通過該詞在不同語境中重複出現而獲得確定。語言學習者對語料資訊的使用，是外語習得研究中的較新課題（Cobb, 1999）。這個研究的一項有用的發現是即使初學者，只要給他提供清晰的學習目標和可以使用的平衡語料庫介面，學生也可以運用這些資訊，來代替在大量的閱讀中反覆遇到該生字詞的過程。Cobb 的研究顯示，使用平衡語料資料的學生與使用生詞詞彙表的學生相比，前者更加擅長把生詞運用在正確的語境中。本研究將以類似的方法來檢視平衡語料庫的應用是否也能幫助美國的中文學生更有效地學習生詞。

研究方法

本研究之參與者為美國大學三年級的 12 名學生。學生分別在電腦上閱讀兩篇新課文，並且各有一個半小時的時間來學習課文中的生詞（附錄 A）。兩篇課文的長度與生詞的數量都相近，學生在閱讀〈課文一〉時，可利用字典或是火狐線上詞典來學習生詞，線上詞典提供拼音和字詞的英文詞義，如圖 1 所示。

學生在閱讀〈課文二〉時，除了可利用字典外，還可點閱生詞所連結的平衡語料庫，每個生詞有 15 到 20 個從平衡語料庫中截取的例句。本研究之語料來自中央研究院現代漢語標記語料庫。學生點擊任何一個生詞，就可以連結到該生詞的平衡語料例句，如圖 2 所示。

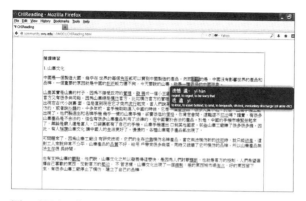

圖1 〈課文一〉：學生可利用字典或是火狐線上詞典來學習劃線的生詞。

圖2 〈課文二〉：學生可利用字典以及點閱劃線生詞所連結的平衡語料庫例句。

　　學生在閱讀與學習生詞時可自行決定是否要用線上詞典或點閱平衡語料的連結來幫助自己理解該生詞的用法。本研究所採用的量表是參考詞彙知識評量表（Vocabulary Knowledge Scale, 或稱 VKS）（Cobb, 2007）。與一般二分法不同的是，這份評量表可以讓學生表達對生詞的循序理解程度。評量可分為四個等級：

　　0 = 我完全不認識這個字詞

　　1 = 我不確定這個字詞的意思

　　2 = 我覺得我知道這個字詞的意思

　　3 = 我完全理解這個字詞的意思和用法

在學生開始閱讀學習生詞之前，已經先就每篇課文的劃線字詞做了一次詞彙知識評量表，以確定這些字詞對大多數學生來說都是生詞。閱讀前的這項評量顯示，〈課文一〉有兩個字詞對大多數的學生來說不是生詞，〈課文二〉有一個字詞不是生詞，這些字詞在學生閱讀後做詞彙知識評量時已被剔除。雖然有些學生已經認得某些字詞，但沒有人表示對某個字詞是完全理解的。在做詞彙知識評量表時，所評量的生詞是沒有語境與例句的，學生只能就生詞本身來做判斷。學生在完成〈課文一〉時就先做〈課文一〉的詞彙知識評量，在閱讀完〈課文二〉之後，就開始做〈課文二〉的詞彙知識評量。學生在電腦上評量自己對每個生詞理解的程度，每一篇課文學生必須評量20個生詞。

研究結果

在所有的學生完成兩篇課文的詞彙知識評量表之後，電腦可計算出每個學生對〈課文一〉與〈課文二〉詞彙理解的平均值。以下的列表可以顯示所有參加此次研究的學生（由英文字母A到L來代替）在閱讀前與閱讀後分別對兩篇課文新詞彙的理解比較。每個數字代表該學生對每篇課文的20個生詞理解的平均值（詞彙知識評量表0-3）。因此，數據越高，代表學生對該課文的詞彙理解評量越高。每篇課文的第三行數字代表的是學生閱讀學習生詞前和學習生詞後所做的詞彙知識評量平均差，這個資料代表學生學習前後對每一篇課文生詞的習得評量，而兩篇課文的學習工具和輔助不同之處就是〈課文二〉的生詞可以連結平衡語料庫。

從表1可以看出學生對兩篇課文各20個生詞的理解在閱讀之後都有顯著的提升。尤其值得注意的是在閱讀之前，有幾個學生的詞彙知識評量平均是零，也就是說這些學生對所有的生詞都完全不認識，這個現象在閱讀之後已經不再出現。學生在學習〈課文一〉的生詞時，是利用火狐線上詞典，在學習〈課文二〉時，可以點閱每個生詞所連結的平衡語料庫例句。就兩篇課文的詞彙知識評量平均差來看，〈課文一〉只有2名學生在閱讀前後的平均差達到2.0（學生E和L），而〈課文二〉則有6名學生（學生D, E, F, G, I和L）。表2顯示學生在學習過兩篇課文的生詞之後所做的詞彙知識評量比較。

由表2的數字可以看出學生對〈課文二〉詞彙的理解平均高過對〈課文一〉詞彙的理解。雖然學生C和J的詞彙理解還是偏低，但〈課文二〉依然比〈課文一〉的稍高一些。兩篇課文生詞理解的評量結果比較可以在圖3中更清楚地顯示。

根據研究結果的分析，學生對〈課文二〉的生詞習得比〈課文一〉稍有效率，其中的差距在學生B、E、I和K的自我評量中最為明顯。但由於參與研究的學生人數只有12人，所以獲取的資料還有更

表1 〈課文一〉閱讀前後詞量知識評量比較

學生		A	B	C	D	E	F	G	H	I	J	K	L
課文一	閱讀前VKS平均	0.8	0	0	1.2	0	1.3	2	2.1	0.4	0	0	0.6
	閱讀後VKS平均	2.4	1.8	1.5	2.6	2.0	2.4	2.8	3	2.1	1.5	1.3	2.7
	閱讀前後差	*1.6*	*1.8*	*1.5*	*1.4*	*2.0*	*1.1*	*0.8*	*0.9*	*1.7*	*1.5*	*1.3*	*2.1*
課文二（連結平衡語料庫）	閱讀前VKS平均	1.3	1.2	0	0.4	0.6	0	0	1.2	0.8	0	0.8	0
	閱讀後VKS平均	2.9	3	1.8	2.8	2.8	2.5	2.8	3	2.8	1.6	2.2	2.8
	閱讀前後差	*1.6*	*1.8*	*1.8*	*2.4*	*2.2*	*2.5*	*2.8*	*1.8*	*2.0*	*1.6*	*1.4*	*2.8*

表2 〈課文一〉與〈課文二〉閱讀後詞量知識評量比較

學生	A	B	C	D	E	F	G	H	I	J	K	L	平均
課文一	2.4	1.8	1.5	2.6	2.0	2.4	2.8	3	2.1	1.5	1.3	2.7	2.2
課文二	2.9	3	1.8	2.8	2.8	2.5	2.8	3	2.8	1.6	2.2	2.8	2.6

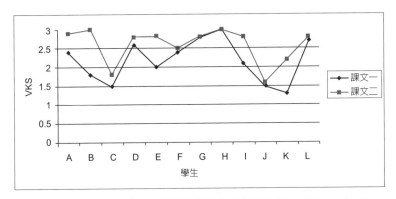

圖3 〈課文一〉與〈課文二〉閱讀後詞彙知識評量比較，〈課文二〉可連結平衡語料庫例句。

精確的空間。此外，在學生做完詞彙知識評量之後，並沒有再做客觀的評估，比方說以口試、填空題或造句來確定學生已理解字詞的意思和用法 （詞彙知識評量表3），也稍微減低了這項研究結果對平衡語料的肯定性。但不可否認的是，所有的學生的自我評量都顯示對〈課文二〉的生詞理解較多，而唯一的學習方法差別，就是〈課文二〉可連結平衡語料庫的例句。

教學建議與結語

此項研究結果顯示學生利用平衡語料庫學習中文生詞的詞彙習得成效似乎比只依賴母語英文翻譯要高。用平衡語料庫中的例句來幫助學生詞彙習得的優點是教師不必花很長的時間準備例句，而學生所閱讀的句子都是真實語料，不但有助於詞彙知識的理解，更可以增進學生的閱讀能力。另一項優點是提供學生一個有效的自學工具，尤其是對那些沒有機會在中文環境中學習的學生來說，平衡語料庫的使用可以讓他們在短時間內接觸一個字詞在不同語境中的用法和意思。平衡語料的使用並不困難，教師甚至可以將平衡語料庫的網址提供給學生，讓學生們自行查閱特地字詞在真實語料中的用法。在學生閱讀了多個例句之後，理論上來說，也較能避免直接將母語意思和用法轉換成中文的錯誤。

然而，如同之前的研究所指出的，使用平衡語料庫來幫助詞彙習得也有其缺點。第一，平衡語料的句子多為短句，學生無法看到完整的句型。其次，由於語料所提供的是真實的材料，有些句子本身就有許多學生不認得的生詞，還有比較複雜的文化背景，這些因素都加深了學生理解平衡語料庫中句子的難度。所以平衡語料庫的使用也許較適合中文高級水平的學生。此外，利用電腦來幫助學生學習中文生詞也較能順應目前日漸普遍的外語學習習慣和趨勢。雖然這份研究結果顯示平衡語料庫是值得利用和推薦給學生的中文詞彙習得工具，我們還需要更多的相關的討論和研究來確定平衡語料對中文詞彙習得或閱讀能力提升的真正效益。

參考文獻

中央研究院現代漢語平衡語料庫 http://db1x.sinica.edu.tw/cgi-bin/kiwi/mkiwi/mkiwi.sh

Cobb, T. (1999). Breadth and depth of vocabulary acquisition with hands-on concordancing. *Computer Assisted Language Learning 12*, 345-360.

Cobb, T. (2007). Computing the vocabulary demands of L2 reading. *Language Learning & Technology, 11* (3), 38-63.

Ellis, N. C. (2005). At the interface: dynamic interactions of explicit and implicit language knowledge. *Studies in Second Language Acquisition, 27*, 305-352.

Everson, M. E., & Ke, C. (1997). An inquiry into the reading strategies of intermediate and advanced learners of Chinese as a foreign language. *Journal of the Chinese Language Teachers Association, 32,* 1-20.

Everson, M. (1998). Word recognition among learners of Chinese as foreign language: Investigating the relationship between naming and knowing. *The Modern Language Journal, 82,* 194-204.

Hayes, E. (1988). Encoding strategies used by native and non-native readers of Chinese Mandarin. *Modern Language Journal, 72,* 188-195.

Jarvis, S. (2000). Sementic and conceptual transfer. *Bilingualism: Language and Cognition, 3,* 19-21.

Jiang, N. (2004). Semantic transfer and its implications for vocabulary teaching in a second language. *The Modern Language Journal, 88,* 416-432.

Ke, C. (1996). An empirical study on the relationship between Chinese character recognition and production. *Modern Language Journal, 80,* 340-350.

Ke, C. (1998). Effects of strategies on the learning of Chinese characters among foreign language students. *Journal of the Chinese Language Teachers Association, 33,* 93-112.

Lin, Y. (2000). Vocabulary acquisition and learning Chinese as a foreign language. *Journal of the Chinese Language Teacher Association, 35,* 85-108.

Yang, J. (2000). Orthographic effect on word recognition by learners of Chinese as a foreign language. *Journal of the Chinese Language Teachers Association, 35,* 1-18.

附錄A

〈課文一〉山寨文化

中國是一個製造大國，幾乎在世界的每個角落都可以買到中國製造的產品。然而遺憾的是，中國沒有影響世界的產品和品牌。一個重要的原因就是中國的創新能力還不夠。今天要說的山寨，就是一種奇怪的中國現象。

山寨其實是山裏的村子，因為不接受政府的管理，發展成一個小王國。所以，山寨和官方是一對反義詞，但是山寨和官方又有很多共同點。因為山寨總是模仿官方，比如模仿官方的管理方法等等，有些時候模仿得還非常成功。山寨經常出現在古代小說裏面，但是直到現在它才突然流行起來。當人們說某一個產品是山寨產品的時候，就是指這個產品是模仿的，或者說抄襲的。十多年前，當手機剛剛進入中國的時候，它是一個奢侈品，很多人買不起。於是，山寨手機工廠出現了。他們製造出和名牌手機幾乎一樣的山寨手機，卻賣很低的價格。你肯定會問，這難道不犯法嗎？確實，有很多山寨產品是不合法的，但也有很多山寨產品利用了法律的，在中國屬於合法的產品。於是，中國的手機市場繁榮起來了，無論是窮人還是富人，口袋裏都有了自己的手機。山寨手機還出口到其他國家。那些山寨工廠賺了很多很多錢。因此，有人稱讚山寨文化讓中國人的生活更好了。慢慢的，各種山寨電子產品都出現了。

可問題來了。因為山寨工廠沒有研究技術，它們的生存依靠模仿名牌產品。當它無法模仿新的技術時，就只能破產。這對工人來說非常不公平。山寨產品的品質不好，給用戶帶來很多麻煩，同時又破壞了它所模仿的品牌。所以山寨產品無法生存很長時間。

也有支持山寨的觀點。他們說，山寨文化之所以發展得這麼快，是因為人們討厭壟斷，也就是官方的控制。人們希望選擇自己喜歡的東西，反對官方的壓迫。不管怎樣，山寨文化出現了一個趨勢：差的東西被市場淘汰，好的東西留下來。有很多山寨工廠停止了模仿，建立了自己的品牌。

〈課文二〉中國環境污染問題

　　無論在電視上還是在網路上，你看到的中國是灰濛濛的，幾乎沒有綠色，特別是在城市裏面，空氣污染特別嚴重。在農村，人們也不夠重視環境，對自然資源的利用不加以控制。我生活在北京，這裏有兩千萬人口，幾百萬輛汽車，而且人口越來越多，汽車也越來越多，每天都會發生堵車。這麼多汽車不僅帶來了空氣污染，同時也帶來了噪音污染。中國的每個城市都想變成紐約曼哈頓，所以整個中國是一個巨大的建築工地和工廠車間：每天有很多舊的樓房被夷為平地，同時又有無數新的高樓拔地起；工廠每天都產生大量工業垃圾，其中有一部分被不負責地排放到大自然中。據說，中國一年用掉的鋼鐵和水泥是全世界的一半，但是建造出來的樓房只有三十年的壽命。說到這裏，我想起了2008年的四川地震，好多無辜的孩子死了，不是因為地震很強，而是因為建造學校的人很不負責，偷工減料。在北京，每年有很多沙塵暴，沙塵暴來的時候，一切都是土黃色的。人們不但不能出門，而且必須把門窗關好，因為空氣裏都是噁心的沙子。

　　今年，中國西南部發生了嚴重的乾旱。很多地方半年多沒有下雨。人們無法正常生活，土地乾裂了，農作物也死了。有人說這是天災，也就是大自然造成的災難，無法避免；也有人說這是人禍，也就是人造成的災難。這次旱災的原因跟森林遭到嚴重的破壞，土壤不能保存水分有極大的關聯。

　　中國環保專家鄭義指出，中國的環境問題根源在於制度。比方說，在西方國家如果一個化工廠向河裏排污水，肯定會受到嚴厲的法律制裁。然而在中國，同樣一件事，只要花少量的錢，就可以賄賂環保官員，他們就會視若無睹。

　　中國人很樂觀，很多人總是說：「都已經很好了，一切都已經很好了。」有很多人不知道別的國家環境怎麼樣，大家對自己的生活環境不是很重視。我去過別的國家，看到他們的生活環境那麼美麗而且充滿綠色，我驚訝的同時也很難過：中國有很多的問題，而大部分人還無動於衷。我父母年輕的時候，人們喜歡到城市裏看高樓；現在，年輕的我們只想逃到大自然呼吸新鮮的空氣。我的朋友勸我不要難過，他說，大的國家就很難管理，小的國家才容易管理。我不太同意，我認為，很難管理並不是說無法管理，成功的可能性還是有的。但首先，我們需要改變，很多很多的改變！

（以上課文摘錄自〈慢速中文〉http://www.slow-chinese.com/）

A Study of Guided Concordance Use on English Vocabulary Learning for Writing by Chinese-L1 College Students

Hsien-Chin Liou
Department of Foreign Languages and Literature, Feng Chia University
hcliou@fcu.edu.tw
Yueh-Chih Lin
Department of Foreign Languages and Literature, National Tsing Hua University
juliettelin@hotmail.com.tw

With the development of computer-assisted language learning (CALL), more and more second language (L2) instructors have recognized the effects of concordancing in helping classroom teaching. Data-driven learning (DDL) (Johns, 1991) enabled by concordancing has been recommended because the corpus and the concordancers provide authentic language models for L2 learners if proper training is given (Yoon, 2011). The look-up procedures with chosen sentences help the learners to notice the rules of word patterns, the constraints of English words, and the discrepancy between L1 and L2. Further, some studies maintain that concordancing may reduce students' common word errors caused by L1 interference (Chen, 2011; Gao, 2011; Liao, 2011). Nonetheless, these studies have not revealed precisely how effectively concordancing can reduce L1-influenced word errors. Learner processes of data-mining and information-decoding need to be investigated while they engage in various concordancing-enhanced writing tasks. The present study investigated the effects of guided concordance use on EFL college students' productive collocation learning and focused on its effectiveness on reducing L1-influenced word errors. A study with the single-group pretest-posttest design was carried out on fourteen English-major sophomores and then a delayed posttest was held to examine the sustainability of the effect. For treatment, a four-week instructional design involved guided scaffolding prompts during concordancing when the participants worked through pedagogical exercises with an online concordancer, *TANGO*. An evaluation questionnaire was designed to understand the subjects' perceptions about the effects of the concordancing process. The data were analyzed by the non-parametric Wilcoxon Signed Rank Sum Test. The results showed that our concordance-based approach enhanced the college students' vocabulary and writing abilities and the effects remained after four weeks. The students' writing and written responses also improved in terms of reduced L1-influenced collocation errors. Most students held a positive attitude toward the instructional design of the study. Implications and future research possibilities are discussed.

Keywords: concordancing, L1 interference, L2 writing, scaffolding prompt

引導式語境共現應用於大學生英文寫作之詞彙學習

劉顯親

逢甲大學外國語文學系

hcliou@fcu.edu.tw

林嶽崎

國立清華大學外國語文學系

juliettelin@hotmail.com.tw

　　隨著電腦輔助語言學習（CALL）的發展，越來越多的二語教學者認同字詞檢索對於協助課堂教學的成效。字詞檢索中的資料驅動學習（DDL）（Johns, 1991）向來為人推崇，是因為若能給予學習者足夠訓練，語料庫與字詞檢索系統能為他們提供真實的語言範本（Yoon, 2011）。查詢的程序與結果能幫助學習者注意詞彙模式的規則、英語詞彙的限制，以及一語與二語的差異。進一步而言，部分文獻認為字詞檢索可以減少由一語干擾所引起的常見詞彙偏誤（Chen, 2011; Gao, 2011; Liao, 2011），然而，這些研究卻未能確切說明字詞檢索對於減少一語干擾所造成的詞彙偏誤，其成效究竟為何。當學習者投入於各種提升檢索能力的寫作任務中，他們的資料挖掘與資訊解碼過程值得研究。本文探究在教師引導下運用字詞檢索系統對於以英語為二語的大學生學習產出性詞彙的效用，特別是對於減少一語干擾所造成之詞彙偏誤的成效。本文採用單組前後測設計的研究方法測試14位主修英語的大二學生，接著採用延宕後測檢視效果的持續性。就處理方式而言，四週的教學設計包含當受試者使用線上的字詞檢索系統 *TANGO* 進行教學練習時，為他們的檢索過程所提供的引導式鷹架輔助。本研究亦設計一份評估問卷以了解受試者對於檢索成效的認知情況，所得資料以無母數統計的魏克生等級和檢定的統計方法進行分析。結果顯示以字詞索引為本的教學方法能夠提高大學生的詞彙與寫作能力，且效果於四週後仍能持續。學生的寫作與書面回應在一語干擾引起的詞彙偏誤上亦有所改善。最後，大部分的學生對於本研究的教學設計亦抱持正面態度。文章最後討論研究啟示與後續的研究方向。

關鍵詞：字詞檢索、第一語言的干擾、二語寫作、鷹架輔助

Introduction

Vocabulary ability is one of the prerequisite skills in second language (L2) writing but to master it proficiently in written texts cannot be easily achieved. According to the psycholinguist (Jiang, 2004), the perplexities in word knowledge often result from the negative influence of L2 learners' first language (L1). Many L2 learners can hardly avoid being influenced by their mother tongue because they tend to associate new word knowledge with their mother tongue. The direct translation found in L2 learners is evidence that the first language affects L2 processing and lexical development. For example, Chinese learners of English have difficulty in identifying English words that could be translated by the same Chinese phrases, like *criterion-standard, accurate-precise, safe-secure,* etc. Before they accumulate enough input and understand the possible interpretations in various language contexts, L1 negative influence (also called L1 interference) may cause collocational problems. Liao (2011) indicates that L2 learners tend to translate target language word-by-word rather than retrieve adjacent phrases all together by using proper collocations. For example, in Chinese-English translation, '我感到頭痛' was translated as **I felt a <u>headache</u>* instead of '*I had a <u>headache</u>*' although the learners had already learned the two verbs. Among various vocabulary difficulties, collocation problems have been emphasized in recent years and exacerbated by the heavy demand for L2 learning. Researchers have found that to memorize collocations, "the strings of specific lexical items that co-occur with a mutual expectancy" (Nattinger & Decarrico 1992, p. 36.), L2 learners often rely on word definition and L1 translation (Chan & Liou, 2005; Liu, 2002; Yang, 2012).

Some studies and pedagogical applications showed that data-driven learning (DDL, Johns, 1991) can provide L2 learners with prolific example sentences as language models. Yoon's review (2011) of twelve studies on concordancing activities confirms that concordance use could assist L2 learners' linguistic aspects of writing once proper training is provided. Yet, one of the major pitfalls of applying DDL for L2 learning is the time-consuming process of decoding many concordance lines to find patterns. To respond to the need for L2 learners, Chang and Sun (2009) developed self-made scaffolding prompts to guide their L2 learners to use concordance lines to enhance proofreading tasks. They empirically demonstrated that the experimental group with the prompts performed better than the control group without any guidance. Perez-Paredes, Sanchex-Tornel, Alcaraz-Calero, and Jimenez (2011) explored a similar concern in their study and suggested that guided corpus consultation is more efficient than non-guided corpus consultation based on the total number of searches and actions performed by their learners.

For English-as-a-Foreign-Language (EFL) college-level writing, little research develops specific concordancing instructions or hands-on prompts to help L2 learners shorten data-decoding time by highlighting language foci among a sea of example sentences. Thus, we aimed to investigate how effectively a guided corpus-based approach could enhance L2 learners' productive collocation use in a writing class, and to survey the users' attitudes toward the instructional design combined with concordance use in order to address the following three research questions.

(a) Can EFL college learners' productive collocation performance be enhanced by guided concordancing training? If so, can the effect last after four weeks?

(b) Can more L1-influenced collocation errors (commonly caused by L1 interference) be reduced given the guided DDL, compared with errors unrelated to L1 influence?

(c) What are the learners' perceptions of the DDL instructional design in terms of their productive collocation learning?

Recent Research on Corpus-Based Teaching of L2 Writing

Corpus-based learning has been popularized in second language teaching because it provides abundant language models to broaden and deepen L2 learners' language knowledge. Thanks to being immersed in rich exposure, authenticity, and data-driven learning, L2 learners take concordances as language resources or language references to check linguistic features and patterns (Yoon, 2008, 2011). Moreover, frequently looking words up in a concordance facilitates L2 learners' induction of grammar rules (Lee & Swales, 2006), to initiate self-corrections (Chambers & O'Sullivan, 2004), and to become used to collocations (Wu, Witten, & Franken, 2010).

Corpus Analyses of L1 Interference and Their Pedagogical Applications

L1 interference, also called "cross-linguistic influence" and "negative language transfer," refers to the negative influence of native language on L2 learners' performance and development in the target language (Hashim, 1999). While producing the target language, EFL/ESL (English-as-a-Second-Language) learners' use of words, sentences, and discourse is inevitably influenced by their mother tongues; L1 lexical interference seems to be more evident in the learners' written English (Bunnui, 2008).

According to Nation (2001), eight types of word knowledge: meaning, written form, spoken form, grammatical behavior, collocation, register, associations, and frequency often hinder L2 learners from conveying meaning clearly. Among these difficulties, collocation problems pose any layer of learning challenges. To memorize collocations, L2 learners often rely on word definition and L1 translation (Chan & Liou, 2005; Liu, 2002; Yang, 2012). However, the two collocation learning strategies often lead to wrong usage in the target language. Taking Chinese learners of English for example: many people put wrong verbs into sentences, like *'Please **open** the computer' rather than the correct verb form '***turn on*** the computer' because both verbs are translated using the same Chinese word, '*kai*' (開), literally 'open'.

Some researchers tried to analyze common collocational errors from various learner corpora, expecting to induce systematic rules of word errors and find the pedagogical ways to solve these vocabulary learning difficulties for EFL learners in Taiwan. For example, Liu (2002) in her M.A. thesis gathered 1100 word errors from IWiLL (Intelligent Web-based Interactive Language Learning), an online platform for Taiwanese learners' learning English reading and writing (Wible et al., 2000). From a one-million word English Taiwan Learner Corpus (*English* TLC), she selected these common word errors by teachers' comments marked on high school and college students' writing. Out of those 1100 errors, 265 word errors were lexical miscollocations. Among 265 items, nearly 96% (233 items) lexical miscollocations belonged to the same phrase combination, Verb-Noun (V-N). Among them, 131 verb pairs were extracted based on WordNet verb files (Miller, 1995) which share lexical semantic relations. Then, 115 verb pairs were categorized into the same verb sets (see her Appendix B: *List of the 115 Verb Noun Miscollocations Categorized by the Verb Files of WordNet*, Liu, 2002, pp. 134-137). These procedures of analyzing the corpus and the classification of word errors indicated that some common word errors occurred following systematic rules based on close semantic relations between Chinese and English, particularly out of the mistakes in writing of the same learner group. Liu (2002) suggested that the V-N miscollocation list could be adopted for L2 teaching purposes.

In Yang's dissertation (2012), she extracted the top 200 most common word errors made by Chinese learners of English from two large EFL learner corpora in order to examine these learners' difficulties of verb learning. One was the 1.5-million-word Taiwan Normal University Corpus (TLEC), consisting of Taiwanese college students' writing. The other was the 1.1-million-word Chinese Learner English Corpus (CLE), covering senior high school students' and college students' compositions (Gui, 2005). She classified the 200 word errors into three categories based on verb transitivity (*Arrive, Agree, Care, Dream, Listen, Reach*), semantic prosody (*Cause, Happen*), and near-synonyms (*Happen/Occur, Say/Tell, Understand/ Realize*) (Yang, 2012, p. 54). The results showed that although there was no clear-cut factor to identify each type of error, L1 interferences and word-by-word translation could be two major reasons. For example, in the transitivity group, the highest error rate was "*Arrive*" (37.2%) because the Taiwanese learners often missed prepositions, such as "*at*" by writing a wrong phrase, like *"arrive an airport.*' It meant that the lack of preposition usage for intransitive verbs in Chinese may lead to the misuse of an English word. Besides, the inappropriate phrases *"realize* the <u>theory</u>' and *"realize* the <u>reason</u>' which appeared in students' writing might result from their L1 direct translation.

Pedagogical Applications of Learner Corpus Analysis or Concordancing Technologies

Two studies of learner corpus analyses of L1 interferences (Liu, 2002; Yang, 2012) contributed to our knowledge about the common errors that Chinese L1 learners may make when writing in English. The findings are worthy of being implemented to reduce L1 interference of learning vocabulary. Based on Liu (2002) and others, Chan and Liou (2005) extracted 36 English word errors from 100 common V-N miscollocations from Chinese college students' compositions. The 36 V-N miscollocations were viewed as the target words and designed into five online exercise units for 32 college students. They furthermore carried out a pretest-treatment-posttest experiment to examine whether concordance-based instructions plus the five online units in the exercises of multiple choice, Chinese-English sentence translation, and gap-filling exercises could improve EFL learners' collocational performance. The results showed that the concordancing approach combined with the traditional classroom instruction could significantly enhance college students' collocation performance, and the effect could remain after two and a half months. Besides, the students liked the approaches and would incorporate them into their future vocabulary learning. Based on these findings, the researchers suggest that more guiding aids, like teacher's involvement, time investment, and material coverage could reinforce collocation learning augmented by concordance use.

Several other Taiwanese scholars are also concerned with their college students' collocation errors as influenced by Chinese, and used concordancing to help alleviate the problem. First, Liao (2011) investigated EFL students' difficulties of learning collocations and suggested general principles of teaching collocations with concordancers. He not only indicated that negative influences of L1 Chinese was one of the most common problems leading to word errors but also pointed out six types of collocation errors made by EFL students in productive language. To solve the vocabulary learning difficulties, Liao (2011) investigated how concordancers enhanced 26 college sophomores' collocational performance by designing cloze translation questions as practices. On average, the improvement between his pretest and posttest attested to the effects of concordance use in learning of English collocations for translation.

Secondly, Chen (2011) and Gao (2011) supported that concordancers could enhance L2 learners' translating ability in retrieving collocations or reducing word errors. Chen (2011) developed a web-based concordancer, *WebCollocate* and compared it with *Hong Kong Polytechnic Web Concordancer* to see which one would more efficiently help both teachers and students quickly locate proper collocations when completing translation tasks. The results showed that through keying their first language (Chinese) queries in a search engine to get the English examples, the concordance users, including both teachers and students, could efficiently retrieve proper collocations. Similarly, Gao (2011) exhibited the benefits of a parallel bilingual concordancer in completing translation tasks by investigating whether his 21 college participants could independently revise their previous produced sentences via using his self-developed Chinese-English concordancer (CERT) instead of an online dictionary (Yahoo Dictionary). The results revealed that the learners in the experimental group (using concordancers) could switch between L1 and L2 more adroitly regarding word choice or word combination. Moreover, while revising sentences, the students in the experimental group also more successfully utilized the concordancer to proofread their awkward linguistic forms. As a result, students polished their writing by eliminating misused words.

To sum up, these studies confirmed the values of corpus analyses of L1 interferences (Liu, 2002; Yang, 2012). Their findings, like the categories of common word errors caused by L1 interference in Liu (2002), were applied for pedagogical purposes (Chan & Liou, 2005). Other researchers also pointed out problems induced in Chinese-English translation tasks as a common type, and regarded concordance-based approaches as viable solutions (Chen, 2010; Liu, 2011; Gao, 2011). By reducing collocation errors caused by L1 negative transfer, English learners could avoid common word errors (Chen, 2011), expand the depth of vocabulary (Gao, 2011), and translate better by reducing collocation errors (Liao, 2011).

Guidance of Concordance-Based Learning

Though some studies showed the benefits of corpus-based approaches, the time-consuming data-decoding process was also a concern (Yoon, 2011). To make up for this major limitation, a few researchers have started to develop scaffolding prompts and hands-on corpus-based activities as a concordance consultation process (Chang & Sun, 2009; Kennedy & Meceli, 2010; Liao, 2011; Perez-Paredes et al., 2011; Yoon & Hirvela, 2004) in order to help L2 learners decode concordance-based information. Yoon and Hirvela (2004) and Kennedy and Meceli (2010) carried out concordance consultation with teacher-guided activities. They claimed that either by teachers or by contextual aids, concordancing guidance should happen prior to the students' hands-on search work for increasing the frequency of using concordancers. Even more, instructors can predict the students' difficulties, for example, L1 interferences based on the analysis of learner corpora, and then encourage students to avoid improper language use by consulting concordancers (Liao, 2011).

Chang and Sun (2009) investigated the effects of self-designed prompts on assisting L2 learners to decipher corpus-based information. The results showed that with step-by-step scaffolding instructions embedded with proofreading activities, 26 high school students' proofreading performances on collocations were significantly enhanced after their four-week training. Similarly advocating teacher's guidance of concordancer use, Perez-Paredes et al. (2011) compared the effects of guided and non-guided teaching methods, and found that their experimental group with specific guidelines before using the corpora had better performance on their designed task than the control group.

These findings emphasized the necessity of guidelines implemented in concordancing classroom use. Both teachers and learners appreciate proper corpus-use guidance leading to effective concondancing. The literature supports that L2 learners are very likely to gain benefits from concordancing in productive collocation learning as long as proper guidance is provided. Thus, the three elements of incorporating corpus-based teaching: teachers' guidance for DDL, corpus-based materials to avoid L1 interference, and proper classroom activities for specific learning groups of L1 background are essential to make concordance use effective. Therefore, in the present study, we investigated the effects of guided concordance use in productive collocation learning, and particularly focused on its advantages for reducing written collocation errors influenced by the learners' mother tongue.

Methodology

This study examined the effects of concordance consultation on EFL college-level English learners' productive collocation learning for writing. A concordance-based approach was carried out in a writing class for four weeks in order to examine whether college students' English collocation usage in writing could be enhanced with the assistance of concordance-based learning materials and designed activities. To fulfill the purpose of this project, a four-week training session was designed and composed of step-by-step concordancing guidance and various pedagogical activities. Fourteen Taiwanese sophomores in an English writing course were the participants. Furthermore, the present study focused on the effects of concordance use on removing vocabulary learning difficulties resulting from learners' L1 influence. Common word errors caused by L1 influence were collected from previous studies and incorporated into our teaching materials. Guided to fix this specific type of word errors by consulting a user-friendly concordancer, *TANGO*, the 14 students' performances before and after the training session were assessed through a test with various question types. They were further assessed four weeks after the treatment ended to examine the retention effect. Finally, students' perceptions of concordance use and of the scaffolding prompts designed for learning English collocations in writing were shown based on the results of an evaluation questionnaire.

Participants

Fourteen English-major sophomores taking a Reading and Writing Course in a Northern Taiwan university served as the participants. They spoke Chinese as their mother tongue, and had learned English over eight years – since the time they were in grade five at the primary school. With an average age of twenty, all of them had English writing experience because they had prepared for College Entrance Examinations where writing was required at their high schools, and they also took English courses which involved training in writing during their first year of college.

Instruments and Procedures

Before taking part in this experiment, the participants signed a consent form to ensure their willingness to be involved in the present study. Then, their backgrounds were recorded by a questionnaire composed of five-point Likert scale items and several open-ended questions. After the treatment, their perceptions on overall concordance use in the present study were collected by an evaluation questionnaire.

The present study adopted a single group pre-posttest design followed by a delayed posttest. The pretest, the posttest, and the delayed posttest contained the same four parts: (a) part I: 25 multiple-choice items, (b) part

II: 12 proofreading items, (c) part III: 10 Chinese-English translation items, and (d) part IV: one 80-word paragraph writing. To examine whether the effects of the concordance-based approach maintained after the treatment ended, a delayed-posttest was designed which was composed of about half of the posttest items. The items in the pretest, posttest, and the delayed posttest focused on specific target words which were based on previous studies that showed students' L1 lexical interference (Chen, 2011; Liu, 2002; Yang, 2012). The first three question types belong to the embedded, selective, and context-dependent design options and the last one is an embedded, comprehensive, and context-dependent composition profile in the framework for L2 vocabulary assessment by Read and Chapelle (2001). The fourth question type, one 80-word paragraph writing, was used to assess how the test-takers used the target words in paragraphs. They needed to write a coherent paragraph by providing a topic sentence and embedding at least five target phrases from the previous three parts.

The main sources of sentences for these question items came from keyword searches of some concordance lines from the British National Corpus. In addition, online dictionaries (Longman Dictionary and Yahoo Dictionary), concordancers (TANGO), and the textbook of this course (Wyrick, 2011) were employed as supplements. Every part of the test contained two kinds of target words extracted from the common word error lists in previous studies which all examined Chinese-L1 students' essays in Taiwan contexts (Chan & Liou, 2005; Liu, 2002; Yang, 2012). Word errors influenced by L1 and the other word errors irrelevant to L1 influence were allocated to items in the pretest and posttest. Both tests were identical, including 52 target words and phrases coming out of the extraction. Three-fifth of the items came from L1-Chinese English learners, and 21 of them common possible errors from all other non-native English learners who may

Table 1

The allocation of target collocations in each question type of the pretest, posttest, and delayed-posttest

Pretest and Posttest	L1-influenced words	Non-L1-Influenced words	Total
22 Multiple-choice items	13	9	22
10 Proofreading items	5	5	10
10 Translation items	13	7	20
TOTAL	31	21	52
Delayed-posttest	L1-influenced words	Non-L1-Influenced words	Total
12 Multiple-choice items	5	7	12
6 Proofreading items	3	3	6
5 Translation items	9	1	10
TOTAL	17	11	28

not share L1-Chinese background. The delayed-posttest contained 28 target phrases extracted from the posttest, including 17 L1-influenced words and 11 non-L1-influneced words. Table 1 shows the allocations of the target collocations in the three tests. All items were the same in both the pretest and the posttest, and about a half of the posttest formed the delayed posttest. The order of the items in the pretest was different than the posttest and the delayed posttest. The participants did not obtain the correct answers after they were tested each time.

The evaluation questionnaire contained 31 items which were used to survey the students' perceptions on the concordancer (the 1st to 11th items), concordancing guidance (the 12th to 13th items), pedagogical activities (the 14th to 27th items), and target collocations (the 28th to 31st items, see Appendix for a complete version).

Treatments

Steps to using *TANGO*. A user-friendly Chinese-English concordancer

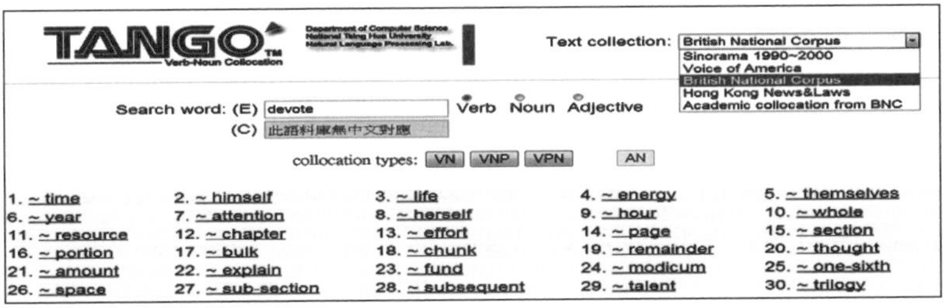

Search word: devote　目前搜尋總筆數：30

1. devote time (46)

But it is sobering to reflect that Bowes could **devote** so much **time** and energy to assembling his huge collections, a task that preoccupied him for many years, without apparently caring that a main source of his wealth, coal, was blighting lives and blighting the country side.

2. devote himself (18)

Up to the age of thirty or so he appeared to **devote himself** mainly to the social life of various celebrated Parisian salons.

3. devote life (13)

A nurse who died of cancer has bequeathed her pony for the use of the terminally ill children she **devoted** her **life** to.

4. devote energy (10)

As for the moody magnetism Method actors **devote** all their **energy** trying to perfect, Allen can take it or leave it.

5. devote themselves (10)

Most of them abandoned their former preoccupations and **devoted themselves** instead to less controversial types of literary study, such as text exegesis.

Figure 1. A screenshot of the concordance, *TANGO*

named *TANGO* was learners' major learning reference tool (Liou et al., 2006; http://candle.cs.nthu.edu.tw/collocation/webform2.aspx?funcID=9). As for consulting steps, users typed a keyword into the search engine, and then selected one of the collocation forms (e.g. VN-verb and noun) and one of the databases (See Figure 1). In seconds, they would receive a list of frequent collocations and they could click on the phrases to read example sentences. L2 learners could read the results composed of chunks of texts that contained the keyword and the collocated words.

Designed guidance. To reduce the learner's time searching, guidance was designed to highlight the discrepancy of the L1 and L2 and to help distinguish confusing meanings of target words. Some researchers believed that with the appropriate instructions and teacher's participation, concordance users could benefit by avoiding too much tedious data-mining (Chang & Sun, 2009; Liao, 2011; Perez-Paredes et al., 2011). Therefore, six sequential questions were designed to help participants to headline the significant grammar rules and linguistic constraints. The first two questions (Q1-Q2) were designed to guide the participants to associate both Chinese and English meanings of the target word. The next two questions (Q3-Q4) were designed to guide learners to identify the part of speech and the language forms. The last two questions (Q5-Q6) had learners generate the rule of language use from model sentences, and encouraged them to place the target words in appropriate contexts.

Pedagogical Activities

To expand the powerfulness of concordance use, four kinds of activities: multiple-choice, Chinese-English translation, proofreading, and paragraph writing were designed as pedagogical activities for classroom practice and homework. The exercise types correspond to the four main question parts in the pretest, the posttest, and the delayed-posttest, which was composed of embedded, selective, and context-dependent designs. For pedagogical purposes, the implementation of the activities could be seen as a meaningful practice to strengthen students' word use in various discourse contexts and to encourage their productive vocabulary ability (Laufer & Girsai, 2008). To accomplish the tasks, first of all, the need to understand the target word sense was activated in order to fulfill the task requirement. While completing activities, they were asked to "search" for words (for the meaning or/and for

Table 2

Data collection procedures of TANGO training

WEEK	CLASS ACTIVITY	DATA COLLECTION
1st week	Orientation	· Consent form · Background questionnaire · Pretest
3rd week	Unit 6: Effective Sentences (i)	*TANGO* Training1 (plus homework)
4th week	In-class writing	*TANGO* Training2 (plus homework)
5th week	Unit 6: Effective Sentences (ii)	*TANGO* Training3 (plus homework)
6th week	Discuss students' writing	*TANGO* Training4 (plus homework)
7th week	Chapter 7: Word Logic	· Posttest · Evaluation questionnaire
11th week	Regular reading and writing activities	· Delayed-posttest

the form) through *TANGO*, and then they were guided to "evaluate" which word contexts in the concordance would be correct. Table 2 shows the data collection procedures including four *TANGO* in class training sessions.

Data Analysis

The statistical non-parametric Wilcoxon Signed Rank Sum Test was employed to compare individuals' scores obtained from the pretest and posttest as well as the scores between posttest and the delayed-posttest. The delayed-posttest was made up of about half of the items in the posttest (in statistical computation, posttest2 yielded from delayed-posttest was a subscore of the posttest1, from posttest). We turned raw numbers into percentages for comparing their performance between the two stages.

First, the answers of the 25 multiple-choice items were scored dichotomously. Once the participants gave a correct answer to each item, they gained one point. Second, the students' collocational performance was assessed based on whether they corrected word errors in the ten proofreading questions. Every question was worth two points. Students who chose the wrong word from two underlined hints gained one point; to gain the other, they also had to provide a proper word to substitute for the chosen wrong word. Third, each sentence in the Chinese-English translation items with two collocations was worth six points (60 for 10 items): 1 point for the overall sentence structure, 2 points for writing the two appropriate collocational phrases, 2 points for translating the accurate key words of each collocated phrase, and 1 point for other grammar aspects like plurals, tenses, and spellings. Fourth, twenty points were assigned to paragraph writing. The test takers' vocabulary performance presented in paragraph writing was measured by two aspects. Ten points were allocated to measure the appropriateness of the five chosen collocations in the sentence context, including their spelling, tense, and target collocations. The other ten points accounted for the content, organization, and language use of the paragraph quality. To maintain raters' reliability, the quality and assessment of writing were read by two raters, and the inter-rater reliability was 0.85, which was acceptable according to statistic standards (Shrout & Fleiss, 1978, p. 426).

To investigate the students' performances of target word usage in writing, all the items in the four types of questions administered in the pretest, posttest, and delayed posttest were classified into two categories: word errors influenced by L1 and other word error types, which were based on supporting theories and studies of L1 interference with L2 learning (Bennui, 2008; Dulay & Burt, 1974; Liao, 2011; Yang, 2012). L1-influenced word errors, commonly observed in our learners, were one major focus of the current study. The categorization of the two types of word errors across the four question types was based on pedagogical concerns; we did not run any reliability check. The percentage of word errors in each category as shown in tests was calculated by the Wilcoxon Signed Rank Sum Test to compare how much the students improved in reducing word errors caused by L1 influences.

Last, we analyzed data from the evaluation questionnaire for understanding students' attitudes toward concordance use. Percentage, the mean of each item, and the mean rank order were computed for all the items designed using the 5-point Likert scale of agreement. As for the open-ended questions, all the participants' responses to each item were summarized.

Results and Discussion

(a) Can EFL college learners' productive collocation performance be enhanced after concordancing training with guidance? If so, can the effect last after four weeks?

Since the sample size was small (N=14), the non-parametric statistic method named Wilcoxon Signed Rank Sum Test was adopted to examine whether learners' collocation performance in English writing improved and was retained after the four-week treatment. Without predicting the results, we referred to two-tailed statistical results. The results showed significant differences between the 14 participants' pretest scores and posttest scores. Positive ranks were 14 while negative ranks were zero. This showed that all participants' collocation performance significantly improved after the treatment. The sum of ranks (105 points) and the Z scores (-3.3) indicated significance ($p < 0.01$) (See Table 3). In addition, the effectiveness of the treatment remained four weeks after the posttest took place. Half of the original posttest items were identical to those in the delayed-posttest and defined as posttest2. Table 4 shows that there was no significant difference between posttest2 and delayed-posttest (z scores = -0.63) and the average

Table 3

Results of the Wilcoxon Singed Rank Sum Test for comparison of gain scores from the pretest and the posttest

		N	Sum of Ranks	Z-score	Sig. (2-tailed)
Posttest-Pretest	Negative Ranks	0[a]	0	-3.3	<0.01 *
	Positive Ranks	14[b]	105		
	Ties	0[c]			
	Total	14			

Note 1: * $p < 0.05$

Note 2: a. posttest1 < pretest   b. posttest1 > pretest   c. posttest1=pretest

Table 4

Results of statistical comparison of gain scores from the posttest2 and the delayed-posttest

		N	Sum of Ranks	Z-score	Sig. (2-tailed)
Delayed-posttest-Posttest2	Negative Ranks	7[a]	42.5	-0.63	> 0.05 *
	Positive Ranks	7[b]	62.5		
	Ties	0[c]			
	Total	14			

Note 1: * $p > 0.05$

Note 2: a. delayed-posttest < posttest2   b. delayed-posttest > posttest2

c. delayed-posttest=posttest2

scores of the two tests were very close. This means that the effect was maintained.

In addition to overall significant improvement and the retention effect, we discovered that the paragraph writing task had the most significant gain in scores out of the four question parts (See Figure 2, in the unit of both the raw gain score and the percentage). This improvement of paragraph writing was also retained in the delayed-posttest.

Figure 3 showed the range and distribution of all fourteen participants' scores and six chosen learners' scores in the pretest. Their average overall score

Gain
scores

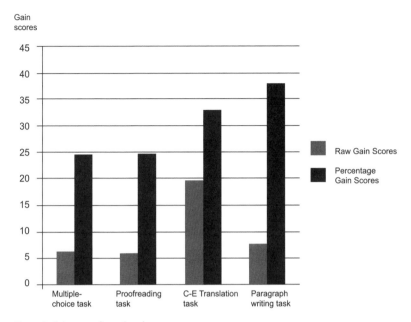

Figure 2. Gain scores for each task

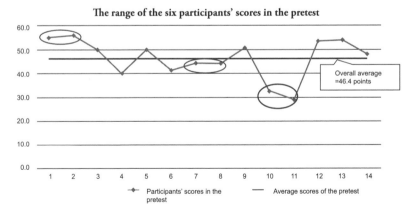

Figure 3. The distribution of the chosen 6 participants' scores in the pretest among the 14

of 14 in the pretest was 46.4% when scores of four question types were combined. We selected six students whose scores were above, near, and below the overall average, 46.4 to show their various writing performance in more detail. The six participants' writing scores with two representing each of the three levels of language proficiency were based on the overall scores of the pretests (6 students = 2 students x 3 levels).

As shown in Table 5, we found that the length of the six learners' paragraph writing had been extended and the students tended to use more target collocations in their paragraph writing across time. The average length had increased from 50 words (in the pretest) to 135 words (in the immediate posttest), and the length was retained in the delayed-posttest (133 words). As for the number of target phrases, the students used less than two collocations on average in the pretest, but they nearly lived up to the expectations of using

Table 5

The length of the paragraph written and the number of the correct target collocations found in the pretest, immediate posttest and delayed-posttest

Pretest overall scores	Student	Pretest		Immediate Posttest		Delayed-posttest	
		Number of words (Length)	Number of target phrases	Number of words (Length)	Number of target phrases	Number of words (Length)	Number of target phrases
55.04	S1	88	2	130	5	99	5
55.81	S2	90	4	165	7	165	5
44.57	S3	47	2	127	4	189	3
44.19	S4	77	1	102	3	88	4
32.56	S5	83	0	202	3	172	1
29.46	S6	0	0	88	5	88	6
	SUM	385	7	814	27	801	24
AVERAGE		≒ 50	**1.5**	≒ 135	**4.5**	≒ 133	**4.0**

five target collocations correctly in the posttest (4.5 phrases) and the delayed-posttest (4.0 phrases).

(b) Can more L1-influenced collocation errors (commonly caused by L1 interference) be reduced given the guided DDL, compared with errors unrelated with L1 influence?

To answer the second research question, we compared the accuracy rates of L1-influenced collocations and non-L1-influenced collocations regarding scores obtained in the pretest, posttest, and delayed-posttest using the Wilcoxon Signed Rank Sum Test. The scores showed that both groups of collocations improved after treatment. Although the correctness of L1-influenced collocations was slightly lower (32.33%) than the other collocations (41.33%) in the pretest, the students improved more on L1-influenced collocations (40.04%) than non-L1-influenced collocations (30.10%) as shown in Table 6.

Table 6

The correctness of target collocations in pretest and posttest

	L1-influenced collocations	Non-L1-influenced collocations
Pretest	32.33%	41.33%
Posttest	72.37%	71.43%
Gain scores (%)	40.04%	30.10%

Furthermore, the statistics demonstrated that L1-influenced collocations and non-L1-influenced collocations between the pretest and the posttest showed a significant difference ($p < 0.05$) (See Figure 4, Table 7). In sum, both types of collocation errors were corrected, and more of the L1-influenced collocation errors were eliminated than non-L1-influenced errors.

In addition to the overall improvement, the reduction of L1-influenced

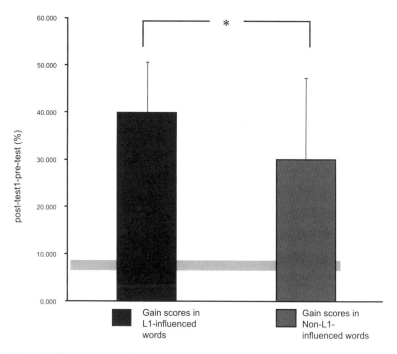

Figure 4. The comparisons between the gains in L1-influenced collocations and non-L1-influenced collocation

erroneous phrases also demonstrated significant differences on written practices (the translation task and the writing task) and the effect remained till the delayed-posttest. Take the translation task for example: after the treatment, nearly all of the students made correct sentence structures and used accurate phrases to translate Chinese sentences into English. They did not avoid translating difficult phrases but adopted more suitable phrases; for example, over ninety percent of the participants translated "認輸" as "*give up*" on the pretest, but they wrote "admit defeats" or "accept failures" on the posttest. From the results of translation tasks, it seemed that the participants successfully learned to identify the differences of confusing English words that

Table 7

Results of the comparison of the gains in L1-influenced collocations and Non-L1-influenced collocations

		N	Sum of Ranks	Z-score	Sig. (2-tailed)
L1-Non-L1	Negative Ranks	3[a]	20.5	-2.01	<0.05 *
	Positive Ranks	11[b]	84.5		
	Ties	0[c]			
	Total	14			

Note 1: * $p < 0.05$
Note 2: a. L1 < Non-L1   b. L1 > Non-L1   c. L1=Non-L1

Table 8

The frequency of target words used in paragraph writing of the posttest

Posttest	The usage L1-influenced words	The usage Non-L1-influenced words
Items	45	27
Percentage	64.28% (45/ (14*5) *100 = 64.28)	38.57% (27/ (14*5) *100 =38.57)

had similar Chinese equivalents instead of just relying on direct translations. With a four-week concordancing-based training, over seventy percent of the students translated 珍惜友誼 as "value friendship" rather than "cherish friendship" or "treasure friendship", both of which contained the same Chinese equivalent, "珍惜."

The increases of using L1-influenced phrases correctly also showed in the paragraph writing, and the effect was extended four weeks after the immediate posttest was held. Calculating the number of words used in paragraph writing, we found that the participants had nearly twice the number of preferences of incorporating L1-influenced target words into their posttest writing (68.28%) than non-L1-influenced words (38.57%) as illustrated in Table 8.

On the pretest, the participants could not identify what collocations were. However, on the posttest the fluency and the accuracy of their writing demonstrated that they were able to apply the target phrases in the right contexts while composing a paragraph. For example, the students originally made errors by referring to "*public service*" as "*the positions of working for government*" and describing talented students with an inappropriate adjective phrase, like "prolific students." However, they clarified the two phrases by embedding them into the right contexts. They finally used "*public service*" to as a substitute for the miscollocation "**public facility*" and replaced "*prolific students*" with a more proper adjective phrase, like "*prospective students*" on the posttest.

The above evidence showed that L1-influenced collocation errors could be corrected with assistance of the concordance-based approach. The training was particularly beneficial in correcting L2 learners' common collocation errors that were caused by their mother tongue (Chinese). It increased students' collocation knowledge and furthermore motivated the students to produce the correct language forms in written language.

(c) What are the learners' perceptions of the instructional design in terms of their productive vocabulary learning?

To investigate the students' perceptions of concordancing, means of their responses to items in the Evaluation Questionnaire were computed. The 31-item questionnaire was designed with 23 items using a five-point Likert scale and 8 open-ended questions. Means of the responses to each item were calculated and then ranked. Some of the students' opinions and comments were summarized. As shown in Table 9, the students showed positive perceptions of the concordance-based vocabulary instruction. After the four-week training, all students became skilled in manipulating *TANGO*

Table 9

Students' perceptions of TANGO

Items	Mean	Rank
1. The speed of Internet is quick enough to use in class.	2.93	7
2. I understand how to look collocations up by the concordancer, *TANGO*.	4.43	1
3. I think concordancing is helpful in learning English word usage.	4.36	3
4. Generally speaking, after using *TANGO*, my English writing has been improved.	3.93	6
5. Looking collocations up by *TANGO* builds my confidence in writing English collocations.	4.21	5
6. From now on, *TANGO* will be one of my language learning tools.	4.43	1
7. I will keep using *TANGO* to polish English writing.	4.29	4

(Mean=4.43) as shown in item 2, and most of them were willing to continue using *TANGO* as one of their language learning tools (Mean=4.43. see item 6) due to its convenience and usefulness. Almost all of the students believed that concordance use would be helpful in learning words (Mean=4.36, see item 3), especially in checking words and learning authentic collocations.

Secondly, concerning scaffolding prompts, most students held a positive attitude toward the eight steps of concordancing procedures and the six sequential guiding questions used in our in-class sessions. Table 10 shows that most students agreed that the eight steps were clear enough to understand how to use *TANGO* (Mean=4.36, see item 13.1), yet the ability to induce grammar rules may take more time (Mean=3.79, see item 13.3). They generally agreed that consulting *TANGO* with the assistance of scaffolding prompts built up their writing confidence (Mean= 4.36, see item 12.7), and using *TANGO* could help them write better (see item 12.4).

Third, students' perceptions of teaching activities and our chosen target

Table 10

Students' perceptions of scaffolding prompts

Items	Mean	Rank
12.4 Generally speaking, after using *TANGO*, my English writing has been improved.	4.29	2
12.7 Looking collocations up by *TANGO* builds my confidence in writing English collocations.	4.14	4
13.1 The (above designed) eight steps are clear for me tounderstand how to look collocations up by *TANGO*.	4.36	1
13.3. I can induce grammar rules by the above steps when consulting *TANGO*.	3.79	10

Table 11

Students' perceptions of teaching activities and chosen target collocations

Items	Mean
28. Overall, the chosen word patterns taught in our class are suitable for me to learn how to make sentences for writing, not too hard nor too easy.	4.00
29. In previous learning, I often made word errors related to the target collocations that I learned in our class.	3.86
30. I guess the English word errors might result from my direct translation from Chinese knowledge.	3.86
31. I believe after learning these target collocations, my writing could be better, as I can use correct English collocations in making sentences.	4.00

collocations were reported in Table 11. Nearly all students (92.85%) appreciated the appropriateness of the target collocations (Mean=4.00, see item 28). They agreed that the target collocations were commonly misused based on their previous learning experiences (Mean=3.80, see item 29). They also admitted that one of the reasons that they made errors on those collocations was due to their reliance on direct translation (Mean=3.86, see item 30). However, they believed that their writing could be polished by removing these common collocation errors (Mean=4.00, see item 31). Therefore, they followed guidance step by step as an essential activity.

Discussion

The effects of guided concordancing on college learners' productive collocation performance and the retained effects. The participants' overall improvements were clearly shown by their increasing scores from the pretest to the posttest. Besides, among the four question types, they made the most improvement in paragraph writing. Without a control group, we can only argue the effects may come from a combination of our designed concordancing treatment plus the students' regular classroom writing instruction. The more encouraging evidence is that the subjects maintained their performance in the delayed posttest even four weeks after the treatment ended. The finding may be attributed to several factors: the design of the scaffolding prompts, the teachers' instant feedback, and an abundance of concordancing practice with the enhancement of the tool, *TANGO*. Both scaffolding guidance and hands-on pedagogical activities served an effective instructional purpose. In agreement with our expectations, according to the students' significant improvement and retained effects, we demonstrated the effectiveness of this concordancing-based approach on college students' productive collocation learning.

Providing steps of concordancing procedures was helpful for shortening L2 learners' consulting time (Chang & Sun, 2009). We designed the scaffolding steps as six sequential guiding questions for helping the students anchor learning objectives. Our first two guiding questions enlarged the students' vocabulary size as well as vocabulary knowledge by urging them to associate words with synonyms, antonyms, and L1-L2 equivalents. The third and the fourth questions assured that the students understood the part of speech of the target words and the collocational patterns. These methods combined with guessing and instant double checking from the concordance reinforced their vocabulary learning more effectively than the method which asked them to directly memorize. After receiving ample examples, the fifth and the sixth questions narrowed down the most common collocations of the target collocations. In the process of answering the two questions, the students were welcome to browse the usage of the target phrases by viewing example sentences so that they could identify the constraints of target collocations.

These scaffolding prompts may help to improve the students' scores from the pretest to the posttest by relating the current knowledge to their prior learning experiences. Before obtaining the new knowledge, they could check their guess, and then reinforce the knowledge by checking collocations through *TANGO*. Therefore, through regular practice, their overall language ability improved and the effect was retained one month later in the delayed posttest.

In the study, the effective instructional design featured ample practice and multiple tasks. The students were allowed to practice these different tasks while they were searching for answers from *TANGO*. This design stimulated them to guess and to process target collocation items from different angles, and provided them chances to carry out their word learning strategies. From simple recognition on multiple-choice items to difficult utilization of produced written language in paragraph writing, the students had enough time to warm themselves up and then were ready to produce language at the end of the practice sessions. First, they could identify how to use the target collocations by reading sentences in the multiple-choices items. Next, after imitating the language use in different contexts, they could start spelling out the collocations' forms in the proofreading tasks. Then, the students were encouraged to use the collocations in sentences in the Chinese-English Translation task. Finally, paragraph writing allowed them to compose target collocations in their writing.

We could ascribe the learning effectiveness as found in the study to the contributions of both learning materials and the teaching methods which were incorporated into the concordance-based approach. We found that the students improved much more in paragraph writing, and this may be because the other pedagogical tasks prepared their readiness and built up their confidence in using the target collocations in writing. In addition, the familiarity with concordance use led them to more efficiently decode word usage among concordance output examples no matter when they accomplished tasks in class or out of class. In short, the sequential scaffolding prompts and pedagogical tasks were helpful for maximizing learners' potential for learning more advanced word and collocation knowledge.

The effects of the concordance-based approach and more correct cases of L1-influenced collocations. We found that concordance consultation had positive effects on correcting both L1-influenced collocation errors and non-L1-influenced errors. Comparing the gain scores from error-free items of the L1-influenced collocations and non-L1-influenced collocations, it was found that the students improved more on L1-influenced collocations than non-L1-influenced collocations (40.04%: 30.10%) as shown in Table 6. We suggest that these results probably arose from the design of the teaching materials which included the source of the target collocations and the choices of pedagogical tasks.

The sources of target collocations came from the contributions of previous learner corpus-related studies (Chan & Liou, 2005; Chen, 2011; Gao, 2011; Liao, 2011; Liu, 2002; Yang, 2012) which assisted us in locating target L1-influenced and non-L1-influenced collocations. The L1-influenced collocations were extracted from previous research on corpus analyses and their applications (Chan & Liou, 2005; Liu, 2002; Yang, 2012). The non-L1-influenced collocations were chosen based on the participants' writing textbook (Wyrick, 2011) and instructors' teaching experiences. With the word lists verified by rigorous studies, the instructors were able to logically predict the students' errors and difficulties in writing. These applications were also used to avoid students' direct translation and reliance on L1 definitions in writing because the chunks of collocational phrases enhanced the L2 learners' writing ability from single words to sentences (Liao, 2011).

In addition to the contribution of the target word lists and collocations, the design of our written tasks may provide practice for learners to activate their productive vocabulary knowledge. Take the participants' performances on Chinese-English translation items for example. The students obviously corrected their mistranslation by learning chunks of English, like the collocational phrases, "*discriminate against*" and "*label...as...*" instead of depending on word-by-word translation, like the wrong phrase "**stick memos.*" In other words, they were able to distinguish between Chinese (L1) and English (L2). Moreover, they noticed that the preposition "*against*" collocating with the key verb "*discriminate*" had no Chinese equivalent. Therefore, while they were practicing translating Chinese into English, they would not always rely on direct Chinese equivalents. Instead, they memorized the whole phrases and wrote English sentences by using linguistic chucks. These benefits were supported by prior studies on the college students whose mother tongues were in common, that is, Chinese (Chen, 2011; Liao, 2011).

What's more, the students showed their successful learning of those target collocations to be influenced by the L1 by using them in paragraph writing. We found that with our designed concordance-based approach, the students preferred to use more L1-influenced collocations in writing paragraphs compared with non-L1-influenced collocations both in the immediate posttest and the delayed-posttest. The reasons why the students preferred to use L1-influenced phrases could be explained by the following.

Memorizing target collocations in the L1 was efficient (Dulay & Burt, 1974) because the students sometimes took advantage of their L1 learning experiences and then focused more on L1-related collocations. The alternatives for collocational verbs in phrases, like "attain/achieve/accomplish goals" and "build/establish friendship" encouraged the students to try them out in writing. That was also why the students were able to remember these phrases and used them again in paragraph writing for the delayed-posttest. Although some of their memories were a bit blurry, they correctly used more collocational phrases which were beyond the target words taught in class. For example, they learned the target phrase "*label...as*" and finally they extended more similar patterns, like "*regard...as*" in their two posttests. This showed that L1-influenced phrases built up their confidence and reinforced their memories so that they could increase the use of the phrases. The stronger support for the effect of our treatment came from the finding that the students were able to keep these abilities as shown in the delayed-posttest.

Participants' perceptions of concordancing with guidance. We found that the participants generally held positive attitudes toward the effectiveness of the current concordance-based approach, including the concordancer, the scaffolding prompts, and the instructional design.

Toward the concordancer, *TANGO*, the students revealed that it brought benefits to their vocabulary learning and writing ability so that they were willing to continue using *TANGO* as one of their learning tools. Because of the repeated practice with clear concordancing instructions, they became familiar with using *TANGO* and then appreciated its strengths. For example, they expressed that *TANGO* was helpful and practical because the concordancer was easy to manipulate. The large amount of collocations and sentence examples were helpful in checking words, learning authentic usage, and making up for the lack of information provided by dictionaries. They also expressed that some difficult sentences could still be comprehended with the aids of scaffolding prompts which helped students to induce grammar rules, extend word banks, and save time in the decoding process (Chang & Sun, 2009). The multiple pedagogical tasks provided a great number of advantages as well. To illustrate, the students had more practice to check their language use and to compare their interlanguage against authentic data. The scaffolding prompts and the various tasks designed in the concordance-based approach enriched their language knowledge because the practice highlighted the language forms that had been misused by EFL learners. Some students also agreed that the target words were suitable for them to reinforce their language ability because they always looked the target words up with *TANGO* even though sometimes they could guess the answers.

The students' strong favor towards concordance use could be ascribed to the easy accessibility of *TANGO*, teachers and students' time investment (Yoon, 2008), and the effective guiding materials. The easy access to the Internet and *TANGO* allowed them to practice anywhere. As the students gradually developed the habit of concordancing, they became more confident in using words in English writing; thus, the concordancer helped them to write better. They completed tasks faster through the assistance of scaffolding prompts which enabled them to decode an abundance of information and thus avoid the time-consuming process. With the effective scaffolding prompts which assisted the concordancing process, the students indicated that they were able to follow steps, focus on forms, and then imitate how the phrases had been used from example sentences in the concordancer. These methods helped them raise the accuracy of words and collocations in writing. The users' familiarity of using the concordancer led to more frequent uses. Once the students' concordancing habits had grown, they could auto-nomously learn new linguistic forms. Without instructional design, they had been guided step-by-step to figure out the blurry conceptions of chosen target words which may be heavily influenced by the L1, and the correct forms that they had learned were reinforced by repeated concordancing practice. Thus, they were willing to continue using *TANGO* as a language reference tool.

Conclusion

The present study investigated the effectiveness of a concordance-based approach on college students' productive collocation learning using a single group pre-posttest design. The study recruited fourteen EFL English-major sophomores as the participants receiving four sessions of concordancing instruction. The purpose was to raise the sophomores' vocabulary/collocation abilities and to improve their writing accuracy. We took cross-language influences into consideration and expected the design to reduce students' word errors due to L1 interference. The results showed that the concordance-based approach was beneficial for college students' learning of target collocation items produced in writing. Students retained improvement for at least a month after the instruction ended. Finally, the students held a positive attitude toward the instruction design. It is suggested that the benefits of learner concordancing are evident in post-instruction performance and retention effects. The advantages may come from looking words up by the concordance program *TANGO* with scaffolding guidance, which was helpful for speeding up decoding procedures (Yoon & Hiervela, 2004), highlighting linguistic foci from contexts (Laufer, 2008), and building students' confidence (Yoon, 2008). The designed materials embedded with target words influenced by the L1 (Liu, 2002; Yang, 2012) can facilitate learning collocations for writing, because they increased the noticing effects for Chinese-L1 EFL learners. The users (students) can distinguish the differences between L1

(Chinese) and L2 (English) and thus diminish more word errors caused by cross-language interferences. Finally, the students' positive feedback is inspiring and encouraging for concordance-based teaching and learning. To some extent, their positive attitudes vouch for their willingness to utilize the learning tool (*TANGO*).

Limitations and Future Research

In the research design, there were two limitations. In our study, we recruited only 14 college students as participants in a writing class. More students are desired to increase representativeness of effects on such learners with a similar background. Second, having a control group is suggested to form a stronger research design (than that in the current study) for future research. More pedagogical tasks can be designed to test different groups of participants, like non-English-major students, in order to expand the values of concordance use in second language writing.

Pedagogical Implications

The contributions of the present study include that (a) abundant language models help students distinguish constraints of target collocations and become familiar with collocational phrases in databases due to the use of *TANGO*, (b) scaffolding prompts help the users shorten time of decoding information in the concordance output, and (c) multiple tasks as concordancing practice facilitate learning in terms of assuring language usage. With positive effects of this approach found in the current study, two implications in second language teaching and learning can be suggested.

First, our concordance-based approach is beneficial because we scaffold L2 learners' language learning with constructive sequences of concordance-based guiding instructions. To be specific, the guidelines lead the students to acquire the target collocations by following the sequential steps in our design: (a) confirming learner's knowledge of word sense, (b) extending the target word to its synonyms, (c) ensuring learner's knowledge of word class, (d) raising awareness of collocation patterns or phrasal units, (e) raising awareness of word usage patterns, and (f) applying all types of word knowledge in context. The effectiveness appeared on both learning and teaching. For learning, a package of concordance-based pedagogical design encourages the students to take responsibility for learning and developing their learning strategies. For teaching, the designed materials incorporated the L1-influenced target collocations may cause noticing effects. Moreover, the materials guided the students to compare and contrast the discrepancies of two languages.

Second, the present study suggests that more explorations into other concordance methodology are necessary. For example, we illustrated how to facilitate concordancing with steps explicitly as done by previous researchers (Chang & Sun, 2009), but we further intertwined guidelines, activities and practices into pedagogical designs. This implied that learner concordancing could be incorporated into other pedagogical methodologies rather than be inflexibly restricted to a single method.

We concluded that a concordancer, like *TANGO*, is a reliable method of combining teachers' involvement and guidance (Yoon, 2008; Yoon & Hirvela, 2004). Teachers play essential roles in incorporating language tools to motivate, to guide, and to support students. These show that the concordancer itself is not omnipotent. How a teacher utilizes the concordancer in instruction should be emphasized. With the teachers' involvement, the learners would be more likely to be benefited by the advantages of prior knowledge, as with their first language acquisition.

Acknowledgements: We would like to acknowledge the funding support in completing the paper under a Taiwan National Science Council project (NSC99 -2410-H-035 -059 -MY3).

References

Bennui, P. (2008). A study of L1 interference in the writing of Thai EFL students. *Malaysian Journal of ELT Research, 4,* 72-102.

Chambers, A., & O'Sullivan, I. (2004). Corpus consultation and advanced learners' writing skills in French. *ReCALL, 16* (1), 158-172.

Chan, T. P., & Liou, H. C. (2005). Effects of web-based concordancing instruction on EFL students' learning of verb-noun collocations. *Computer Assisted Language Learning, 18* (3), 231-250.

Chang, W. L., & Sun, Y. C. (2009). Scaffolding and web concordancers as support for language learning. *Computer Assisted Language Learning, 22* (4), 283-302.

Chen, H-J. H. (2011). Developing and evaluating a web-based collocation retrieval tool for EFL students and teachers. *Computer Assisted Language Learning, 24* (1), 59-76.

Dulay, H., & Burt, M. (1974). Errors and strategies in child second language acquisition. *TESOL Quarterly, 8,* 129-136.

Gao, Z-M. (2011). Exploring the effects and use of a Chinese-English parallel concordance. *Computer Assisted Language Learning, 24* (3), 255-275.

Gui, S. (2005). A survey of preposition usage of Chinese English learners. In H. Z. Yang, S. Gui & D.Yang (Eds.), *Corpus-based analysis of Chinese learner English* (pp. 226-245). Shanghai: Shanghai Foreign Language Education Press.

Hashim, A. (1999). Crosslinguistic influence in the written English of Malay undergraduates. *Journal of Modern Languages, 12* (1), 59-76.

Jiang, N. (2004). Sematic transfer and its implications for vocabulary teaching in SLA. *The Modern Language Journal, 88* (3), 416-432.

Johns, T. (1991). Should you be persuaded: two examples of data-driven learning. In T. Johns & P. King (Eds.), *Classroom Concordancing. English Language Research Journal, 4,* 1-16.

Kennedy, C., & Miceli, T. (2010). Corpus-assisted creative writing: introducing intermediate Italian learners to a corpus as a reference resource. *Language Learning & Technology, 14* (1), 28-44.

Laufer, B., & Girsai, N. (2008). Form-focused Instruction in second language vocabulary learning: a case for contrastive analysis and translation. *Applied Linguistics, 29* (4), 694-716.

Lee, D., & Swales, J. (2006). A corpus-based EAP course for NNS doctoral students: moving from available specialized corpora to self-compiled corpora. *English for Specific Purposes, 25*, 56-75.

Liao, B.S. (2011). 大學生中譯英搭配詞能力與錯誤之探討。*English Teaching & Learning 35* (1), 85-122.

Liou, H. C., Chang, J. S., Chen, H. J., Lin, C. C., Liaw, M. L., Gao, Z. M., Jang, J. S., Yeh, Y. L., Chuang, T. S., & You, G. N. (2006). Corpora processing and computational scaffolding for an innovative web-based English learning environment: The CANDLE project. *CALICO Journal, 24* (1), 77-95.

Liu, L. E., (2002). *A corpus-based lexical semantic investigation of verb-noun miscollocations in Taiwan learners' English*. Master Thesis. Taiwan: Tamkang University.

Miller, G. A. (1995). WordNet: A Lexical Database for English. *Communications of the ACM, 38* (11), 39-41.

Nation, I. S. P. (2001). *Learning Vocabulary in Another Language*. Cambridge: Cambridge Press.

Nattinger, J. R., & DeCarrio, J. S. (1992). *Lexical Phrases and Language Learning*. Oxford: Oxford University Press.

Perez-Paredes, P., Sanchex-Tornel, M., Alcaraz-Calero, J. M., & Jimenez, P. A. (2011). Tracking learners' actual uses of corpora: guided vs. non-guided corpus consultation. *Computer Assisted Language Learning, 24* (3), 233-253.

Read, J., & Chapelle, C. (2011). A framework for second language vocabulary assessment. *Language Testing, 18* (1), 1-32.

Shrout, P. E., & Fleiss, J. L. (1979). Intraclass correlations: uses in assessing rater reliability. *Psychological Bulletin, 86* (2), 420-428.

Wible, D., Kuo, C.H., Liu, A., Tsao, N.L. (2000). An investigation in using WordNet to automate the correction of language learners' collocation errors. Unpublished manuscript. Taipei.

Wu, S., Witten, I. H., & Franken, M. (2010). Utilizing lexical data from a Web-derived corpus to expand productive collocation knowledge. *ReCALL, 22* (1), 83-102.

Wyrick, J. (2011). *Steps to writing well* (11th ed.). Boston: Wadsworth.

Yang, H. H. (2012). A corpus-based study of EFL learner difficulties with verb. PhD dissertation. National Taiwan Normal University. Taipei, Taiwan.

Yoon, H., & Hirvela, A. (2004). ESL student attitudes toward corpus use in L2 writing. *Journal of Second Language Writing, 13* (4), 257-283.

Yoon, H. (2008). More than a linguistic reference: the influence of corpus technology on L2 academic writing. *Language Learning & Technology, 12* (2), 31-48.

Yoon, H. (2011). Concordancing in L2 writing class: An overview of research and issues. *Journal of English for Academic Purpose, 10*, 130-139.

Appendix: The evaluation questionnaire

Chinese Name: _____ **English Name:** _____ **Gender:** _____

Email: _____

PART 1: Perceptions of the concordancer (*TANGO*)

1. The speed of Internet is quick enough to use in class.   SA A U D SD

2. I understand how to look collocations up by the concordancer, *TANGO*.
   SA A U D AD

3. I think concordancing is helpful in learning English word usage.
   SA A U D SD

4. Generally speaking, after using *TANGO*, my English writing has been
   improved.   SA A U D SD

5. Looking collocations up by *TANGO* builds my confidence in writing
   English collocations.   SA A U D SD

6. From now on, *TANGO* will be one of my language learning tools.
   SA A U D SD

7. I will keep using *TANGO* to polish English writing.   SA A U D SD

8. There are some pros and cons for me to use *TANGO* to work on word
   usage.
   Advantages:_____.
   Disadvantages:_____.

9. From now on, if I have access to a computer with internet, in addition to
   looking collocations up by online dictionaries, I will consult *TANGO* to
   check word usage.
   ☐ YES   ☐ NO
   The reasons:_____.

10. Have you met any difficulties when you were using *TANGO*?

_____ (Be specific)

11. If *TANGO* could be updated, which function do you expect?

☐ Pronunciation ☐ English sentences with translations in Chinese

☐ Online practices ☐ The complete texts of extracted sentences

The reasons:_____.

PART 2: Perceptions of the concordancing guidance

12. In class, we went through the 6 steps to complete the translation items.

Q1: What English words do I associate with the following Chinese phrases?

付出_____努力 _____完成_____目標_____

Q2: How would I translate the following words? (Write in Chinese)

contribute _____ donate_____endeavor _____

achieve _____ accomplish _____ target _____

Q3: Start consulting TANGO, which forms would I try to search for?

(A) Verb + Noun

(B) Verb + Noun + Preposition

(C) Verb+ Preposition +Noun

(D) Adjective + Noun

Q4: Which verbs can precede "efforts" and "goal"?

(1)_____+ effort (2)_____+ goal

Q5: Click the above two phrases and copy one example sentence from TANGO for each.

(1) (~effort) _____

(2) (~goal) _____

Q6: How would I translate the Chinese sentence into English?

為了成功，她盡力付出努力以完成目標。

_____

12.1 Q1 encourages me to associate a group of English words with the same Chinese meaning. For example, when I tried to translate "努力," Q1 helped me list "effort, endeavor, and diligence."   SA A U D SD

12.2 Q2 helps me to learn more similar English words that I have not learned before.   SA A U D SD

12.3 Q3 helps me to identify part of speech (詞性) of words
SA A U D SD

12.4 Q4 helps me to select the proper language form from *TANGO*.
SA A U D SD

12.5 Q5 saves my time because I do not have to browse all examples in *TANGO*.   SA A U D SD

12.6. Q6 encourages me to test out the word usage I learned from *TANGO*.
SA A U D SD

12.7. Overall, these designed guidelines are good for me to consult *TANGO* and acquire word patterns effectively.   SA A U D SD

13. Look at the following 8 steps of concordance use.

---

1. Enter key words into search engine (e.g. "effort")

2. Decide upon the part of speech (e.g. Noun)

3. Choose the database (e.g. BNC)

4. Tick one collocation form (e.g. Verb + Noun)

5. Search the collocational phrase (e.g. "make ~")

6. Click on the authentic sentence

   (e.g. *"Susan **made** an **effort** to imagine what it would be like to live a settled life with a partner she saw every day."*)

7. Identify the language usage (e.g. "make efforts to Vr" or "make an effort to Vr")

8. Accomplish the task

13.1 The above eight steps are clear for me to understand how to look collocations up by *TANGO*.   SA A U D SD

13.2 If I forgot how to look collocations up by *TANGO*, I will refer to the above instructions and then practice them again.   SA A U D SD

13.3 I can induce grammar rules by the above steps when consulting TANGO.   SA A U D SD

PART 3: Perceptions on pedagogical activities

14. While practicing consulting *TANGO* in class, I followed guidelines step by step instead of skipping the instructions or guessing answers randomly. SA A U D SD

15. When I practiced answering the above questions, I came up with predicted answers in Chinese and then I check the English collocations by *TANGO*.   SA A U D SD

16. While consulting *TANGO* in class, did you any other resources to answer questions?

☐ YES   ☐ NO

The resources are: _____

17. Although I am not familiar with some words (e.g. pungent odor) in multiple-choice items, I still can find the correct answers by consulting *TANGO*.   SA A U D SD

18. After practicing Chinese-English translations with *TANGO*, I learn phrases that I might misuse, like "admit defeat" (rather than "*accept defeat*").   SA A U D SD

19 After practicing Chinese-English translations with *TANGO*, I learn how to use phrases **more precisely**, like "recite poetry" which is better than "memorize poetry."   SA A U D SD

20. The items from proofreading tasks help me to differentiate **subtle usage** between phrases, like "expand one's horizon" and "expound one's views."

SA A U D SD

21. The items from Proofreading tasks help me notice the minor errors concerning **word pattern**, like "retreat *into* a distance" (rather than 'retreat *back a distance').   SA A U D SD

22. I tended to think of the Chinese meaning of the target English words, and then their word usage, and work on corrections in proofreading tasks. This often leads to mistakes.   SA A U D SD

23. In addition to the target phrases in each question, I can discover **other grammar rules**. For example, besides learning the phrase "*seek one's inspiration*," I also find that '*inspiration*' is an uncountable noun. '
SA A U D SD

24. In addition to the target phrases in each question, I can learn **more collocations**. For example, besides learning the phrase "*seek one's inspiration*," I also remember other phrases, like '*arouse* one admiration,' '*stir* one's imagination,' '*raise* one's expectations.'   SA A U D SD

25. How much time does *TANGO* Homework take you every time.

_____

26. Would you accomplish *TANGO* Homework 4 faster than Tango Homework 1?

☐ YES   ☐ NO

Because: _____

27. Whenever I do my homework, I consult *TANGO* by following the guidelines step by step.

☐ YES

☐ NO

Because: _____(You can choose more than one answer.)

(1) I do not know how to use *TANGO*.

(2) The questions are too easy to consult TANGO; I can answer some of them right away.

(3) I tried, but I have difficulties in finding correct answers from so many sentences.

(4) This learning tool is not suitable for my learning style.

PART 4: Perceptions on target words

28. Overall, the chosen word patterns taught in our class are suitable for me to learn how to make sentences for writing, not too hard nor too easy.
    SA A U D SD

29. In previous learning, I often made word errors related to the target words that I learned in our class.   SA A U D SD

30. I guess the English word errors in item 22 might result from my direct translation from Chinese knowledge.   SA A U D SD

31. I believe after learning these target words, my writing could be better, as I can use correct English words in making sentences.
    The reasons: _____.   SA A U D SD

國家圖書館出版品預行編目（CIP）資料

大學語言課程教研薈萃：第二語言讀寫教學研究論文集 / 李明懿，
雷貝利（Barry Lee Reynolds）主編 . -- 初版 . -- 桃園市：
中央大學出版中心；臺北市：遠流, 2017.11
面； 公分 . --
部分內容為英文
ISBN 978-986-5659-16-5（平裝）

1. 語文教學 2. 教學研究 3. 文集

800.3   106016576

大學語言課程教研薈萃
第二語言讀寫教學研究論文集

主編：李明懿、雷貝利（Barry Lee Reynolds）
策劃：國立中央大學語言中心
執行編輯：曾炫淳
編輯協力：簡玉欣

出版單位：國立中央大學出版中心
　　　　　桃園市中壢區中大路 300 號

　　　　　遠流出版事業股份有限公司
　　　　　台北市南昌路二段 81 號 6 樓

發行單位／展售處：遠流出版事業股份有限公司
地址：台北市南昌路二段 81 號 6 樓
電話：(02) 23926899　傳真：(02) 23926658
劃撥帳號：0189456-1

著作權顧問：蕭雄淋律師
2017 年 11 月 初版一刷
售價：新台幣 300 元

如有缺頁或破損，請寄回更換
有著作權·侵害必究 Printed in Taiwan
ISBN 978-986-5659-16-5（平裝）
GPN 1010601498
YLib 遠流博識網 http://www.ylib.com E-mail: ylib@ylib.com